WAY OF THE WITCH

WITCHES OF NEW YORK
BOOK 6

KIM RICHARDSON

KR PUBLISHING

Way of the Witch, Witches of New York, Book Six
Copyright © 2023 by Kim Richardson
Cover designer: Karen Dimmick/ ArcaneCovers.com
All rights reserved, including the right of reproduction
in whole or in any form.

www.kimrichardsonbooks.com

WAY OF THE WITCH

WITCHES OF NEW YORK
BOOK 6

KIM RICHARDSON

KR PUBLISHING

CHAPTER 1

They don't want Shay. They want you.
Okay, so these were not the words I was expecting, coming from my angel father Matiel's mouth. It took my brain a few seconds to jump-start back to reality.

Once I reoriented myself to the present moment, I couldn't help but feel like a character in a cheesy action movie. I mean, what kind of line was that? It sounded like something straight out of a nineties' Schwarzenegger flick.

I stood in my apartment on the thirteenth floor of the Twilight Hotel, which I now used mostly as my office and to hang out with the gang. I was supposed to be doing that now, celebrating my little sister Shay's recovery from the Mark of Death curse that the evil sorceress Auria had bestowed upon her, instead of ogling the angel who stood in front of me.

My hold on Shay relaxed, but I was still holding on to her. I wasn't sure if that was for her or more for me. Shay's head tilted up, and I felt my little sister's eyes on me.

I never looked away from my father. "Me?" I repeated like an idiot. And then, of course, followed by the usual, "Are you sure?"

Matiel exhaled heavily like he'd been holding his breath this whole time. "I'm afraid so. Yes. They want you. Not Shay."

Movement caught my eye, and I turned to see Valen walking to the door of the apartment. At first, I thought he was leaving to give us some privacy, but then the giant shut the door and walked back, cutting off the loud, happy conversations from the hallway. Now they were but incoherent muffles.

Valen's focus was on my father as he positioned himself back against the wall just off the kitchen, leaning with his arms over his ample chest. His expression was carefully blank. No way to tell what he was thinking.

My gaze darted back to my father. "I'm guessing from that guarded expression that they don't want to give me a halo?"

A muscle flicked along my father's jaw. "No."

"My own set of wings?"

Matiel blinked.

Ah. "They want me dead. Am I right? Because I'm part angel? But then, that would make Shay a target as well." I gripped her shoulders, feeling her tense. She'd been through enough. The kid needed a break. She deserved a break and to be a kid for a while.

"You being my child is partly the reason, but not in the way I initially assumed," said Matiel after a moment, his features tight. "The legion isn't attempting to obliterate human-angel hybrids, like Shay or any other child of both species. They don't seem to be interested in them."

I screwed up my face. "Just how many other half-breeds are there?"

"More than you know."

"Not all yours, I hope." The idea that Shay wasn't my only half-sibling was daunting.

Matiel shook his head. "You and Shay are my only children." His eyes lowered to my little sister. "I had hidden her from the legion because of what she is and what she can do with her celestial magic, the sun's power. But as I learned, she is of no interest to them." His eyes met mine again. "They seek you. Just you."

"To kill." Again, he didn't answer, but he didn't need to. "Why me? I can't even do magic in daylight," I said, frustrated. It wasn't entirely true. I could still conjure up a mean teardrop of starlight. But you get it. Still, this had to be a mistake. Yes, I was a Starlight witch, which was rare, but my magical abilities weren't up to par with a powerful White or Dark witch.

My father shook his head, looking frustrated. "I'm not sure. It could be something we haven't seen yet. Something you have, something *inside* you that hasn't manifested yet."

I snorted. "I'm a forty-one-year-old witch. I've

3

come into my powers a while back. Years ago. Apart from my starlight, there's nothing else. I can't *do* anything else. Nothing's changed. I haven't discovered anything new about my powers." As soon as the words escaped my lips, I knew that wasn't entirely true. I had been able to fly using my starlights as jet packs. But it wasn't really that different, just the same magic used in an altered way. It wasn't new magic by any means.

"I can't do White or Dark magic," I continued. "Trust me, I've tried." The memory of my failed attempts as a twelve-year-old to conjure elemental magic with the local witch kids came back in a flash. They'd all laughed when I couldn't call forth the most basic of flames like them. "I'm as dry as a human in that department. So, why are they after me?"

Matiel was silent for a moment. His expression was cautious as he said, "I don't know. Whatever it is, they consider it a threat."

My brows reached my hairline. "This doesn't make sense." A faint feeling of apprehension slid under my skin at how he'd said it. Letting go of Shay, I propped my hands on my hips, rummaging through my mind to come up with a logical explanation as to why the Legion of Angels would be after me. According to my father, it had nothing to do with me being his daughter—well, not entirely. It was something else. But what? The fact that they weren't after Shay did make me feel better, but it also added to my confusion. She was a hell of a lot more powerful than me. But they weren't after her. They wanted little ol' me. This was nuts.

Shay shifted next to me, and I could see the longing on her face. She was eager to be with her father, yet she seemed uncertain that it was an option, like I was keeping her from him. Okay, so maybe I was. But since she wasn't at risk of suffering the angels' wrath, I didn't see why I should keep her away from him.

"Go see your dad," I said softly and gave her a nudge forward.

With a burst of energy, Shay ran across the room toward her father, throwing her arms around him in an embrace.

"Hey, peanut," Matiel said as he planted a kiss on the crown of his daughter's head.

The sight of Shay hugging her father—*our* father —was a nice distraction to the real reason he was here. I didn't know if his visit would be the last in a long time, and I didn't want to bring it up. I didn't want to disappoint Shay. Let her have her moment with him because who knew when he'd return.

I looked over at Valen. He was watching me, and a play of emotions crossed his face. I knew that look. He was anxious, afraid *for* me. Having a Legion of Angels after you wasn't like combatting a wicked vampiress or a mad sorceress. This group wasn't something I'd ever faced before. They were other-worldly beings with otherworldly fighting skills and weapons. Unknown territory for me. Could I even defeat them? Or even just one? Could I even match them in combat? If they came at me during the day, I was a goner.

My father couldn't have given me worse news.

Valen's body shifted and took on a defensive stance, his expression full of menace. His face was set in an intimidating snarl as if he was ready to fight anything that might threaten me. I knew he would. He'd protect me with his life. That was just the kind of man, giant, he was. But what could a giant do against a Legion of Angels?

"I need to sit down." I walked over to the empty armchair and let myself fall. Something was different in my apartment. And that's when my eyes fell on the green-gray carpet. It was still ugly, but it was new. The black scorch marks left by my failed attempt to call my angel father were gone. Not that it mattered now. Guess Basil would bill me for that soon.

Valen pushed off the wall and came to stand next to me. He reached over, and I felt the warmth of his hand on my shoulder. The brief touch sent a message that I wasn't in this alone. He was with me on this, no matter what.

Matiel moved over to the couch and sat, and Shay jumped to the spot next to him. I wanted to laugh at just how cute and happy she was, but I couldn't find it in me. My body was tight with tension like a rubber band stretched too far.

"You know," I began, looking between my father and Shay on the couch facing me. "I don't know if I could have been hit with worse news. I mean, what could be worse than a Legion of Angels wanting me dead. Right?"

At that, my father stared at his hands, and the expression drained from his face. One moment, there had been blissful happiness shared with my sister, but the next, it had simply vanished, leaving his features cold as wild panic crossed his eyes.

I leaned forward in my chair. "I don't like that look on your face. What are you not saying?"

"It's not the Legion of Angels that's after you. Well, not exactly," he said, still staring at his hands. I felt Valen's weight shifting next to me as Matiel looked up and met my gaze. "It's the Assassins' Guild of Angels."

I had a brain-fart moment. And then. "Excuse me? There's an Assassins' Guild of Angels?" I imagined a group of black-clothed men climbing up walls with long, gleaming swords like ninjas from hell.

Matiel folded his hands on his lap, and I noticed Shay had lost her smile, staring at me with wide eyes. "Yes," answered my angel father.

"And *why* is there an Assassins' Guild of Angels? I mean, I thought angels were supposed to protect and heal and do all that angel stuff."

"There's a lot you don't know about us," said Matiel.

"No shit."

When I met Matiel's eyes, he stared at me momentarily, frustration and sadness sharing space on his features. "They are killers. They exist to eliminate threats to the balance of power in heaven and on

7

earth. If someone or something poses a significant danger, the guild will send their best assassins to take care of it." Matiel's voice was low and serious, and I felt a shiver down my spine.

My mind was reeling. I had never heard of anything like this. Assassins were supposed to be human, not angelic beings. Okay, not entirely true. I'd heard of paranormal bounty hunters, which were kind of like assassins for hire. Mercenaries. But the idea that angels out there were hired as killers was insane.

Yet, there was Matiel, telling me they did exist.

Valen put a hand on my shoulder again, and I leaned into him, feeling for a moment like I was back in the safety of his arms. The Assassins' Guild of Angels sounded like something out of a horror movie, not something that actually existed in the world. But as I looked into Matiel's eyes, I could see the truth.

"They are highly skilled in combat and assassination," the angel continued. "They are ruthless. Amoral. And care nothing for mortals. They wouldn't even think twice about taking your life."

"I can imagine," I breathed. I could imagine a lot.

"You don't want to face them. Trust me."

"Well, it's not like I have a choice. Do I?" I gave my father a hard stare, and he looked away. It was his fault I was in this mess, in a way. He had disobeyed the legion's laws and had sex with my mother, but that was a whole other story.

I frowned, trying to wrap my head around the

concept. "So, the legion's released their dogs because they think I'm a threat to them? How? I'm just a mortal witch. Nothing more."

Matiel sighed heavily, his expression pained. "I understand this is a lot to take in."

"You think?"

"The fact that they are after you means you have become a threat to the balance of power. Something about you has them… concerned."

"What?" I raised my hands. "What can I possible have that can threaten them?" I asked, feeling a sense of disbelief. I was just a witch with angel blood. Why would the Assassins' Guild of Angels even bother with me?

Matiel shook his head. "I don't know."

"What *do* you know?" Yeah, my voice was high with emotions, but I was tired from the ordeal with Freida, and this was just not the relaxed environment I had hoped for.

My father's brows rose, the only indication that he was irritated by my tone. I didn't care.

"They believe you are a threat to them," he answered finally. "That is all I know. Your existence is a violation of the laws of the angelic realm, just as Shay's is. But that's not the reason. It's something else. Something only you possess."

"I feel so lucky." A mix of fear and anger bubbled up inside me.

"And I know," continued Matiel, "that the Assassins' Guild has been given orders to eliminate you."

I felt my blood run cold as Matiel's words sank in. "Wonderful."

"I'm sorry," he said softly.

"When?" demanded Valen, speaking for the first time. "How many?"

My father's gaze flicked to the giant. "I'm not sure."

Irritation flared. "Guess."

"Ten," answered the angel. "Ten of their best assassins."

You'd think ten wasn't such a big deal. Given that it'd be nighttime, I could defeat ten witches or other paranormals, but we were talking about *angels*. Trained assassin angels, no less. Immortal celestial beings of immeasurable power. The odds were not in my favor.

"When will the assassins come looking for Leana?" asked Valen. The slight scruff around his face created a provocative silhouette, giving him an alluringly mysterious and sexy-as-hell look.

Matiel looked at me and said, "Anytime. They've already been given leave."

My father looked around the room nervously as if he was afraid of something lurking around us. He shook his head, and muttered under his breath. "After all these centuries... I should have known they would try something like this."

I let my head fall into my hands. "Guess I can't take a few days off." Nope. Not when I had angel assassins looking for me.

"Do they know where she is?" Valen's voice was hard, and I looked up.

Matiel shook his head. "Not yet. They tried to get that from me while I was… indisposed… but I managed to keep that secret."

He looked at me. If he was expecting a thank-you, he was going to be seriously disappointed.

"It won't take them long to find you, though," continued my angel father. "I suggest you look for another accommodation. And you should keep moving. A different safe house every day."

"No," I replied firmly. "Tired of running. We've done enough running. If they want to find me, they can find me right here. I'm guessing I can't expect any help or protection from you?"

I stared at my angel father, not understanding what crossed his face. He was still a stranger to me. Unlike Shay, I hadn't known of his existence until about a month ago. She'd had years to get to know her dad.

My father's expression shifted as he observed me. I didn't know him well, but I could see his disappointment in my answer. He wanted me to live. That part was obvious. But I wouldn't run. And he knew he couldn't make me. No one could.

"Take this." He reached inside his jacket and handed me what looked like a silver ring.

I frowned as I took it. The metal felt cool in my palm, and I could see a twist of intricate markings that looked like sigils etched into the sides. "Is this ring supposed to protect me? How? Will it give off a blinding glare? Amaze angels to death?"

"It will grow warm at the presence of them."

Just when I was about to tell him that he was an angel, and the ring was still cool, I felt a prick of magic, and then the silver ring glowed and grew warm against my skin.

"It will warn you when an angel is near." My father sighed. "It is the only thing I can do."

I pursed my lips. "Not a hell of a lot. Unless this ring can make an angel-shield or something, it might give me a heads up, but I'll have to fight them on my own."

"If I try to intervene, if I try to stop them, they will execute me," said my father.

Shay's intake of breath was loud in the sudden silence, her eyes wide with fear. Her mouth was forming words, but she didn't speak them. She was stuck between seeking her father's protection and knowing that if he stepped in, he would likely perish.

I wouldn't do that to an eleven-year-old kid. "It's fine. I wouldn't ask you to do that."

Matiel nodded, relieved, but his eyes were sad. "The Assassins' Guild of Angels is not something to be taken lightly. They are ruthless and efficient. They will stop at nothing until their target is eliminated."

My mind was reeling with the information, trying to make sense of everything.

Matiel gave a small nod, his expression pained. "I'm sorry, Leana. I wish I could do more to help you."

Valen let out a soft growl as he spoke. "I won't let them hurt her," he said firmly with vehement eyes.

I was touched by Valen's devotion and willingness to protect me, yet I didn't wish to be the cause of anyone else getting in harm's way.

Shay spoke up, her voice quiet but determined. "I can help too. I have my magic."

I stood up, shaking my head. "You need to focus on school. That's it. I'll leave you now so you can spend some time with each other. I'm sure you have lots to talk about."

Shay screwed up her face. "Where are you going?"

"For a walk. I need to clear my head." I wanted to ask Matiel when we'd be seeing him again, soon or not, but I had a feeling just making his appearance now had cost him. I didn't want to bring it up in front of Shay.

"I'll walk you out," said the giant beside me.

I turned around, not bothering to say goodbye or thank my angel father. I was too pissed off, upset, anxious, and too many other emotions for me to even think about parting politely.

I was barely aware of leaving the apartment and walking through the group of festive paranormals on the thirteenth floor as I made my way to the elevators.

My mind just wasn't in the mood for a celebration. The Assassins' Guild of Angels was after me, and I had no idea why.

Welcome to my life.

CHAPTER 2

I barely slept a wink. I drifted in and out of consciousness all night, tossing and turning, dreaming of ninjas dressed in black with black wings, crawling up the walls and attacking me. Mostly hitting me in the face with their wings. Weird dream.

When I finally decided to get out of bed, I was drenched in sweat. I'd have to wash the sheets. But first, I needed a shower.

After my father's visit, I'd walked the city streets, Valen next to me. I hadn't said a word for about an hour and had traveled all the way to Central Park, where I'd planted my butt on the grass, staring out at the lake. All the while, the giant followed me like a silent, huge bodyguard. I knew he had followed me to protect me, first from the angel threat, but I knew he was also there for moral support. He didn't ask me any questions. In fact, he was just there, waiting for me in case I needed to talk, which I didn't. Not at the time.

But it was nice just having him there, comforting.

And then, after what felt like hours, I said, "Let's go home."

We walked back without any angel sightings, or angel assassins, and had returned to the hotel to find Matiel still with Shay, which was good. I wanted her to have some time alone with her dad. I was sure she had lots to say about her school and her new friends.

They finally said their goodbyes, me just staring and not saying anything at all until Matiel did his angel exit thing and just vanished before our eyes. Then we all clambered back to the large apartment over Valen's restaurant, After Dark, and went straight to bed. My body was tight with tension in every step. The assassins hadn't found out where I lived yet, but I knew that wouldn't last.

I had no idea what to expect. I assumed they would resemble my father, meaning they would be more humanoid than perhaps a four-legged demon creature, though demons could also be humanoid in appearance.

But the truth was, they could look like anything or anyone. Take any shape they desired. They could jump me anywhere at anytime.

My phone beeped, and I grabbed it from the night table to see a new text message.

Catelyn: *You okay? You looked upset yesterday.*

Me: *Yes. Long story. Angel assassins are out to kill me. Tell you all about it later.*

Catelyn: *What? That's crazy. I'm here if you need me. We're staying for another couple of days or so.*

Me: *Thanks.*

I smiled. Strange how Catelyn had been my mortal enemy a few days ago, and now she was concerned about me. I was glad she was staying around for a few more days. I might need her help. One giant was good to have around. Two were even better while facing angel assassins.

I knew Elsa and Jade had been concerned at my less-than-usual enthusiasm about the party they'd organized for Shay, but I'd brushed it off as nothing as I'd headed out of the hotel. I didn't want to ruin their fun, though I knew I'd have to tell them sooner rather than later. If angel assassins were after me, I was going to need all the help I could get.

The silver ring my father had given me sat on the same night table, next to where my phone had been. I stared at it. It was large, a man's-size ring, and I doubted it would fit on my slim fingers.

Resolute, I tried every finger on both hands—my right fingers were slightly larger than my left—but in the end, the ring was loose on each finger.

"I do have big thumbs." I slipped the ring around my right thumb. It fit. "Well, there you go."

I sat there, staring at the ring, feeling... different? Was it just my imagination, or did I feel the slightest hint of electricity coursing through my veins and limbs? Or was my mind simply playing tricks on me? Was it only an imagined response to my father's claim that I would feel different?

After a record-breaking shower, I got dressed and found Shay eating her breakfast at the kitchen island.

She turned in her seat to look at me. "You're late."

"I didn't sleep well." I made a beeline for the coffee machine, thrilled that Valen had made a fresh pot. "When did Valen leave?"

Shay shrugged. "I don't know. Ten minutes ago?" She shoved a spoonful of cereal into her mouth.

I turned around and leaned on the counter. "Did you have a nice time with your—our father?"

Shay nodded. "Sorry about the assassins. That sucks."

I didn't know why, but I choked out a laugh, with some coffee spilling down the sides of my mouth to my chin. It sounded so absurd, so crazy, just as Catelyn had said, to have a guild of killer angels after me. Worse was not even knowing the real reason. Just that they were after me, to kill me. Swell.

Shay's face wrinkled at my reaction. "You're weird."

I wiped my mouth with a clean dish towel. "Isn't it wonderful? Take after my mother."

Shay blinked. "What are you going to do? About the assassins?" Her green eyes were focused on my new thumb ring.

It was my turn to shrug. "Not sure. I guess I'll have to beat on some angels."

"But what if they come during the day?" asked my little sister, clearly frightened.

Good question. "If I can figure out what about me threatens them, maybe I can make a deal."

Admittedly, it was lame, but I had thought about

this all night, trying to come up with ways to keep the angels from killing me.

"I can help," said Shay, her eyes round with that cute determination. "I have magic."

"I know." I tossed back the last of my coffee. "Let's go. We'll talk more on the way."

"Valen wants you to text him before we leave," said Shay as she hopped off her stool and walked over to the entrance.

I pulled out my phone.

Me: *Off to take Shay to school. I'll let you know if I see any angels.*

The three dots that followed told me the giant had his phone on him.

Valen: *I'm coming with you.*

Me: *No. I don't think they know where we are. Not yet. I'll let you know when I'm back.*

Valen: *Are you wearing your father's ring?*

I stared at the ring on my thumb, knowing it wouldn't do much good.

Me: *Yes.*

Valen. *Okay. Be careful.*

It took about eight minutes to walk Shay to school, me wishing I had eyes in the back of my head so I could see an assassin sneaking up on me, and Shay bouncing all the way to Fantasia Academy.

But as we arrived, and Shay dashed up the stairs to wave at me from the front doors, next to that oily, skinny male faculty member called Cosmo, no ninja angels had presented themselves. So far, so good.

I watched Shay disappear into the school building, feeling a sense of relief wash over me. I knew she was safe within those walls, but I still couldn't help but worry about her. After all, she was just a kid, and even though Matiel had said that the angel assassins were after *me*, it didn't mean they wouldn't use Shay to get to me.

I turned around to walk back to the hotel, my mind racing with the possibilities of what could happen next. I needed to find out as much as I could about the angel assassins, or just angels in general. The more I knew about my enemy, the more prepared I'd be when they came for me.

I'd admit it. I knew next to nothing about angels. I'd learned a hell of a lot more about demons since they were a constant nuisance, especially when the lower demons feasted on humans and paranormals. But angels? That was an entirely different beast.

And I had a lot of work to do. First, I'd check with the Merlin database and read everything they had on angels. If that wasn't enough, there was always the Gray Council archives here in New York City.

I texted Valen to tell him that Shay was safely at school, and I was on my way back. I knew the giant was worried about me, and he had every reason to be.

As I walked down Fifth Avenue, the sidewalk crowded with the bustle of humanity, I felt a sudden prickling at the back of my head—the feeling I usually got when someone was watching me.

I halted, my heart crashing against my chest as I spun around slowly, trying to detect where the feeling was coming from. A human woman bumped into me, mumbling a few curse words as she continued. I caught the words "bitch" and "idiot."

"Manners are free," I shouted back at her, and she proceeded to flip me the finger over her shoulder.

I love this city.

Apart from that assault, I couldn't sense any paranormal energies nearby. Just the regular human senses as New Yorkers went about their daily business. No angels, as far as I could tell.

I exhaled. "I'm losing my mind."

Despite this, I couldn't shake the feeling of being watched. That probably had something to do with Matiel's warning that assassins were hunting me. So, naturally, I saw them everywhere and nowhere.

"Yup. Still losing my mind."

I kept going. My senses were on high alert, knowing I didn't have much in terms of magic to protect myself. But I did have something, despite its size.

I raised my hand and stared at the ring that encircled my thumb. Nothing was special about it except for the pretty sigils etched into the metal. And it wasn't giving off any signals yet. I took that as a sign that the angel assassins hadn't found me. Yet.

With that in mind, I made my way back to the Twilight Hotel without incident, though still feeling the creepie-crawlies at the back of my neck. I rolled my eyes at myself. Losing my touch? Yeah, right. More like I was getting soft in my old age. Maybe I needed to switch to decaf and start knitting sweaters for my imaginary cats.

When I pushed open the hotel doors, I was greeted by the lobby's grandeur—high ceilings, lots of glass windows, and a blend of gray paint with rich red accents. As soon as I stepped inside, I felt a wave of magical energy wash over me. That familiar pulsing sensation reminded me that the area was protected by a ward.

"That's her!"

"Here she is!"

"I can see it already! Her face is perfect for the camera!"

I looked over at the commotion, and my eyes fell upon a small man with a puff of snowy hair and a matching white beard. He had round glasses perched on his nose, making his eyes appear abnormally large, like an owl's. His dark suit was striking against his pallid complexion. Basil, our hotel manager, and my boss. That, in itself, wasn't odd. What was strange was the way he was beaming at me. He *never* smiled at me. And now he stared at me like I'd just won employee of the month.

Okay, this was *so* wrong.

Next to him stood a cluster of three twentysomething paranormals. All females. The shortest one had a mass of brown locks tied in a messy knot on top of her head and glasses designed for someone twice her size. Next to her was a dark-skinned female with short hair who looked like she'd taken a pair of scissors and done it herself. The tallest was pale like she'd never set foot outdoors and had lived most of her life in an attic, spending her days with her nose in a book.

One thing was for sure. I'd never seen them before. They weren't tenants. Guests, maybe? Yet they were all gawking at me like they knew me.

Their eyes were bright with excitement, and their bodies practically vibrated with energy. Their faces lit up as they saw me. I felt a twinge of unease, not sure what was going on. It didn't take a genius to realize they weren't here for a room.

I clenched my jaw. Basil was up to something.

"Ah, Leana. There you are, my dear." Basil waddled over to me, his arms outstretched in welcome. Yeah. Like that had ever happened before. "I've been waiting for you for over a half hour. Where have you been?" He looked over his shoulder at the group of young females. His face stretched into another one of those false grins. They moved forward, following him as a unit, as though they were attached at the hip. Their eyes never moved away from me. Creepy.

I narrowed my eyes at the little witch. "You know I walk Shay to school in the morning. What's up? All that smiling must be hurting your face."

"What? Ha ha. You're so funny." Basil let out a false laugh that looked painful as he glanced at the group of young paranormal females. The energies they were emanating were a combination of witch and shifter.

"What's going on?" I asked, trying to keep my

voice steady, but their presence was starting to annoy me.

Basil chuckled, his eyes crinkling at the corners. "She's such a tough one, real rough around the edges." Again, with the fake laugh.

The trio of young females closed in on me like they'd just spotted a unicorn. Their faces were full of wonder, their eyes wide and unblinking and their mouths agape. They were so close, I could feel the heat of their breath on my skin. I got a real good whiff of their perfumes mixed in with the scent of wildflowers, wet dog, and possibly horse.

As they gazed at me with wonder, I couldn't help but feel like a prized exhibit at a zoo. I half expected them to start throwing peanuts at me as if I were a performing elephant.

Basil leaned forward and whispered, "Just go with it."

I gritted my teeth. "What. Did. You. Do?"

"Leana, I'd like you to meet Daisy, Dina, and Demi." Basil gestured to the group of females, though I had no idea who was who. I'd already forgotten most of their names.

"Hi!" They waved as a unit, still watching me with their disturbing gazes. I was going to have nightmares for weeks.

I opened my mouth to answer, but Basil cut me off.

"I have a proposition for you, my dear," he said to me. "An offer you can't refuse. You'll thank me for it."

I frowned, still not understanding what he was talking about. "What offer?" I asked, crossing my arms.

Basil beamed at me. "We're going to be on TV! Isn't it wonderful? We're showcasing the hotel and all of its splendor."

"It's my YouTube channel," said one of the girls, the small one with the glasses. *"The Supernatural Lounge."*

"Youtoo is what all the younglings are into these days," said a smiling Basil as he propped his hands on his hips.

I nodded. "Yes. I know all about YouTube. But isn't that more of a human social media platform? I didn't think we paranormals were into that?"

The same female nodded. "We are. Everyone watches it. We've got ten million subscribers. We put on a weekly show."

"Huh." I watched the group closely, knowing that whatever this scheme was, it would be bad for me. "I still don't understand what's it got to do with me." And why did I get the feeling I was about to hate it?

"Leana. Hey." I turned my head to see Jimmy rushing over, a dark suit wrapped around his lean frame. His hair gleamed in the lobby light, and his eyes were wide and apologetic. "Sorry. I wanted to warn you."

I frowned. "Warn me about what?"

As one, the three females pulled out what looked like their cell phones suspended by those selfie sticks —all aimed at me.

Basil flashed his teeth my way. "Everyone will want to stay at the Twilight Hotel after this. We'll have to turn guests away," said the hotel manager, and he clapped his hands a little too enthusiastically. "You're the new face of the Twilight Hotel."

Oh, crap.

"We're here to make an episode on the Starlight witch," said the one with the glasses as she stepped forward, shoving her phone in my face. "And you, Leana Fairchild, are going to be the star!"

Well, fuck me.

CHAPTER 3

When the group of young females had said they wanted to film an episode with me for their *YouTube* channel, I had no idea it meant they would be following me *everywhere* I went. I had three new shadows.

It was as if I had my own personal paparazzi, except instead of being hounded by the likes of TMZ, I was being followed by a group of intense young women armed with iPhones.

Which explained why they were in the elevator with me, filming me with the video app on their phones as we ascended. I always thought of myself as the boring, introverted type. Nothing was special about what I did on a daily basis. Okay, well, that wasn't entirely true. Since I came to stay at this hotel, my life hadn't stopped being eventful.

Still, I wasn't one to like being filmed. Hell, I didn't even like to have my picture taken. This was all very surreal and foreign to me.

And I hated it.

Besides, I was a very private person. I didn't want strangers getting a glimpse of my life.

"I'm not doing it," I'd told Basil before stepping into the elevator. "Find someone else."

Basil's face turned an ugly shade of red. "You *are* going to do it," he said through his teeth and fake smile. "Because if you don't, you're fired."

My lips parted. "You can't fire me for not wanting to have some strangers following me everywhere with their phones in my face. I have rights." Not sure I had a case, but I was throwing it out there.

The hotel manager narrowed his eyes and pointed a grubby finger in my face. "You listen here," he said, his voice carefully low. "This is the best promotion for the hotel money can buy. The Gray Council's on board. Everyone's on board. And you'll be on board if you still want to have a job."

Irritation flared, and I imagined grabbing the tiny white witch by the neck and squeezing—really, really hard. "Some things about my life need to be kept secret. I don't want the entire world to know who I am."

"Everyone knows you're a Starlight witch," said the same female with the glasses.

"It's not a secret anymore," said the one with the dark skin.

"You see." Basil raised his brows in triumph. "Everyone knows who you are. So there's no issue here. And they're interested. They're interested in you and what you do for the hotel. And you're going to be polite and let these girls follow you. Give them all they want. That's an order."

An order? That's it. I was going to strangle him. "And if I don't?" I saw Jimmy shifting uncomfortably from the corner of my eye.

Basil slid a finger across his neck. "You will," was all he said to me. He spun around and addressed the young females. "I look forward to seeing us on TV." And then he was gone.

"I'm really sorry about this," said Jimmy, his voice low so only I would hear.

"It's not your fault."

"Uh…"

I stared at the assistant hotel manager. "Jimmy?"

Jimmy's cheeks darkened as he stared at the floor. "It was my idea."

I swore. "Please tell me you're joking." I liked Jimmy. I cared about him, but I was about to strangle him too.

He shrugged. "I saw their channel. I thought it would be good promotion for the hotel. You know, I'm always looking for ways to promote the hotel. I never thought they'd want to focus just on you. If I'd known Basil was going to force you, I would have never mentioned it."

"Too late for that." I glared at Jimmy, whose face was apologetic, and marched across the lobby, my temper on the verge of exploding. I felt it slip as the three females piled into the elevator with me, all smiles and intrigue.

After a moment, the elevator dinged, and the

doors slid open. I stepped onto the thirteenth floor, cringing on the inside as I saw the regular tenants wandering about.

"Okay, people," said the same girl with the glasses, and I turned around to look at her over my shoulder. "This is where the magic happens," she said into her phone's camera. Her eyes widened as she added, "This is the thirteenth floor."

She moved her selfie stick around, showing the hallway and doors. "This is where Leana battled all those demons single-handedly and where she saved all these poor, pathetic lives." Again, she moved the camera over a few confused tenants. I caught sight of Barb rushing into her apartment and slamming her door. Smart witch.

Technically, the battle had happened on the roof, but I wasn't about to correct her.

The same paranormal female snapped her fingers at the other two. "Dina. Demi. Get some interviews with those two," she said, pointing to a confused Mr. and Mrs. Dankworth.

"Should you be doing that?" I asked who I presumed was Daisy with the glasses. "They didn't sign up to be on your channel. You need their permission. Right?"

Daisy pushed up the glasses on the bridge of her nose. "My viewers want to experience what it's like to be the Starlight witch in this hotel. We need to interview real people and hear their stories. Hear what they say about *you*."

The fact that she didn't answer my question

wasn't lost on me. I looked over at Mr. and Mrs. Dankworth. Seeing their confusion and unease only strengthened my anger toward this group, but I bit my tongue. Would Basil fire me if I tossed them off the roof? Probably. I needed my job. I needed the money.

I let out an exhale that sounded more like a growl and marched across the hallway to my old apartment.

I crossed the apartment, making my way to my desk near the window. I glanced around, seeing only Julian in the living room. Jade and Elsa were not here. Good. I needed to sit down and do some work, find out everything I could about angels, which was something I should have done a while back when I first discovered I had an angel father. But life had a way of keeping me distracted. Like fighting off Dark witches and crazy sorceresses and trampires. Those kinds of distractions.

I had a group of at least ten angel assassins on my tail, well, according to my father. I needed to know if angels had any weaknesses, something that could help me defeat them. My dearest papa could have helped in that department, but he'd just vanished after spending time with Shay, and I didn't know when he'd be back—or *if* he'd be back. I knew just showing up this time had been difficult, which meant I was on my own.

I pulled out my chair and sat down at my desk, the leather chair creaking under my weight. I reached for my laptop, opened it up, opened a browser, and logged on to the Merlin database.

I typed "angel weaknesses" into the search bar and began scrolling through the pages of results.

"Who are your shadows?" asked Julian as he looked over from the couch. "And why are they filming us?"

Damn it. Part of me wished they'd stayed in the hallway. I turned in my seat to answer, but Daisy beat me to it.

"We're from *The Supernatural Lounge*," she said as she strolled through the apartment, her voice filled with conviction like they were a household name. "We're doing an episode on Leana." Dina and Demi crowded around her, though I still didn't know who was who.

Julian turned in his seat to face them. "I've heard about you. Yeah. I've seen your show. The one with the boogeyman in that kid's closet. Man, that was some scary shit. It was awesome."

"We know," answered Daisy.

I had to resist the urge to roll my eyes. Oops. I rolled them.

Daisy carefully turned on the spot, aiming her cell phone's selfie stick like a sword. "This is where Leana used to live. And this is where she'd cook her meals, and here is where she used to sleep." She stepped into my old bedroom, Dina and Demi right behind her doing the same thing with their phones.

I didn't live here anymore, but I still felt like this was a violation of sorts. Invasion of privacy.

"This is the bed where Leana and that *hot* restaurant-owner giant got busy," I heard Daisy say, followed by the giggles from the other two.

Heat rushed to my face. Okay, so they'd done their research. I wasn't thrilled that they knew about Valen and me. I didn't think he'd like having his paranormal race discussed so openly like that—to ten million viewers, no less. Granted, most of those viewers were humans who thought the show was rigged, obviously. Still, I was certain they also had paranormal viewers like Julian.

Daisy stepped out of my old bedroom and made her way over to Julian. "Can you tell the viewers who you are and what your relation is to Leana?"

A smirk materialized on Julian's face, the type of expression he had probably mastered over time to charm women into showering him with their undergarments. "Julian. And I'm a friend. I also happen to be an *excellent* potion-and-poisons witch. But I have many *other* talents."

Now I rolled my eyes openly.

"So, you and Leana battle demons together? What's that like? Our viewers want to know," asked Daisy, her phone in Julian's face, though the witch didn't seem to mind it at all. In fact, if I were to guess, it looked like he was enjoying himself.

Julian cocked his head to the side, looking smug. "A few times, I didn't think we'd make it."

"Really?" Daisy snapped her fingers at Dina and Demi, and the two females rushed over and pointed their phones at Julian.

"Tell the viewers about that," continued Daisy. "Tell us how you barely escaped the clutches of a great *horned* demon."

I spun back around and ignored Julian's response. I was glad he was taking over. I didn't mind at all that he loved all the attention, but I hated attention. I also had the feeling he knew this and was helping me by giving the ladies what they wanted for their episode.

I stared at the computer screen. Surprisingly, the Merlin database had more information on angels than I thought. I learned there were three different types of angels. First, were regulars, like, say, my father, who were sometimes considered guardian angels, responsible for the well-being of humans and all other beings such as us paranormals.

Next, were the archangels, which were of the highest rank. They governed and served as commanders in the Legion of Angels and made up the Council of Ministers.

And then there were the assassins.

I couldn't find where it said if they were regular angels or archangels. Archangels were more powerful, so having archangel assassins wasn't going to be easy. Not that regular angels would be, but you get the general idea.

The more I read, the more I realized that angel assassins were basically just that—angels hired to kill. More like ordered to. The only difference was that they were trained in the Assassins Guild of Angels.

As I delved deeper into the texts, my heart raced with fear and curiosity. The Assassins Guild of Angels were known for their deadly skills and unwavering loyalty. Awesome.

I couldn't find much on angel weaknesses. A passage read "Though immortal, if an angel loses its soul, it would die a true death." What the hell did that mean? I found another small section discussing some weapon that may or may not kill an angel.

The Merlin database didn't give me much. Looked like I might have to pay the Gray Council archives a visit.

It wasn't like the Assassins Guild of Angels had a headquarters in the city, either, where I could just show up and argue my case. Did I even have a case? I still had no idea what I'd done to deserve a death wish. I was part angel. So freaking what? From my understanding, Shay and I weren't the only ones. Angels had been bumping uglies with humans and paranormals for thousands of years. It wasn't a recent thing. So why all the attention on me? What made me different from all the other half-angel offspring? Nephilim, or whatever?

I didn't know, but I wasn't going to find out.

"Why are you doing research on angels?"

I jumped in my seat. Daisy leaned over my shoulder, her phone roaming over my laptop screen. I'd never heard her approach. Being that close to her, I could get her witchy readings. She was a witch. A Dark witch, from the light vinegar aroma rolling off her.

I leaned back and glared at her. "That's none of your business." The last thing I needed was a group of strangers interfering with my work. Or rather, my life.

"Our viewers want to know," she replied, like my comment had no merit. "Why angels? Have you seen an angel?" She pointed her phone in my face.

"No."

"Are you looking for an angel?"

"No."

"That's not what it looks like to me." Daisy looked over her shoulder and motioned for Dina and Demi to come over.

"I don't care what it looks like to you."

"She's looking for an angel," said Daisy, talking over me.

"No way," said the dark-skinned one leaning over with her phone. "So angels are real?"

"Angels are *so* real," said the other pale female as she joined her group at my desk. "Leana. Tell us what it was like to meet a real angel. Our viewers want to know."

"Your viewers want to know?" I clenched my jaw. Basil might have given them carte blanche to follow me around, but they didn't have permission to all my life details. I wasn't about to share with the world my angel origins.

I opened my mouth to politely tell her to fuck off, but a voice beat me to it.

"What's going on here? Barb said there were journalists?" Elsa stormed through the front door, her posture erect and authoritative. She wore a pleated green skirt, orange garden clogs, and her reading glasses stabbed into the top of her blazing red hair.

The three—let's call them YouTubers—abandoned me and met Elsa with their phones aiming at her like wands.

"We're from *The Supernatural Lounge*. Maybe you've seen our channel on YouTube," informed Daisy.

Elsa looked like she was trying to decide whether she knew what YouTube was or not. "I don't recall, no."

"And *who* are you? What's your relationship with Leana?" Daisy placed her phone right up in the older witch's face like she was looking for blackheads.

"Our viewers want to know," said the paler one, who was either Demi or Dina.

Julian snorted. "This is awesome," he said and sipped his coffee.

I made my angry eyes and flicked a finger at him. "Don't you even start."

Elsa froze for a moment, and just when I thought she was going to tell them off for me—I loved her for these kinds of things—she smiled and brushed back a strand of her wild red hair. "How do I look?"

Oh, hell no.

"Amazing. Your red hair is going to pop on screen," said the tallest of the group.

Elsa's cheeks touched pink. "Thanks," she said, raising her chin, one hand clamped around her locket. "My name is Elsa. I'm known on the thirteenth floor as the witch who speaks her mind and gets things done."

"Were you at the Battle of the Thirteenth Floor?" asked Daisy. When Elsa didn't reply, though she stared with a confused expression, Daisy added, "With the demons? You know, the battle of the demons here in the hotel?"

"Oh, right. Yes, yes, of course, I was there," answered Elsa, finally making the connection. "We fought side by side against those foul creatures."

"Who fought side by side?"

We all turned to see Jade rolling in on a pair of roller skates. Jade was dressed in her usual eighties' attire. Today she wore an acid-washed jumpsuit, and her blonde hair was pulled up with an over-the-top red bow.

The YouTubers and I stared at Jade as she pulled off a perfect pirouette and halted next to Elsa. Julian whistled appreciatively, but I just rolled my eyes —again.

"What'd I miss?" asked Jade, her eyes flicking over the YouTubers who were still gawking at her.

"Journalists," I said, my voice dripping with sarcasm.

Jade blinked and then, "Oh my god. I know you. I love you guys! You're from *The Supernatural Lounge*."

Yup, if one of us had to be a fan, Jade would be it.

Daisy and the other two didn't look fazed by Jade's fangirling. "Who are you, and what's your connection to Leana? Our viewers want to know."

Jade's face turned the color of the bow on the top of her head. "I... I'm... uh..."

Daisy frowned at Jade's lack of an answer. "The roller skates. What's up with that?"

"Umm." Jade stared at her skates. "I don't know. I like them. And they make me taller. What battle?"

Again, Daisy didn't seem interested in that answer. She grabbed her phone, tapped a few times on the screen, and then pointed it back at Jade. Yeah, she just deleted that section.

"Why is Leana researching angels?" Daisy inquired with a professional air.

"You're researching angels?" Elsa eyed me with that questioning frown I'd gotten to know over these past few months.

I pursed my lips. "Not exactly."

"Is it because of Shay?" Jade's brows were high on her forehead.

"Shay? Who's Shay?" Daisy pointed her phone my way.

"No one," I said, rising from my seat and getting ready to stuff those phones down each of their necks. I closed my laptop and moved away from the desk.

I was glad they didn't know of my little sister, and I was going to keep it that way. I narrowed my eyes at Jade, who clamped her mouth shut, clearly having understood my meaning. Shay was off limits to them.

The dark-skinned YouTuber flashed her phone in Jade's face. "Were you there at The Battle of the Thirteenth Floor?"

"Uh… the one on the roof?" came Jade's reply.

The three YouTubers lowered their cameras and conversed for a few seconds. And then, "Tell us about the battle of demons on the roof," said Daisy.

I kind of zoned out as Jade recalled the events of us on the roof, battling demons while trying to close the portal simultaneously. I made my way to the kitchen and poured myself a glass of water. I set the glass on the counter and stayed by the island, listening.

"Tell us more about this Rift. What does it do? Can it open at any time? The viewers want to know," said the dark-skinned female.

My temper was rising. I needed to work, do some more research on angels. I needed to pay a visit to the Gray Council archives. No way would I let these YouTubers come with me. They wouldn't even be allowed in. Nope. I needed to sneak out of here without them seeing me. I needed to find a way to ditch the three females.

I needed a distraction.

I met Julian's stare. He must have recognized that look on my face, the one that said, "I needed to flee," because the next moment, he nodded in the direction of the door.

Then the male witch cleared his throat and said, "I can tell you a lot more about that Rift."

At that, the three YouTubers turned their backs on me and hurried over to Julian to get his version of events.

It was the distraction I needed. *Thank you, Julian.*

Without a word to Elsa or Jade, I backed away slowly at first, but as soon as I reached the threshold of the apartment door, I bolted.

Laughing all the way down the hall like a crazy person, I jumped into the waiting elevator and pressed the lobby number.

Again, I laughed by myself all thirteenth floors down. Just as the elevator settled, the doors swung open, and I was running.

I didn't see Basil anywhere. I didn't even take a moment to harass Errol at the front desk. I just wanted out. To put as much distance as I could between me and those YouTubers.

I pushed open the doors and rushed out of the hotel. I should be talking to Valen. Yes. I needed to tell the giant about this group. At least to warn him.

I made for the restaurant, but something in the alley between the hotel and the restaurant gave me pause.

It wasn't so much a specific thing but more how it made me feel.

My new ring pulsed with heat and buzzed with energy.

A draft of the scent of citrus hit me. A woman, as far as I could tell from her slight build, stood in the alley between the buildings dressed in leather that reminded me of dragon scales. A long sword was strapped down the column of her spine. Yup. A freaking sword. Long, black hair spilled down her back past her waist. Her skin was fair, from what I could see. And just like my father, her skin gave off a brilliant glow, as though light illuminated her from inside.

An angel—correction—an angel *assassin*.

She hadn't seen me yet. She glanced from the hotel to the restaurant, her head cocked to the side like you'd see a dog do when it was trying to make sense of what its owner was telling it.

Suddenly, her body stiffened, like she'd sensed something.

And when she turned around and smiled, I knew that something was me.

CHAPTER 4

My father was the only other angel I'd ever encountered, so I had no idea what to expect. Except for the major fact that she was sent here to kill me.

Her face was human, blessed with unnatural good looks, and with the darkest eyes I'd ever seen. They were almost black. Her features and stare were unsettling, like how a mountain lion watched you from a tree before it leaped at you and went for your jugular.

She was shorter than me, but I doubted that would make a difference. This wasn't a normal foe. She was immortal. It was worse than facing a demon because I had no leverage. I didn't know how to defeat an angel. I'd never had to fight one before.

The angel female reached behind her back and pulled out her sword. "I thought I smelled the stink of Nephilim."

I gave my armpits a sniff. "I did sorta wing it in

the shower this morning. I might have forgotten a few bits."

I was a bit concerned at the prospect of some humans wandering our way or glancing into the alley to see some crazy woman with a sword. Guess I'd deal with it If it came to that.

Damn it. Here I was facing an angel, an angel *assassin,* and all I had on me were my clothes and my wits. If I screamed Valen's name, would he hear me? "What do you want?" I figured stalling for time was a good idea while I figured out a plan.

The angel assassin sneered. "To end you."

"Lovely."

I took a deep breath and tried to focus. I had to think of a way to defeat her or at least escape. I knew I couldn't fight her head-on, not with her sword and immortal strength. I had to use my brain. But at the moment, it was suffering from a major mental block.

"Why?" I asked, stalling for more time. Hey, you never knew. She might actually tell me why the Legion of Angels wanted me dead. I could work with that. My father hadn't given me much. A part of me wondered if he knew the real reason but wasn't at liberty to tell me.

The angel raised an eyebrow, holding her sword in one hand. The sides gleamed in the sunlight. "Why what?"

Hmmm. Had the legion sent me a daft angel? "Why do you want to end me? Look, if you're gonna smite me, could you at least tell me why? I mean, as far as I know, I've never done anything to your

Legion of Angels. Hell, I'd never even met an angel before I met my father just a few weeks ago. Maybe you've got it wrong?"

The angel looked at me as though I was a puppy who just peed on her expensive shoes. "Of course not. Because you're a Nephilim," she said, as if it was obvious.

I sighed. "I know that, but why does that matter? I'm not the only one. Why me?"

The angel just stared at me, her expression as blank as my bank account. "Because Nephilim are abominations. You are the offspring of angels and humans, a forbidden union that defies the laws of nature and God. You are a stain on the purity of creation, and you must be eradicated."

"You're just full of rainbows and sunshine this morning."

She smiled. Her grin chilled me on a hot morning. "I'm an assassin."

"So I've heard." I needed to get more out of her. "But I didn't choose to be a Nephilim. I was born that way."

The angel lowered her head. "I don't care."

I took a few steps back, my hands slowly moving to my sides as I looked over my shoulder to the street behind me. The human crowds didn't take notice of us. Too busy with their own lives to stop and watch what would appear to be just two women chatting in an alley. Although one with a sword.

I couldn't fight her with my magic or my bare

hands. So I did what any smart witch would do in my place.

I knelt and grabbed that rock next to my shoes, the size of my palm.

The angel laughed when she saw the stone in my hand. "What are you going to do with that?"

"This."

I let my stone fly. And by a miracle, it hit her right smack in the middle of her forehead with a thud.

"Ha!" I fist-pumped the air.

The stone fell to the ground with a dull thump. The angel blinked at me. Irritation flickered behind her dark eyes. "What was that? Did you think you could stone me to death?"

I shrugged. "If it'll work, hell, yes."

She grinned at me, her teeth unnaturally straight and white. "It won't."

I didn't reply, instead focusing on the task at hand. I had to stay alive long enough to figure out why this angel had been sent to kill me, and devise my escape.

But then the angel did something unexpected.

She reached around her belt, pulled out a long dagger, and tossed it at my feet. "I don't like to kill unarmed opponents. There's no honor in that."

I stared at the blade at my feet. "I like the way you think. But you shouldn't be trying to kill me. Period." With my eyes on the angel, I knelt and grabbed the blade. It was surprisingly light and looked as though it was sharp enough to slice through metal.

"We all live by a code," she answered.

"Yeah, no cheesecake after ten p.m." I knew the odds of me beating this angel weren't in my favor, even with the help of that dagger, but I wouldn't let this angel kill me without a fight. "I don't suppose I can talk you out of it? I can pay you. Whatever you want."

The angel let out a scornful laugh. "You cannot bargain with an angel assassin, Nephilim. Your fate is sealed."

I exhaled, shaking my head. "You know, I'm getting really tired of people trying to kill me all the time. I have a life, you know."

The angel cocked her head. "It is your destiny. You were born to die."

I frowned. Destiny? Fate? That was a bunch of bull. I refused to believe that I was just some pawn in a cosmic game. "Destiny can kiss my ass. I'm in control of my own life."

"We shall see." The angel smiled, and then she charged, her sword raised high. I sidestepped her attack, blocking what was surely a killing blow with the dagger, and then ducked and leaped back.

The angel paused, surprised by my move. She hadn't expected me to be skilled with a weapon apart from the magic I couldn't really use. I smirked, knowing I had just bought myself a little more time.

The surprise on the angel's face filled me with confidence. "Didn't see that coming. Did you?"

"You're not as defenseless as you look," she said,

a note of respect in her voice. "Good. This might not be so boring after all."

"Thanks for noticing," I replied, twirling the dagger in my hand.

The angel stared at me. "You will never win. You can't best me."

"Maybe not," I said. "But I'll die fighting."

The angel laughed, but it was a bitter sound. "It would be better to accept your fate and die quickly."

I tapped my lips with a finger. "Let me think about it—yeah, no."

"Suit yourself." The female angel lowered herself in an attack stance and lunged at me, sword swinging.

Oh, shit.

I knew I'd been lucky with the first round, so I did the only thing that came to mind.

I ran like hell.

I made it to one of the parked cars in the alley and used it to put some safe distance between us. When I looked up, the angel was already next to the car. She held her sword high, and she brought it down.

I felt the air move around my face, and the tip of her sword nearly brushed my nose as it came down hard on the hood of the parked car. I heard the sound of the tearing of metal, and then half of the hood collapsed.

Damn. That was some serious metal in that sword. And that could have been my face.

"Nice sword," I said.

The assassin smiled. "I know."

I stared at her from behind the mangled car. I was running out of options. My magic was useless against a being of pure divine power, and my physical strength was no match for the angel's superior strength and speed.

I knew I had to act fast.

"Ha!" I fake-karate-kicked with my leg, hoping to catch the angel off guard. She stumbled back, surprised by my sudden move. Taking advantage of her momentary confusion, I lunged at her with the dagger.

But the angel was quick. She parried my attack easily and kicked me in the stomach, sending me flying backward toward the alley. I hit the ground hard, feeling the breath leave my lungs.

The angel approached me slowly, a smirk on her lips. "You can't beat me, Nephilim," she said. "It's not your fault. You should have never been born."

I glared at her, refusing to show any weakness as I scrambled to my feet. "Fine. But I'm prettier."

Confusion flashed across the angel's face. "Your mortal beauty can't save you."

"No. But it was fun saying it."

I gripped the dagger tightly. Desperate, I called to the power of the stars, focusing on the energy of the stars high above me and feeling the energy coursing through my veins.

Yes! I lifted my hands, and... nothing. Not even a drip.

"Yeah. I got nothing."

The angel stepped closer. "Was that supposed to scare me?"

"No. But it was supposed to distract you."

With one swift motion, I lunged forward, trying to catch her off guard again. The angel reacted promptly, parrying my attack easily before countering with another swift kick to my chest. I stumbled back, trying to catch my breath.

The angel was ruthless, her movements fluid and graceful. I could barely keep up with her as she attacked again and again, her sword whistling through the air. I dodged and weaved, trying to find an opening but couldn't. She was too fast, too skilled.

And at any moment, I knew I was about to lose my head.

I thought of Shay at that instant. If I died, she'd lose a sister. But there was Valen. And I knew should anything happen to me, he'd protect her.

I barely had time to block the assassin's strike as she came at me without pause. I caught her sword with that dagger, blade on blade.

I kicked out my leg, and it connected, pain reverberating up my thigh. I knew I'd hit her hard. She yelped and stumbled back, and I spun around, avoiding the strike of her sword skewering me.

"So you *can* feel pain," I said. "Interesting."

In a burst of swiftness, the angel came at me, swinging her sword with a kind of vampire speed that was truly impressive. Her strikes were fueled with skill and precision, not anger and emotion. She was well-trained.

But I wasn't going to give up just yet. I had to find a way to turn this fight around. And then I saw an opportunity. The angel had left her side exposed for just a moment, and I seized the chance. I lunged forward, my dagger aimed at her heart.

But she was too damn quick. She spun around, catching my wrist with her free hand and slamming me against a parked car. Pain exploded through my body as my back hit the metal, and I cried out in agony. The dagger fell from my hand, clattering to the ground.

The angel pressed her sword to my throat. "You have lost," she said, her voice cold and emotionless.

I glared at her, refusing to give up. "How much?"

"How much?"

"How much did you get paid for my head? What do you get?"

The angel raised an eyebrow, intrigued by my words. "Your mortal mind wouldn't understand."

I hissed as her sword cut the soft flesh of my neck. "Not money. Power? Rank? Yeah. It's all about power and rank with you people. Isn't it?"

"Perhaps. But you'll never know."

And that's when things got worse.

"Leana!"

Shit. I craned my neck, looked behind the angel, and cursed.

Elsa and Jade came rushing into the alley. And following closely behind were the YouTubers, their phones and selfie sticks pointing in my direction.

Daisy snapped her fingers at the other two. "Quick. I don't want to miss a thing."

The young females got close and then halted, their feet planted as they directed their phones at us, just as I felt the clang of magic in the air. Jade and Elsa's magic.

I had no idea if the angel would attack others who weren't on her kill list. But if Jade and Elsa assaulted her, she would, without a doubt, retaliate.

The angel glanced over at the source of the disruption, her focus on me forgotten for a moment.

I took advantage.

I stomped on her foot, felt her sword slip from my neck, and lunged forward, my hands reaching for her eyes. She dodged effortlessly, moving with an agility that was beyond human.

"You're not even trying," she taunted, her sword glinting in the light.

"Trust me. I am." I gritted my teeth, feeling a pull of magic coming from the witches. "Stay back," I yelled at them. "You can't fight her."

"We won't let this shifter kill you," cried Elsa.

"She's not a shifter," I howled back. "She's an angel." I heard the intake of breaths from the witches and the YouTubers, but I kept my focus on said angel.

My victory was short-lived, though. The angel retaliated with a powerful blow that sent me crashing into the ground. I felt the breath knocked out of me, and I struggled to get back on my feet.

I knew I couldn't beat her. That was obvious. Not during the day, at least. And I feared the longer we were at it, the higher the chances were my friends would get involved and do something stupid. I needed to hide until the cover of night.

That's it.

I darted into the throng of humanity, bolted down the alley, and headed south.

"Leana!" I heard Elsa holler behind me as I sprang onto East Thirty-Ninth Street.

Footsteps neared, the assassin's footsteps, and I threw myself into the human crowd. Cars honked at me as I dashed across the busy street. A car slowed as I approached.

This was it. My opportunity to pull off a signature Hollywood car-hood-slide move.

I held my breath and sprang into the air, gauging the distance between me and the side of the car—

And missed.

The air left me as I hit the moving car with my gut.

Ouch.

"Get out of the street! You just scratched my car, you stupid bitch!" cried the owner of the car I'd just assaulted with my gut.

"Sorry," I wheezed, and wobbled my way to the other side of the road. Just as I reached the sidewalk, I turned around, having sensed the angel before I saw her.

Yup. She was smiling. The smile of a winner.

"Not sure what you tried there, but I believe you scratched that expensive car," she said, walking leisurely toward me.

"I felt a little reckless." I had nowhere to run now. I was screwed.

She raised her sword. "Time to die, Neph—"

A city bus came rushing through and plowed into the angel.

Whoopsie.

The bus put on the brakes, but by the time it stopped, it had moved another fifty feet.

I stared at the mangled body of the angel, not knowing how to feel about that. She *had* tried to kill me. It was why she was here. But she was an angel, and I had mixed feelings about that. What happened to people who kill angels? Well, technically, I hadn't killed her, but still. Yet, did angels even die? Weren't they immortal? Had her soul died when the bus ran her over? All these questions needed answering.

"Holy shit. You just killed an angel."

I glanced up to see the YouTubers rushing over.

"Quick, get some footage of the dead angel," ordered Daisy, snapping her fingers at her two friends.

I watched, sick to my stomach, as the two females started to film the dead body of the angel next to a group of human onlookers doing the exact same thing with their phones.

I shook my head. Something was seriously wrong with the world.

I turned away, disgusted by the scene.

"You think she's dead?" Elsa appeared next to me, slightly out of breath. Jade was staring at the twisted remains of what had once been the assassin, looking like she was about to be sick.

"I don't think anyone can live with a neck bent like that. Even an angel." I glanced at the angel's face again, smeared with blood, her lifeless, dark eyes staring at nothing. It had happened so fast, I was still trying to wrap my mind around what had just happened.

"Are you all right?" asked Elsa, her tone filled with worry.

"No," I said, my stomach churning. Because how could I be?

I'd just killed an angel.

CHAPTER 5

Okay, I killed an angel. Technically it had been an accident. The bus had killed her by running her over. But I'd played an inadvertent part in her death. She'd chased me across the street, paying no attention to the oncoming traffic, and it had cost her.

An assassin sent by the heavens to kill me, and now she was dead. Talk about a screwed-up turn of events.

As an immortal, I wasn't sure if she was *dead* dead, like she'd suffered her true death or whatever they called it. Perhaps just her human body had died, and she'd returned to get a replacement. The fact was, I didn't know how it all worked. Or maybe if she died on Earth, that was the end of the road for her? Who knew.

Still, I didn't have the luxury of time to ponder the specifics of angel mortality. If one assassin had already found me, the nine others would surely follow. I had to figure out a plan. I needed to figure out my next move because I knew this time I'd gotten lucky and cheated death, but the next time I wouldn't be so fortunate.

One thing was for sure. I was in serious trouble. Killing an angel was a big deal, even if it was accidental. Nobody killed angels. Angels were the good guys. But were they?

Despite my uncertainty, it wouldn't be long before other angels came after me, pissed that I'd killed one of their own.

We'd waited for the human first responders to arrive at the scene: me, Elsa, Jade, and the three YouTubers, who were still filming the gruesome scene, just as a handful of human onlookers.

I'd watched as the paramedics declared the angel female dead, hauled her broken body onto a gurney, and covered her up with a white sheet, which only made me feel worse. They had no idea she was an angel and that no one would come to claim her. But it also told me something important. Angels *could* be killed. Well, at least on this plane of existence, they could be put out of business.

"Let me get this straight," said Elsa, standing, facing me in the kitchen back at my apartment on the thirteenth floor. "That woman was an angel assassin sent by the Legion of Angels to kill you? Am I getting this right?"

"Yup." I set my coffee mug on the counter. "Number one. Nine more to go. Yay."

Jade blinked at me like I'd lost my mind. "How do you know all this?"

"Courtesy of my dearest angel father," I said and quickly recounted the events of last night when he'd showed up.

"That's why you'd left without saying goodbye." Elsa drummed her fingers on her coffee mug, a frown formulating on her forehead. "And he can't help you? At all?"

I shook my head. "Doesn't look like it."

Elsa exhaled. "What's the use of having an angel father if he can't even protect you from his own people?"

Good question. "That's what I'd like to know." I pulled out my phone and texted Valen.

Me: *Need to speak to you. It's important. Hotel apartment.*

Jade leaned her elbows on the counter. "How did they find you so fast?"

I'd thought about that. "I don't think they did. I have a feeling they've been looking for me for a while now. Maybe they followed my father's essence? Who knows. But more will come. That I know for sure."

"And they're not interested in Shay?" Elsa was shaking her head as she threw those words around. "Strange how they want you dead, but your sister holds the real power. And you don't know why? Your father doesn't know?"

I sighed, not feeling the snub in my abilities and what a dud I was because it was true. "I'm not sure.

Part of me wants to believe him when he said he didn't know. The other part thinks he's lying through his teeth."

"Why would he do that? He loves you," said Jade as though that should be obvious to me.

I stared at her, not sure how I felt about that. I'd never heard those words being uttered before about my father. "He said it could be something about me that I haven't seen yet. Like something about me that hasn't manifested. I don't know. It sounds crazy. This whole thing is crazy."

"Could he be talking about magic?" asked Elsa, that quizzical brow returning.

"Could be," I answered, "but witches usually come into their powers in their early teens."

"Maybe you're a late bloomer," laughed Jade. "I was."

I snorted, though something was truly unsettling about the notion that something was different about me that I wasn't aware of. I didn't like it. And apparently, it was going to get me killed. Wonderful.

It wasn't as though I could reach out to my family to question them about that side of my DNA. With my mother's and grandmother's passing, I had no family left, except for Shay and Matiel. If there had been something about my mother's side of the family, I was at a loss. Yet I had a feeling it had more to do with the angel side, not the witch side. But who knew? I might be wrong about that.

"Does Shay know?" Elsa's gaze was intense. "About the assassins?"

I nodded, feeling my chest squeeze at the thought of what that little girl had gone through recently. "She was right next to Matiel when he told me. I won't tell her about this incident. I don't want to scare her. She's been through enough. She needs normalcy back. At least for a little while. Please don't mention it to her."

"We won't," agreed Jade, nodding in Elsa's direction, who gave a nod as well.

"Thank you." I bit my lip, trying to control the frustration building inside me. "There has to be something. Some way to protect myself. Like a spell or something?"

Elsa hesitated before speaking again. "There might be a way."

I straightened my back, intrigued. "What is it?"

Elsa tapped her mug before answering. "It's a protection spell. It will make you *invisible* to the angels. Well, from what I heard."

My heart started racing. "I take it you've never done this before."

"No."

"But *can* you do it?" This was the best news I'd heard since my father first told me about the assassins guild.

She nodded. "I can. Yes. But it's not easy."

My phone vibrated, and I picked it up, seeing Valen's text.

Valen: *On my way.*

"It requires rare ingredients and a lot of power," answered the older witch.

"Can you guarantee the spell will work?"

Elsa shook her head. "No, I can't. I've never done it before, but I've read about it. And there's no spell I can't perform if done correctly. But even then, it's not a guarantee. The angels are powerful beings who might find a way to break through the spell. I just don't know."

I weighed the pros and cons in my mind. On the one hand, I needed protection. On the other hand, I didn't want to put myself or anyone else in danger. But what choice did I have?

I leaned forward, ready to take the risk. "I don't care. I need protection. I can't live my life looking over my shoulder and waiting for the next assassin to come after me. I need to take control of the situation. I'll do whatever it takes."

"Me too," said Jade. "I mean… I want to help."

I gave Elsa a smile. "I have faith in your abilities. I really do. You can do this," I told her, but it was more for me than for her. "If it can shield me for a few days and give me time to figure out why they're hunting me in the first place, I'll take it."

Elsa splayed her hands on the counter, her expression serious. "Okay," answered the witch. "I'll get right on it. I'll need time to gather the ingredients. In the meantime, you should lay low. Don't go out unless it's absolutely necessary."

I wanted to tell her that angels could just as easily come inside but thought better of it.

"But remember… once it's done, it only lasts for a limited time."

"That's fine," I said quickly. "If it can give me a few hours a day, that's good enough."

Jade cocked her head. "What are you going to do?"

I bit my lower lip. "Not sure. My father can't help, and it's not like I can contact him for anything. What I need is to ask another angel why they're after me."

"And how do you plan on achieving this?" asked Elsa, her brows skeptical.

It was the only thing I thought about after facing the angel female. "The way I've always done it. By winging it." I took a breath, waited until I had their full attention, and then said, "I'll have to trap the next angel assassin."

Elsa's mug exploded with a loud crash as it hit the hard floor. "Cauldron help us. She's lost her damn mind."

"I haven't. I thought it through." Not exactly, but I had been throwing around the idea in my head at the sight of the dead angel.

"You're not serious?" Jade stared at me like I'd just torn up her Duran Duran poster.

"I am." My pulse throbbed with excitement as my plan formulated before my eyes. "It's the only way. I'll trap them and force them to tell me *why* they want me dead. I need to know. And once I know, I'll be able to make sense of all of this and maybe get the legion to stop hunting me. Maybe we can make a deal."

"We don't *make deals* with celestial beings," said Elsa.

"I will."

"I don't like it." Elsa muttered a spell under her breath. The air chimed with magic as the shattered pieces of her mug rose from the floor, proceeded to the wastebasket next to the kitchen sink, and dropped into the bin. "How do you plan on doing this? Angels aren't stupid. And these ones are trained assassins."

"I'm going to use myself as bait."

Elsa cursed, and Jade smacked her forehead with an open palm. Hard.

"This plan of yours is getting worse each time you open that mouth," accused Elsa.

I leaned forward. "It's going to work. But obviously, I need to do it at night. I barely escaped today." I looked at Elsa. "So as soon as you have that spell for me, I'll use it during the day, and then I'll set my trap at night. Maybe even tonight. Yes, tonight."

"Do you want to die?" Elsa's voice was dangerously low.

"No."

"What's the rush? Can't you wait a few days?"

I shook my head. "No. I might not have a few days." I pointed out the window. "Another angel assassin might be coming at me in the next ten minutes."

Jade groaned. "Don't say that."

"It's the truth. My time is running out. And the sooner I trap an angel, the sooner I can get some answers. And the closer I'll be to figuring out what the hell is happening."

The two witches looked at me. Concern etched on their faces. I knew they cared about me, and I appreciated their caution, but I couldn't let fear hold me back. I had to be proactive and take charge of my own fate. Damn it.

Jade sighed. "I hope you know what you're getting into."

"I do," I lied firmly. "Look. I have to try something. I can't just sit around and wait for them to kill me. Grab life by the balls and all that."

Elsa crossed her arms, looking skeptical. "And how do you plan on luring them into this trap of yours?"

"I haven't thought of that yet," I said, a sly smile spreading across my face. "I'll have to fight them. That's obvious."

Jade's eyes widened. "You're going to fight them?"

I nodded. "A fight is inevitable. They won't come willingly into my trap."

Elsa shook her head, but I could see the glint of admiration in her eyes. "You're brave. I'll give you that. But stupid."

I stood up, feeling energized by their support. "I have to be."

"Stupid," repeated Elsa.

"I can't keep living in fear. I need to take control of my life."

"I don't like it either," added Jade. "It's too dangerous. What if you get hurt? Or worse, what if they kill you? These are angels. Powerful beings."

I shook my head. "I know. I won't let that happen. I'll be careful. Plus, I'll have you guys watching my back."

"But what if they're not alone?" asked Elsa, worry outlined on her face. "What if they have backup?"

"I'll deal with it," I said confidently. "It's not like I have a choice. I have to do this."

Jade sighed. "I don't like it, but I'll support you. I'll help in any way I can."

"Thank you," I said, feeling grateful for their willingness to help me. I was blessed to have found such good friends.

Elsa nodded. "And I'll finish the spell as soon as possible. But, please, be careful. Don't take unnecessary risks. And don't do anything stupid."

I grinned at them. "Me? Stupid? Never."

Jade laughed. "You're more out there than an eighties' perm."

With a plan in place, I felt better, determined. I was going to trap an angel assassin and get the answers I needed. It was dangerous, risky, and possibly deadly, but it was the only way I could see an end to this madness. And with Elsa's spell, at least I had a fighting chance.

The sound of shoes hitting the carpet floor reached me. Daisy, Dina, and Demi came waltzing into the apartment. Their eyes zeroed in on us standing around the kitchen island.

"The Three Stooges are back," I muttered. I scowled at the group of young women who'd barged into my apartment. "I thought Jimmy had detained them," I whispered under my breath.

Jade's face wrinkled in suspicion. "Doesn't look like it."

"Leana. How does it feel to kill an angel?" Daisy marched right up to me and pointed her damn cell phone in my face. "Our viewers want to know." At my reluctance to answer, she pressed, "Tell our viewers."

"Fine. I will." I smacked her phone out of my face harder than I had thought. The device sailed across the kitchen and fell to the floor with a loud crash. Was it broken? Possibly. Guess what? I didn't care. She could bill me for it.

Without another glance at her, I walked away, my mind spinning with my so-called plans for tonight.

But there was just one major problem.

I'd have to tell Valen. And I knew he wasn't going to be happy about it.

CHAPTER 6

Valen walked into the apartment above his restaurant in less than three minutes. His posture was explosive, and I knew he was worried.

"What's going on?" asked the giant as he crossed the living room area and came to stand next to me by the window overlooking the street below.

I'd texted him again to meet me at "our" apartment instead as I'd stormed out of the Twilight Hotel. The YouTubers didn't follow. Good. My emotions were running high, and I couldn't be responsible for smacking their heads together. And I really, *really* wanted to do it.

I stared out the window. "I think I might get sued." I had only busted a phone, but you never knew. People were overly sensitive these days.

"What?"

I shook my head. "Nothing." I pulled my attention to Valen. "Listen. Something happened."

Valen looked me up and down, seemingly examining me for signs of bruises or injuries, evidence of the "something." "Does it have to do with the sirens I heard?"

"You do have good hearing."

"And?"

I took a breath and hooked a thumb at myself. "I killed an angel."

Valen's expression was unreadable. He just stood there, staring, and I wasn't sure that was any better than an explosive display. "An angel that came after you to kill you?"

"You *have* been paying attention." I rubbed my eyes, trying to rid myself of the image of the contorted angel body in the middle of the street. It wasn't working. I swallowed down the bile that rose in the back of my throat.

Valen grabbed my shoulders and spun me around. "Are you hurt? Did they hurt you?"

"Yes. No. I mean, *yes,* she hurt me. She nearly kicked my ass." And she would have killed me if not for some dumb luck.

Valen let me go. "So, how did you kill her?"

"I didn't." At his confused expression, I added, "The bus did. I ran into the street to try and get away from her because, you know, she was kicking my ass. And then she just got whacked by an oncoming bus. I wasn't sure angels could be killed that way. Turns out that they can." Which was good, in my case.

Valen let out a breath and rested his chin on my head. "You were lucky."

"This time," I answered, feeling a knot of nerves

along the back of my neck, "I don't think I'll get that lucky again. As soon as the other assassins learn what happened, it'll likely get worse."

Valen leaned back to look at me. "What can be worse than nine other angel assassins?"

I shrugged. "Fifty? A hundred? My father guessed they sent the best ten. That doesn't mean that's all they have. I'm pretty sure this Guild of Assassins has trained a lot more than just ten angels since they've been operational." Probably thousands.

Valen took a deep breath and ran his hand through his thick hair. "This is bad."

"No shit," I replied. "I mean, is that angel I fought today *dead* dead? Or does she come back later in a new body? All these things I wished my father would have told me before he took off again." I wasn't sure if he was being dismissive on purpose or if he truly wasn't aware of how this guild operated.

At that moment, I felt the same tingling currents as before, along my arms and legs, but now the sensation seemed to originate from my middle. Could this be the change my father had warned me about? But then again, it could be just cramps. Could be nervous diarrhea.

"You think you'll see him again soon?" asked my sexy giant.

I shook my head. "No. I think it was a struggle for him to come see us yesterday." My eyes went to the kitchen. "I need a glass of water." I walked to the kitchen and poured myself a tall glass of water. With all that fighting and running, I was parched.

"Did the ring help?" Valen crossed his arms over his chest, eyeing the silver ring wrapped around my thumb.

I swallowed. "A bit. All it did was pulse and give off a warm feeling. But that's it. Not like it could create a shield or a glamour to make me invisible to them. About that," I said, taking another sip of water. "Elsa and Jade are going to help with a spell that will make me invisible to the angels. Maybe not *completely* invisible but harder to track." Which was better than nothing. And I had a whole lot of nothing at the moment.

Valen just blinked, seemingly cool and collected. But I knew better. He carried that posture that was nothing but relaxed nonviolence until he struck out and pummeled you to death. Giant tempers.

I sipped the last of the water and put the glass in the sink. "It's going to take a while to finalize the spell. So in the meantime... I need to figure out what I'm going to do."

I still needed to bring up my super plan of trapping an angel, to Valen. I knew he wouldn't take it lightly. He'd probably try to talk me out of it too. Maybe bust a few walls in the process. But what else could I do?

Yup, he would hate it. So I just said it. "I have a plan."

Valen's eyebrow twitched.

Here we go. "The plan is... to trap an angel." I raised my hands in surrender at the storm brewing behind the giant's eyes. "Before you get all Neanderthal and start breaking things, hear me out. Okay?"

Valen's left eye started to twitch. Not a good sign.

"Trapping an angel is the only way I'll get answers since Matiel wasn't helpful. You were there. He doesn't know why the legion is after me, or at least that's what he says. Maybe he can't tell me more for whatever reason. Which leaves me without many choices."

A muscle pulled along the giant's jaw. Damn.

"I caught a Dark, chain-smoking witch before. How hard can trapping an angel be?" I laughed. He didn't.

"Okay. Bad example. The point is, I need to figure out why they're after me in the first place. And then I can hopefully put a stop to the bounty on my head. Without that, without knowing why, I'm screwed. I'll never be able to stop them. I can't live like that."

Valen's stance stiffened, and I could almost see the tension rolling around his shoulders. "What you're suggesting is crazy. No. Insane."

"Tell me about it, but I'm running out of time and options." I stared at Valen's deep, furrowed brow, noticing it sinking lower and lower.

"How will you set this trap?" asked the giant.

"By using myself as bait."

Valen took a breath through his nose. "But you don't know when they will appear. They can show up at anytime. Day or night."

"I know. But I am hoping they're having, like, a halo-meet since I've vanquished one. That I'm not as easy a target as they thought. Should give me some time to prepare." If I was right, and going with my gut, that meant I'd see another angel possibly tonight. And I'd be ready for it.

"How, exactly, are you going to trap an angel?"

I pursed my lips. "With a powerful spell. I've seen it in one of those old tomes from the Gray Council archive. The same book I used to summon Matiel." And failed. "It's not that complicated. A circle. A few sigils. You know… the usual." I smiled, trying to lighten the mood. It wasn't working. I didn't mention the part where the angel subject would have to step *into* the circle for the trap to work. Mostly because I still hadn't worked out that part yet.

Valen was shaking his head. "I don't like this."

"Neither do I. But it's the only way. Please let me know if you have any bright ideas to share."

A knock came from the door, and we both stiffened.

A growl sounded from Valen's throat, and if I didn't know any better, I would have guessed him a werewolf.

"Ease down, big boy." I raised a brow at the giant. "I doubt an angel assassin would knock. It's probably Elsa or Jade." Had they finished the spell? That would be great.

I made to move to answer the door, but Valen stepped forward and got to the door before I'd made two steps out of the kitchen.

The giant swung open the door.

Daisy, Dina, and Demi stood on the threshold.

The three females all went wide-eyed as they took in the giant's impeccable physique, rugged good looks, and that incredible alpha vibe he gave off. It was almost a cologne and very irresistible to us females.

Daisy blinked a few times, like bringing herself out of her stupor, and pointed a phone with a cracked screen in Valen's face as she said, "Are you the giant Valen? Leana's boyfriend? What's it like to be a giant? Our viewers want to—"

The door slammed in her face.

Valen proceeded to lock the door before turning to face me.

A snort escaped me. "That was awesome. You're incredibly hot while slamming doors in the faces of those pretty young women." Women who were half my age with perky breasts, tight bodies, and cellulite-free thighs. Yeah, that made me all warm and tingly inside.

A sly smile formed on Valen's lips. "Mmm. How hot?" The giant prowled closer, his low tone sending my skin ablaze with goose bumps.

I grinned, rolling my eyes over his muscled, immaculate body. "Damn hot."

As I stared up at Valen. I couldn't help but feel a little intimidated by his broad chest and bulging muscles. I mean, I wasn't used to being with someone who could crush me like a grape if they wanted to, but it was also *very* exciting.

But as he leaned in for a kiss, I forgot all about his size and got lost in the moment. His lips were soft and surprisingly gentle for someone so big. He was also extremely talented with that tongue. My eyes practically rolled into the back of my head.

"Who knew giants were such good kissers," I said, pulling away momentarily to catch my breath, my lady bits pounding.

Valen chuckled, his deep voice rumbling through his chest. "You haven't been with the right giant," he said, pulling me back for another kiss.

I wrapped my arms around his massive shoulders, feeling tiny in comparison. "Well, I guess I lucked out, then," I said around his mouth.

Valen let out a snarl as his dark eyes filled with mischief. "You haven't seen nothing yet," he said, leaning in to kiss me again.

"I'm not that easy," I scolded, pushing him away playfully.

The giant flashed me his teeth. "I know you want me."

"Nope," I teased, stepping away from him, but I couldn't stop the grin from spreading across my face or the throbbing from my nether regions.

Valen stalked toward me. He had this predatory glint in his eye that never failed to send shivers down my spine. I liked it.

I let out a squeal as I ran around the kitchen island, knocking over a stack of cookbooks as Valen growled playfully behind me.

"Come here, you little minx," he said.

"Come and get me, giant." I giggled as I ran toward the couch, narrowly avoiding an end table.

"Oh. You bet your sweet ass I will." Valen

laughed, his eyes twinkling mischievously, and then he lunged.

Clever and agile as the witch I was, I tried to leap over the couch, missed, and fell face-first into the cushions with my butt in the air. Not exactly the dismount of a sexy champion but certainly memorable.

A hand slapped my ass. "You're making this *way* too easy," said the giant.

The next thing I knew, strong arms grabbed my waist and hauled me up, and I was crushed against a rock-hard, warm chest, his lips hot and eager as they met mine.

"Gotcha," he whispered, nuzzling my ear before planting another kiss on my neck that had me purring like a cat.

For a moment, I forgot about everything else. The world narrowed down to the taste of his mouth, the feel of his body against mine, and the way his hands roamed over my skin with an intensity that left me breathless.

Then my foot slipped on the rug, and we both went tumbling backward, crashing onto the couch. I couldn't help but burst out laughing as we landed in a tangle of limbs, my hair spilling over his face.

Valen grinned up at me, his eyes shining with amusement. "I see you're trying to make this interesting," he said, his voice low and husky.

"I'm an interesting witch."

He chuckled and leaned in to kiss me again, one hand sliding up to cup my breast through the fabric of my shirt. I moaned into his mouth, arching into his touch, and he took that as a cue to deepen the kiss. I could feel his arousal pressing against me, and it only made me want him more.

Valen's hand slipped beneath my shirt, tracing the lines of my curves as his lips moved down my neck. "You're so beautiful," he whispered, his breath hot against my skin.

"You're not so bad yourself," I teased, straddling him.

Valen's hands roamed freely over my body as we kissed fervently, our bodies pressed tightly together. "I've been waiting all day for this," he breathed, his voice heavy with desire. He rolled off me, scooped me up into his arms and carried me to our bedroom.

"The way you move your tongue like that… are you sure you're not a vampire?" I joked, running my fingers through his messy hair.

Valen grinned down at me, his eyes dark with desire as he set me on the bed. "Positive. Just a very, very good kisser."

He wasn't wrong. I laughed and pulled him in for another kiss, our bodies melding together as we made love with wild abandon. The room was filled with the sound of our moans and the creaking of the bed as we explored every inch of each other's bodies.

And for a little while, all thoughts of angel assassins evaporated from my mind.

For a little while.

CHAPTER 7

"Are you hungry?" asked the sexy male specimen in our bed.

I rolled over on my stomach, admiring those dark, intense eyes. "After all that work? Yeah. I could eat."

Valen gave me a smug smile. "I'll be right back." The giant swung his muscled legs out of bed, and I couldn't look away from his sculpted, naked body. Trust me. You would have looked too. "I've got some really nice Sicilian pasta downstairs that I think you'll like," he said, tugging up his jeans.

I propped my head on my arm to get a better view. "Hurry up. I'm not finished with you."

Valen flashed me one of those smiles that made my blood sizzle and my heart squeeze. I'd never get tired of those smiles.

"Be right back." The giant grabbed a shirt and disappeared out the door.

I lay back as I heard the apartment door shut, feeling a bit more relaxed and surprisingly focused after the round of scream-at-the-top-of-my-lungs sex I just had. Apparently, multiple orgasms are good for clarity. Who knew?

As I lay there, my body still vibrating with the aftermath of those happy endorphins, I checked my phone. The digital clock said two forty-three.

"Time flies when you're having fun," I mumbled, dropping my phone back on the night table.

I swallowed, my throat dry, most probably because of all that screaming. Never in a million years did I think that one day I would meet such a kind, clever, and faithful man whose skill in the bedroom had to be considered wizardry. But here we were, together. And I couldn't be happier.

Smiling like a fool, I hauled my legs off the bed and ventured into the kitchen for a glass of water. Seeing the same glass I'd used before, I filled it up and took a sip.

The floorboards creaked behind me, and I flinched.

"Back so soon?" I asked, turning around.

Okay, this was when things turned weird.

First off, it *wasn't* Valen standing in the kitchen. It was a stranger, a male stranger.

And as the scent of citrus and the cold, familiar energies hit me, I knew he was an angel.

The second part? I was buck naked. Yup. All my bits enjoying the apartment air.

Then I realized my father's ring hadn't given me a warning. I checked my hand. The ring wasn't there.

It must have slipped off my sweaty thumb and was somewhere in the bed.

The angel male snickered as he observed my naked body. Had I been in my twenties, I would have been mortified about my nakedness in front of a stranger—a *male* stranger, no less. In my forties? I stuck out my chest, pressed a hand on my hip, and said, "You're early."

"You're naked," said the angel, that smile still lingering on his thin lips. He had slick black hair, matching dark eyes, and a three-piece suit that looked like it belonged to a Mafia boss from the 1940s. The exquisite suit contrasted his plain, can I say, ugly face. With a crooked nose, he looked like he had been in one too many fights. I couldn't see any weapons on him, but that didn't mean he wasn't carrying.

Crap. Now I was in a pickle.

"Let me guess," I said. "You here to kill me?"

"I am."

"News flash. I killed one of you this afternoon. I'm not so defenseless. Granted, I wasn't naked, but still. I offed one of you. That has to count for something."

The angel rolled his shoulders. "Aliel was weak. Her skills as an assassin were pitiful. Left much to be desired."

I thought she was a badass, but I kept that to myself. "Can I ask why? Why you want to kill me?" I doubted he would give me a straight answer, but I had to try.

"You can." The angel blinked. "But I'm not here to discuss the matters of you vile Nephilim. I'm just here to kill you."

"Wonderful." I set the glass of water on the counter, my heart pounding as I tried to figure out a way that would keep me alive until Valen came back. But I had nothing.

It looked like I would have to fight this angel— naked. Meh. It could have been worse. Like *he* could've been naked too. Now, *that* would have been worse.

The fact that I was naked didn't bother me. What bothered me was that I hadn't set up my angel trap yet. Damn.

But all thoughts of said trap evaporated as I went into self-preservation, self-defense, hell, *survival* mode. I reached out and pulled one of Valen's kitchen knives, the largest, from the knife block on the counter.

"That won't save you," said the angel, his voice annoyingly calm.

"Maybe not," I said, gripping the knife. "But I might stick it into you a few times. And that'll make me happy."

The angel laughed, actually laughed. "You're funny. I think I'll keep some of your teeth as trophies."

Ew. My lips parted. "You keep trophies of your marks?" That was seriously disturbing.

"All angel assassins do," he answered, like that

was obvious. "It helps us relive the experience over and over again."

"Like a serial killer who returns to the crime scene to get his thrills." This angel assassin was starting to creep me out.

The assassin reached into the folds of his jacket and pulled out a long, thin silver blade. His face twisted in wicked glee, like the idea of killing me brought him great joy.

I went down into a crouch.

The angel came at me.

I ducked and spun, slashing out with my kitchen knife at his abdomen. Pain exploded from my side and left arm as the angel tackled me. I slashed my knife out with a powerful stroke. My arm jerked, and I knew I'd hit something. I looked up to find the angel staring at the hole in his expensive jacket.

"Ha. And you said I was defenseless."

The angel regarded me calmly. "Never said that."

"But you were thinking it."

The angel stretched his mouth widely and showed off his pearly whites. He sprang at me with startling quickness, his eyes flashing. He leaped at me like a feral cat, slashing with his angel blade that could have severed easily through bone and flesh. I ducked past his blow, but not fast enough.

He brought his fist down onto my face. Stars plagued my vision as I stumbled. My cheekbone howled in pain. I reeled back and kicked with all my strength, hitting him in the knee. I heard a crack, and he stumbled back.

I felt the warm trickle of blood from my nose, and I blinked the wetness from my eyes as the shape of the angel came into focus before me.

Even with the angel essence that flowed in me, my starlights, I was no match for a full angel, much less a full angel assassin. He was way faster than me, stronger, and dodged my attacks with fluid ease like I was nothing but an annoying child.

My head throbbed, and I felt it swelling up like a balloon. I stumbled, barely aware of my legs that were miraculously still supporting me. A boot slammed into my stomach, and the air shot out of me. I fell to my knees and spat a mouthful of blood, but I was up in a heartbeat, still holding on to that kitchen knife, still naked.

"I'm going to cut out that pretty little throat," snarled the angel male, making a show of his sharp blade. "You understand? Half-breed bitch?"

I raised my blade to his face. "Yeah. Don't think so."

"I shall enjoy cutting up your pretty flesh," said the angel, taking a step closer. "Peeling it off you from the inside out."

"A peel does a girl wonders on her face." I flung the kitchen knife at his head.

The angel was so swift that it scraped his cheek rather than wedging itself between his eyes. Oopsie.

The angel touched his cheek. "Creatures like you give us angels a bad reputation. Lowering ourselves and bedding human females. But soon, you will be dead, and all will be well again."

"Creatures like me?"

"Nephilim are detritivores." The angel's expression changed. It was only for a second, but at that moment, I saw furious rage, arrogant pride, and violent bloodlust on his face.

Anger replaced my fear. "I could say the same about angels."

His upper lip twitched. "And after I kill you, I shall enjoy the fruit of what I was promised."

I spat the blood in my mouth. "How about a big… uh… *no*. Then I'll shove that fruit up your ass."

I stole a look over my shoulder to the window. If only it were nighttime, I'd have this damn halo freak on the floor, begging for his angel life.

The angel grinned. "The sun won't go anywhere for another six hours," he said, reading my thoughts. "You have no magic. No power. You have nothing, and you are nothing."

I shrugged. "I've always thought I had a great ass. That's something."

The angel twirled his blade. "Perhaps I'll keep it as a souvenir, along with your teeth."

Okay, gross. "I thought angels were supposed to be the good guys. Clearly you're not."

The angel shrugged. "Good. Bad. Right. Wrong. These words are subjective, no?" The angel paused for a moment before continuing, "It's all about perspective."

"Nope." I wouldn't agree with anything that came out of that angel's mouth.

"You talk too much, half-breed whore."

"You're the one who's talking."

"I'm going to enjoy cutting out your tongue." A low growl rumbled in the angel's throat.

I stifled a shiver. I knew he meant it. "Aliel might have been weaker than you, but at least she had more class."

I knew I had hit a nerve when the angel lost his smile. "You know nothing, Nephilim."

"Leana."

"And today, you will die, never knowing the real reason why."

I felt like my heart was going to explode. "So, tell me. Tell me why!" I shouted. My anger flared at the look of amusement on his face. I was really starting to hate angels.

The angel clicked his tongue. "I don't think I will. I'd rather you die like the ignorant mortal bitch you are."

I made a rude gesture with my finger. "You're a dick."

The angel sneered and then lunged for me again. Breathing hard with effort, I let my instincts flow and managed to avoid his killing strike. I dropped to the ground and rolled, tears in my eyes at the searing pain and fatigue in my body. How many minutes had gone by? Two? Three? Not nearly enough.

Sweat poured down my forehead and stung my eyes. A boot slammed into my stomach, and I cried out. Before I could move, the angel brought his fist down onto my face. Black spots exploded behind my eyes. I heard the angel laugh as I crawled on all fours like a beast, trying to escape.

He grabbed my leg and yanked me back. Struggling against the angel's grip, I kicked out, and by the goddess, I hit something solid.

With my legs free, I rolled to my feet, staggering as a wave of nausea hit me.

I was going to die. The angel was going to kill me. Play with me. At first, that part was obvious, but then I would die.

I would never know why the legion was after me. I'd never see Valen or Shay again.

Terror like I'd never felt before took over. As the angel neared, I kicked and punched blindly. Every movement was met with tremendous effort. My muscles burned with exertion.

The angel pulled back and sneered. "Give yourself over to me, and I promise a quick death."

"No, thanks. I'd rather go down fighting. I might not be able to defeat you, but I can, sure as hell, give you a few thrashings to remember me by."

The angel gave me an incredulous look. "You mortals always want to play the hero. It's pathetic. And so overdone."

My breath escaped my lungs in a slow groan, my lips trembling so hard I had to clamp down to keep the sound inside. My skin was sticky and wet with my own sweat and blood. I was so tired.

"It would be more honorable to give in and die," encouraged the angel. "Rather than..." He waved a hand at my naked body. "This."

"Screw you," I shouted.

"You are a mistake," he said in a tone of intense satisfaction. "And now I'm going to rectify that."

I heard the sound of shuffling footsteps, and I looked up to find Valen rushing forward. Magic sparks—literally—shot from his body as he transformed into his giant shape and lunged at the angel. Thank god his apartment's ceiling height was over twenty feet, giving the giant enough mobility, something that had occurred to me in the past as improvements he'd made to the building after he bought it.

The angel's eyes widened in surprise. The only time I'd seen it. And I even saw a bit of fear.

He raised his dagger, but it was all over even before it leveled with Valen.

Massive fists pummeled. It happened so fast. All I saw was the giant's fists making contact with the angel's head. In a blur of movement, the giant tossed the angel's body across the apartment. It hit the wall at an impossible speed, followed by a horrible crunching sound.

I stared at the angel, the angel's body, and the grotesque way his neck was bent at an impossible angle, the side of his face smashed like a strawberry pie. Yup. Valen had killed him.

I pressed my hands on my hips. "'Bout time you showed up," I said, coughing. "I'm starving."

CHAPTER 8

"It's a body spray?" I lifted the bottle in the moon's light, seeing a fluorescent pink liquid inside.

"I prefer body *mist*," said Elsa, her locket around her neck glinting in the moonlight.

Jade nudged Elsa. "The pink was my idea. No one wants to spray their bodies with poop-brown liquid."

I gripped the bottle in my hand. "And when I spray myself with this… stuff, it'll make me invisible to angels? Over my clothes?" Not sure why I asked that. It was obvious that I wouldn't strip down naked to spray myself. Or was it?

Elsa flicked a finger at me. "This *stuff* is called Angel Repellent."

"Like mosquito repellent?" I laughed.

"I came up with the name," continued the older witch, ignoring my comment. "Barb and I worked all day on this."

"And me," interjected Jade.

"And Jade." Elsa pointed to the bottle. "You'll feel a little tingle at first. Maybe a sting like when you apply glycolic acid to your face."

"You made me acid in a bottle?" I stared at her.

Elsa rolled her eyes. "Of course not. But for the spell to work, you'll feel some minor tingling. That's all. Only a few sprays. Three will do. And you'll be invisible to angels."

I grinned, impressed. I didn't doubt Elsa's magical abilities, especially not when adding Barb and Jade to the mix. I knew this stuff was going to work.

"How long will it last? This angel repellent?" If it helped keep me hidden from angels, I'd bathe in it.

Jade looked at Elsa before answering. "Two to three hours. That's the best we could do on such short notice. So it's better that you keep spraying it over you every few hours."

I nodded. "Got it."

"So do we hide or something?" Jade looked around the roof of the Twilight Hotel, where I'd decided to stage my trap-an-angel scheme.

I'd thought about that. "No. I don't think that'll keep them from showing up." The angels didn't seem preoccupied with the wave of humanity we were surrounded by. They only cared about their mark. Me.

"They might not even come." Catelyn stood by the roof's edge, unfazed by the dizzying drop down to the street below. Giants. Guess that was one of the perks of being a giantess. You had no fear of heights, no fear of anything, really.

"They'll show up," growled Valen from across the rooftop. He was staring out at the city lights, his features hidden in the semidarkness.

After Valen had reduced the male angel to mush back at his apartment, he'd called a few of his buddies to take the body away. And by buddies, I mean my favorite werewolf Arther. Okay, *not* my favorite, but better for him than contacting the Gray Council. I did not want them knowing I had angel assassins after me. Who knew. They might take that as a sign that I should be killed and try to off me themselves. Yup. Better to keep this on the down-low.

I was extremely grateful to have not one but *two* giants with me. If things went amiss, at least the giants could crush the angel to smithereens.

The gang was all here. All except for Julian, who'd volunteered to look after Shay. After I'd decided to come clean and tell her about the two angels, she was adamant about helping me with my plan. Of course, she was.

"You need me," she'd said. "You need my help."

"It's too dangerous," I told her, my chest squeezing at the resolve on her face.

It was hard to say no to that kid, especially when she was so determined to help me. I saw in her eyes that she cared. She loved her big sister.

But I couldn't risk getting Shay hurt. She'd been through enough. It was time for her to enjoy some well-deserved time with friends, which was why Julian had offered to take her with him to Cassandra's, where the twins were just out of their minds, thrilled to have Shay stay with them. Probably to dress her up in one of their princess gowns. The thought of Shay in a big yellow dress made me laugh.

Yet she'd stomped her feet all the way out of the apartment once Julian had come to fetch her. She was mad. I got it. I'd be angry, too, if I were her. But she was safe. One less thing to think about.

I exhaled and walked back to the small area rug I'd brought from my apartment on the thirteenth floor. I knelt and pulled it back, revealing the chalk circle and symbols I'd drawn a few minutes ago.

The air moved next to me as Elsa lowered herself. "So this is an angel trap? Interesting."

"According to the book, yes," I said, my eyes moving over to the chair where I'd settled the old tome—the same tome I'd used to summon my angel father and failed. I knew I'd done the spell right. Just someone on the "other" side had tampered with it.

Elsa's eyes roamed over my circle. "And all you have to do is—"

"Get the bastard to step inside the circle." It sounded easy enough. Hell, it sounded great in my head. But we all knew things in life were never easy, especially not for me. Nope. Getting this angel to step in that exact spot would be a challenge. But I was ready for this challenge. This time, I was prepared.

Plus, the night sky was peppered with stars. It

was a clear night. And my starlight had a full tank of magic mojo.

"Let's say, hypothetically, your plan works," began Elsa. "Do you really think the angel will answer your questions?"

"It's a risk I'm willing to take," I answered. "I won't let them out until they do. So, yeah. I think they will." I surely hoped they did. "I need to know why they want me dead. And it can't just be because I have an angel father. It doesn't make sense. This is something else."

"Do you feel any different?"

I looked up at Jade, standing above me and Elsa. "What do you mean?" I knew exactly what she meant.

"Well," said Jade with a shrug, "your father said this was something in you that they want. Something that hasn't materialized yet. So… do you feel different now than before?"

"Like menopause?" I laughed. "Ow!" I rubbed my arm where Elsa had hit it.

She scowled at me. "You wait till you get the hot flashes and the sudden weight gain that, no matter how much you exercise or starve yourself, won't go away. Then we'll see who's laughing."

"Okay. Okay." I tried to keep my face blank. "And to answer your question, Jade. No. I don't feel any different. I'm not getting any sudden urges to kill or even just harm others. I don't feel sick or tired. I feel exactly the same."

Yes, that was a lie. But I didn't see what good it

would do to tell them that I started to feel "tingles." It could be nothing. It could be a virus. I didn't want to alarm anyone. At least not yet, not until I was certain.

Jade was still watching me. She crossed her arms over her chest. "What about your magic?"

"What about it?"

"Does *it* feel different to you? Maybe a shift in it? A disturbance in the force?"

"This isn't *Star Wars*, Jade," scolded Elsa. She looked at me. "Though she does make a good point."

"Thank you," said Jade proudly.

Elsa grunted as she lowered herself onto her butt. "From what you told us about what your father said, I feel as though this has everything to do with your starlight."

"I'm not the only Starlight witch that has ever existed. There are others. Have been others."

Elsa watched me and said, "Not *your* brand of starlight."

"Come again?" Okay, now I was confused.

"Well." Elsa shifted her weight until she got more comfortable. "Starlight witches are bonded to their own specific group of stars. Right? Yours is the Alpha Centauri, and Shay is the sun. And the others are different stars."

"Yes. That's right."

"You never draw your powers from the same stars," said Elsa. "I believe whatever this is, the reason why the angels are after you... is *because* of your specific group of stars. Your *particular* brand of Starlight magic."

"Yeah. Maybe." It made sense. And perhaps it was the only theory I had at the moment that made any sense as to why the Legion of Angels wanted me dead. It had to do with my special brand of Starlight magic. "But I'm still not sensing anything different with my magic." Not entirely, and nothing that would contribute to the Legion of Angels wanting to end me.

"Maybe it hasn't happened yet," said Jade, her gaze intense, "but it will."

I don't know why, but a shiver ran through me at her words. I didn't like not knowing something was different about me, that something was about to change. What if this change was bad? What if I became another person? What if I became evil? Was this the reason why the angels wanted me dead? Because I would become some wicked, dark Starlight witch?

A hand squeezed mine. "Don't overthink this," said Elsa. "I can see it all over your face. We don't know what it is or how it'll manifest. Try not to worry yourself to death."

"You're not the one who's about to transform into something," I said.

"It doesn't mean it's bad."

"It doesn't mean it's good either." Not when the Legion of Angels had sent their best assassins to take care of me. Yeah. That didn't settle well. All the more reason to get one of their angels to blab. I needed to know. More than ever.

I felt eyes on me and looked over to find Valen's dark gaze on mine. It was hard to read his face from across the rooftop but not the tightness in his posture and the fists he was carrying around, like at any moment he was going to make holes in the roof.

The more I thought about what Elsa and Jade had said about my magic, the worse I felt. But it wasn't time to linger in despair or to have a freak-out moment. I needed to focus. I needed to get that bastard angel in that circle and get some answers. And I'd do just about anything to get them.

Jade mumbled something, and when I glanced back at her, I saw her stuffing her phone in her pocket.

"What's going on?" I pulled back the rug, made sure it covered all the chalk marks, and stood.

Jade was shaking her head, her expression filled with annoyance. "It's those damn YouTubers. They're looking for you. They won't give Jimmy a moment's peace."

I cocked a brow. "You've changed your tune. I thought you liked them." Maybe they were putting the moves on Jimmy and batting their eyelashes. Yeah. I bet that's what they were doing.

"I did. I do. They just… ugh. They annoy me right now," she added with a wave of her hand.

I laughed. "You're jealous."

Jade's lips parted as Elsa snorted. "I am *not*."

Even in the semidarkness, I could see Jade's face darkening.

"You are." I dusted my jeans. "But I wouldn't be if I were you. Jimmy is totally into you. You're perfect for each other." I wanted to say that he loved her because it was obvious to anyone with a brain, but I didn't want to embarrass her further.

Jade beamed. "I know. But I still don't like it. How long are they staying? Do you know?"

I stared at her. "They're staying in the hotel?" That was news to me.

"Yes. Jimmy told me."

It explained how they just kind of showed up everywhere. "I'm sure as soon as they have enough footage of whatever, they'll move on." Hopefully. The last thing I needed was for this group to get my "transformation" on video and then put it online for the world to see.

Because my witchy instincts told me that whatever was about to happen to me would happen soon. Why else were the angels so adamant about terminating me right now? That was the only explanation for their urgency.

"I need to sit down on something that doesn't crush my coccyx." Elsa pushed to her feet and made her way to her folding chair, Jade following her.

I watched them go, my thoughts scattering around my brain like scared little mice. As they settled into their seats, Elsa flipped through the pages of that large tome I'd brought, trying to come up with a plan to get the angel to step onto the rug while I said the spell. Easy peasy, right?

Valen had not moved from his spot across the roof. His gaze was still trained on me, and a chill ran through my body. What was he thinking? Could he sense the shift in my magical abilities? Was he afraid it would change me and turn me into someone else entirely?

I was glad my father had shown up, for Shay's sake. Yet his presence only increased my anxiety. All he did for me was instill me with unrest. With worry. And part of me wished he'd never told me about this thing about me that hadn't manifested yet.

"I'm forty-one," I muttered. "I'm too old for this crap."

But as I paced back and forth, my mind kept wandering back to the possible transformation that awaited me. What if it was something so drastic I couldn't handle it? What if it turned me into a monster, something that made me a danger to everyone around me? The thought alone made me feel sick to my stomach.

But I couldn't dwell on it. I needed to focus on trapping an angel and getting the answers I needed.

Catelyn was off to the roof's edge again, staring below at the wave of humanity. I was glad she was here. She wanted to help, more than anything, after the trial by combat and the Freida debacle. It was over, and I didn't want to bring it up. We'd moved on.

But now, with this impending change in my

magic and the angel assassins, I needed all the help I could get. And that included Catelyn and Valen. Valen, by looking at him, wished none of this was happening.

I wished that too.

After I stuffed the angel repellent in my pocket, I took a deep breath and walked over to him, trying to ignore how my heart raced in my chest. As I reached him, a gust of wind swept through the rooftop, sending my hair flying in all directions.

He looked at me, his eyes softening just a bit. "We could have done this tomorrow. Elsa's spell would have given you some time to get some much-needed rest."

I smiled at him, my blood warming at the mere thought that he cared about me. "You've healed me. With those giant sexy hands rubbing all over me," I teased, though part of that was true. His magical hands had done their thing, but he had actually healed me with his healing right after he killed the angel.

Valen's eyes danced with mischievousness. "You know what I mean. You didn't have to do this tonight."

I shrugged. "Maybe not. But I wanted to get this over with. I want to know why they want me dead. The sooner I do, the sooner I can figure out what to do and get on with my life without having to look over my shoulder."

Valen was silent.

We felt a sudden shift in the air, and a cold breeze lifted my hair.

I looked up into the sky, seeing the dark, nearly black clouds snuffing out the stars. A raindrop hit my forehead. "Wonderful."

"Looks like rain," Elsa called out from her chair.

"I know," I howled back at her. "Weird. That's not what the forecast said. It was supposed to be a clear night." This was another reason I wanted to take advantage of the perfect conditions while my Starlight magic was at its peak.

Three more drops hit my forehead, just as my father's ring, which I'd found in our bed and put back on right after my angel fight, pulsed with warmth.

My heart leaped in my throat, and I spun around on the spot, searching for the bastard angel.

And then I saw him.

But there was a problem.

It wasn't just *one* angel assassin standing on the opposite side of the rooftop.

There were three.

CHAPTER 9

I stared at the angels. All male. One wore a dark suit, similar to what the one in Valen's apartment had worn. Though that one had dark eyes and dark hair, this angel was pale with fair hair and eyes and shoulder-length bleached-blond hair pulled back in a ponytail. The other two were built like professional bodybuilders, their dark clothing struggling to contain all of their muscles. And they were identical —as in identical twins—with long red hair kept neat in a braid and matching long red beards. They both had their cheeks and ears pierced with metal studs. The one on the right had a pockmarked face and a long scar running over his left cheek down to his ear. Apart from that, it was like staring at clones.

Okay. I was surprised to find three, and I didn't care to hide that from my features. Worse, how the hell was I going to trap one while I had to worry about two others trying to cut off my head?

The night air was cold, and I shivered as water

droplets began to hit my head and shoulders. My chest clenched with sudden worry. Had the angels changed the weather to keep me from accessing my starlights fully? Were they capable of such things? No idea.

"Nephilim," shouted one of the red-beards, a large, grumpy finger pointed at me.

"Angel," I grunted out, mimicking his movements. Was it me, or were these guys not the sharpest tools in the celestial shed?

He smiled, revealing a few missing teeth. "You're dead."

I smiled back. "Not like I haven't heard that one before. I see you brought reinforcements this time." I never thought angels could look this ogre-like, brutish. I'd always imagined them as the picture of perfection, like my father, well-groomed and with chiseled features. The fair one, maybe, but the other two looked more like trolls than angels.

I felt Valen's magic press against me as he transformed into his giant self. "Care to explain why there's a bounty on my head?" I called out. What? Might as well give it a shot.

"You're an abomination. The oracles have predicted your demise." The angel's features were chiseled from stone and ice, though his voice was soft and almost soothing.

I frowned. "Right. Like that makes sense. Speak mortal, will you?" Uncertainty tightened my stance. I didn't like hearing about oracles and prophecies. I was never one to believe in all that stuff. I always believed in making your own luck, your own destiny. Yet this talk of predictions gave me the heebie-jeebies. I didn't like things that were out of my control. Like my life. *I* was in control of my life. Not some random angel or oracle.

Despite my feelings, part of me *wanted* to know what those oracles predicted. I had a feeling there was more to this than he was letting on. Why did the oracles even bother with me? Because, for some reason, *I* was important.

The same angel pulled a long sword from his back as though it had just magically appeared. "We're here for you, Nephilim." He waved his sword at Elsa and Jade and then pointed it at Valen next to me. "But if the others interfere, they will die. Makes no difference to us. A few less demon half-breeds in this horrid world, the better."

"Who you callin' demon half-breed, you miserable angel," yelled Elsa. "You can shove those wings up your halo if you think we're going to run away."

I couldn't see any wings, but I agreed with her. The air shifted, and I felt a tingle of magic spreading over the rooftop like a mist. Elsa's and Jade's magic.

Jade stepped next to Elsa, a united front. A wave of energy washed over me, sending a cold chill down my spine. Power filled the air like a wild river, its current strong. Their clothes and hair shifted in an invisible breeze as their lips moved and their hands made sweeping gestures. My skin prickled with excitement as the surge of power grew, emanating from the witches' strength and magic.

The roof vibrated below my feet as Catelyn, now in her giant form, came to stand at my left. The woman, the giantess, was impressive. Not as large as Valen, but close. She could scare the eyebrows off lots of men. Yet the angels didn't seem bothered at all by my friends. Maybe it had something to do with the fact that the two red-beards were probably close to seven feet tall.

I looked at one of the twins. "You sure you're not half-breeds? Like your mama was a troll or something? You've got that big-and-dumb thing going for you."

I heard Catelyn laugh. Yeah. *Love* her. She always laughed at my stupid jokes.

One of the twinzies broke apart from the group, hunched and prowling like a predator. He, too, reached behind his back and yanked out—not a sword—but the biggest hammer I'd ever seen. He raised it in my direction. "You know you're going to die. You're all going to die."

I gave a one-shoulder shrug. "So you say."

"Any last words?" He laughed, his brother joining in their merriment.

God, I hated these guys.

I tapped my lips with my fingers in thought. "Uh… can't think of anything at the moment. So, no."

The red-bearded angel squinted suspiciously, his nose crinkling as if something unpleasant had wafted beneath it. "Why are you smiling?"

"Life is short. Better smile while you still have teeth."

Again, Catelyn gave a snort. *"You're killing me."*

My grin widened. "I try."

But the angel assassins didn't look impressed with my witty comments. Yet they looked… pleased. Just like the other two angels I'd faced. Pleased at the fact that they were about to end my life.

I glanced at the sky and frowned as more raindrops fell over my face. The sky was still covered. When I looked back at the angels, their faces were lit up with a naughty kind of smile, like when someone's done something bad and managed to escape without being caught, like stealing an item off your shelf.

I pointed up to the sky. "Was this you?"

"Yes," answered the fair angel, pleased with himself. "You can't access your magic without the stars. Without them, you are… weak. Powerless. A dud. Just like a human whore."

Maybe not a hundred percent, but I could still reach some, like maybe, fifty percent. I wanted to keep them thinking I was magicless without a clear sky, but one thing I didn't appreciate was that they seemed to know a hell of a lot about me while I knew next to nothing about them. I really needed to have a chat with my father.

I shifted my weight in an attempt to hide the fact that I was reaching out to the stars. I had no idea if the angels could sense that. I wanted to keep them ignorant of the fact that I still had a connection to the stars. Though small, it was still there.

"So you tampered with the weather. Isn't that cheating? It isn't a fair fight if you take away my weapons."

The angel just gave me a cool smile. "I'm an assassin," he said as though that explained everything. Maybe it did. I pegged him too smart to be caught in my angel trap. He was watching me like he knew or guessed we'd set some trap, all of us waiting on the hotel's roof. Guess that left Tweedledee or Tweedledumb.

"Let's kill them," said the red-beard on the left. "I want to check out that nightclub, Red Room, and hit a few human whores before we leave. Nothing like human tussy."

He didn't say tussy, but you get the idea.

The red-beards laughed, and then the brothers did some sort of fist-bump with their elbows. Really hated these guys.

I cocked a hip. "You angels lack manners. Funny, here I thought you were the civilized ones. Guess I got that part wrong. You're nothing but thugs sent by the heavens."

The pale angel frowned, his eyes glowing with inner power. Ooooh. He was mad. Good. He made a clicking sound with his tongue, and then the three of them charged.

All at me.

Excellent.

The two red-beards came at me first, their hammers drawn and ready to strike.

I had to act fast. My mind raced as I tried to come up with a plan. I knew I couldn't take on all three of them at once, so I had to find a way to separate them.

I stepped back, tapping into my starlight. I felt a tug. Not much, but enough to use as a distraction or push them away.

But I didn't need to.

The air moved around me. Then the two giants lunged forward and met the red-beards' attack. Like two massive walls of muscle, Catelyn and Valen struck hard. The twin angels were caught off guard and staggered back, surprised by the sudden interference.

Valen landed a hard punch on the twin with the scarred face, knocking him to the ground. Catelyn, on the other hand, grabbed hold of the other angel's hammer and twisted it out of his grasp. He stumbled back, fury flashing in his eyes.

"You big bitch," he snarled. "Give me back my hammer."

Catelyn held his hammer with both hands. *"Come and get it."*

And then he charged.

I stared, amazed for a moment at his ability to avoid Catelyn's massive kicks and fists. Something silver caught my eye, and then a small dagger materialized in his hand. He moved close and stabbed Catelyn in the thigh in quick succession.

The giantess roared in pain and lashed out,

missing the damn angel as he leaped back, a crazed expression on his face. Catelyn covered her thigh with her hand, blood oozing between her fingers.

Bastard.

From the corner of my eye, Valen dodged the other twin angel's hammer strike and spun around, kicking him in the backs of the knees. The angel stumbled forward but managed to rotate and slammed Valen in the chest with his hammer. I was surprised when the giant stumbled back. Clearly, these angels were blessed with supernatural strength, more so than any paranormal I'd ever seen. The angel twins were brutes and fought with equal brute force.

I really, *really* hated these guys.

I glimpsed over across from me, rain hitting my face. The pale angel stood and watched the scene play out, his eyes flickering with a strange light. He seemed hesitant to attack, or maybe he was just waiting for his opportunity for a break—an opening to attack me.

Yeah, I wouldn't give him one.

He caught my eye and smiled, a cold smile that set my teeth on edge.

Sweat and breaths fogged the air as Valen brought his massive fists down on the angel twin. The angel raised his hammer, blocking each strike. With a sudden burst of speed, the angel lashed his hammer at the giant. Valen leaped back, barely missing that blow and just managing to keep his footing. But he'd moved to the left side of the roof, giving the pale angel the opening he was waiting for.

The fair angel hesitated for a moment longer. His eyes shone with his angel magic. And then he charged.

Damn, he was fast, and he moved with the speed of a vampire, just like the other two angels. His movements were fluid, as if he was a black blur and not even there. Blink, and you'd miss him.

I crouched low and tapped into my starlight, but nothing came. Damnit. Despite the lack of energy flowing through me, I still had use of my limbs. Would I kick or punch? Whatever came first to me.

A ball of fire hit the pale angel in the chest, and he fell to his knees. Tall orange flames licked around him, burning the angel.

"We witches aren't so weak and useless."

Elsa and Jade approached side by side, orange fireballs dancing around their hands. Elemental fire. Nice. Even nicer was the fact that the angel was also five feet to the left of the rug with the angel trap beneath it.

Now, if only I could get him to move three steps to the right…

Elsa noticed the rug and gave me a nod, having read my expression. We needed to move that angel into that circle.

I started forward, Elsa and Jade moving closer to the angel.

Laughter reached my ears. Then the angel stood

up, and the fire that blazed around him crackled one last time before it vanished completely.

Oh, crap.

The angel wiped down his suit like the fire had soiled it. "You witches will never learn. You cannot defeat me with your little magic tricks. I'm an *angel*," he said, as though that clarified it.

"Maybe you've never faced witches like us," Elsa replied, her voice laced with confidence.

"I have. And I killed them."

The angel charged at us, his eyes radiating power. But we were ready for him.

A violent gust of wind shot out from Elsa's hands, knocking the angel off-balance. I rushed over, grabbed the rug, and yanked it back just as Jade hurled a bolt of lightning that struck him in the back. He screamed out in pain and stumbled backward into my circle.

Without a second to lose, I called upon the power of the stars, channeling it into my hands. Pulling on my starlight, I said the incantation, "Let the loss of freedom be unwitting, into the circle, to do my bidding!"

I felt a tug on my insides as the magic circle was set. There. The trap was activated. The angel was ensnared within the circle.

"Gotcha," I said with a grin. "I trapped me an angel. Ha. Look at me go. That wasn't so hard."

"Good work, Jade," said Elsa, and then the two witches high-fived each other.

I looked over at Catelyn and Valen, still locked in battle with the two angels. Both fought with incredible grace. The angels themselves were formidable adversaries, boasting great strength and stamina. They parried and lunged at Catelyn and Valen with practiced ease, blows and thrusts almost blurring into one. I wanted to help, but right now, I had my hands full.

The pale angel glared at me as he stood up slowly. And then he laughed.

Yeah, that wasn't usually a good sign.

"You must be the stupidest Starlight witch that ever was," he said, his voice low and cold.

My temper bubbled to the surface. "I don't have time for name-calling. How about you start by telling me why the legion wants me dead."

The angel shook his head slowly. "I shall not."

"You have to," I pressed. "*I* control you. You're trapped. You have to do my bidding."

The angel looked at his feet and then back at me. "Am I?"

I stared at the chalk circle in horror. Raindrops had muddled its outer edges, and part of it had already been washed away.

Uh-oh.

And then the angel stepped out of the circle.

CHAPTER 10

Okay, now was a good enough time to panic.

"Run!" I howled.

In a blur, the angel lashed out. I heard Elsa cry out as he stabbed her with his sword in the shoulder. The blade glistened with her blood when he pulled it out.

"No!" Jade thrust out her hands. A bolt of purple energy hit the angel's chest.

But it had barely any effect. The angel laughed again, his eyes flaming with power. He struck out, hitting Jade across the face. I caught a glimpse of her eyes rolling in the back of her head before she went down. The angel raised his sword for a killing blow.

"Stop!" I rushed forward. "It's me you want. Leave them alone."

The angel surveyed me a moment, and then he surprised me by actually turning my way and away from Jade. She was unconscious and would have a killer headache tomorrow, but I was truly worried about Elsa. She was on the floor, deathly pale and clutching her shoulder. The amount of blood pouring out had bile rise in the back of my throat.

The air was thick with rain and the horrid sound of fast thrashing fists pounding on soft flesh. Again. And again. And again.

I flicked my gaze up and saw flashes of red and sweeping arcs of the steel of hammers. I saw Valen, wild and attacking with the grace of a skilled killer—a giant killer. The red-beard angel swung his hammer at the giant with agility and speed, not of this world. He looked like a damn cartoon character leaping around the giant with no sense of gravity, as though his height and build meant nothing.

I didn't like it. Nor did I like the blood leaking from the multiple wounds on Catelyn's side and her thigh. She still hung on to the other angel's hammer. And when my eyes landed on him, he had not one, but two blades in his hands. Both were stained with her blood.

Yes, Catelyn was a giantess and was equipped with supernatural strength. But she wasn't trained as a fighter, not like Valen. I had to keep reminding myself that she was practically an infant in terms of being a paranormal. She lacked the combat skills Valen had.

Fear hit. What if these angels defeated us? What if my super, ingenious plan of trapping an angel ended up killing those I cared about? I couldn't live with myself if they all died because of me.

My heart shattered as I thought of Shay. If we were all killed, who would look after her? Julian?

The sound of my blood hammered wildly in my ears as I pulled my attention back to the pale angel bastard.

The angel pointed his sword at me as though indicating I was next. The bloody tip made my stomach churn. His eyes glowed with that same inner power, angel power.

"You witches are nothing. You can't contain me with your trinkets. I am an angel, and I will not be held by your weak magic."

I gritted my teeth. I would not show this damn angel—assassin—fear. "If not for the rain, I would have trapped you. And your angel ass would have been mine. We both know it."

The angel smiled, his eyes locked on to me. "You thought you could trap an angel with that chalk scribble?" he chuckled, a smug look on his face. "You Starlight witches are so naïve."

"Then why don't you enlighten me? Tell me more about these oracles. What is it about me that scares you? That's right. Your superior selves are afraid of me. Might as well tell me. I am about to die, right? How about you give a witch some information before you slice off her head?" It was worth a shot. The dude was an arrogant bastard, and those loved to boast about their accomplishments.

I heard Elsa whimper from behind the angel, and my heart shattered a little more. She was losing a lot of blood. If I didn't get her to Polly soon, or even Valen, she was going to die.

While the angel was pondering my question, I

flicked my gaze to the sky. The rain was coming down softer, like a mist, but the sky was still covered in dark black clouds. No stars peeked through them.

I needed a plan or a break in the clouds. I needed to keep the bastard talking.

The angel snickered. "You think I'm going to tell you anything, witch?" He took a step closer, his bloody sword still pointed straight at me. "You're nothing. Just a mere mortal with a little bit of power. You don't stand a chance against the legion."

I narrowed my eyes, my grip on my starlight weakening. "Are they all cheaters like you?"

The angel smirked. "Oracles can be a little… over-dramatic with their prophecies. They tend to get a bit carried away with their predictions."

I took a deep breath, trying to ignore the fear gnawing at me. "I like drama. What was the prophecy?" I heard a cry of pain. It didn't sound like Valen or Catelyn. I was hoping that was one of the red-beard angels.

"You believe you can outsmart us. Don't you?" he said, his voice laced with amusement. "You have no idea what you're up against."

"I know enough," I replied, keeping my voice steady. "I know that you and your legion want me dead, and I know I have something inside me that scares you. Something powerful enough to scare a Legion of Angels."

The angel raised an eyebrow. "And what do you want to know? Because I will end your life," he said, surprising me. Yeah. This guy was arrogant.

I hesitated for a moment but then decided to take a gamble. "Answers," I said. "Answers about who I am and why I'm so important to you. Am I about to change? Will I become something else?"

The angel studied me for a beat, as though weighing his options. "You are not as stupid as I thought," he said finally.

I frowned. "I'll take that as a compliment." Just then, a scream cut the air, and I stiffened. Catelyn. But I couldn't look away from the angel. I had to keep him talking.

"But I can't give you the answers you seek," he said, his voice loud over the cries and thumps of battle behind me. "They are not mine to give. I'm just here to kill you."

"Then whose are they?" I demanded.

The angel's smile turned sinister. "That is not for you to know, witch. You are merely a pawn in all of this. You won't live long enough to see it through."

My blood boiled. "I am not a pawn. I am a person with free will, and I refuse to be used as a tool. I'm in control of my life. Not your legion."

The angel chuckled. "Ah, but that's where you're wrong. In this world, everyone is a pawn. Even angels."

"Fine. I'm a pawn. A pawn in what game? What's going to happen to me?"

"I can't tell you that. It's forbidden," he replied.

"Well, I'm not giving up that easily," I said, standing my ground. "There has to be a way to make you talk."

The angel snickered. "You're more persistent than I thought, but you're wasting your time."

I took a deep breath, calming myself and thinking through my options. I couldn't let this angel defeat me, not when so much was at stake. Shay's safety, Elsa's life, and my own destiny were all on the line. I needed a plan, and I needed it fast.

But my brain was a vast empty shell of nothing.

"Now, enough talking," said the angel, his posture shifting as he held his sword before him. "I have another mark to kill tonight. It's time for you to die."

He lunged at me with his sword, and I barely managed to dodge it. I tapped into my starlight, feeling a smidgen of a response. It wasn't much. But I was going to use it.

I hurled a blast of starlight at the angel. Okay, so it was more of a droplet. A pretty droplet. It still did the job.

It hit him in the neck. Yes, I was aiming for his face, but it did what I wanted. He stumbled and lost his focus. And then he laughed.

The angel ran his fingertips along his neck. "Was that the extent of your powers?"

I gritted my teeth in frustration. I knew I had to do something, and fast. The angel was too powerful, and if I didn't act quickly, he would kill me and everyone else I cared about. "I am not a mockery," I spat out. "I am a Starlight witch, and I have powers beyond your comprehension." Yeah, that was a bit much. I wiggled my fingers to add a little drama.

The angel laughed again. "Your powers are nothing compared to the legion's. You are a mere speck in the grand scheme of things."

With my fingers clenched into fists, I glared at him, my anger giving me strength. I refused to let this angel get the better of me. I needed to keep him talking, to distract him long enough for me to come up with a plan. A plan would be good right about now.

"I may be a Starlight witch, but I won't be underestimated. I have more power than you realize," I said, my voice firm.

The angel sneered. "A *female* witch. We are divine beings of light and power."

I shrugged. "I'm half angel. The same power flows in my veins."

At that, the angel scowled, and the grip on his sword tightened. "You are repulsive. An atrocity. Your very existence is abhorrent," he spat.

Okay. Here came my plan. "You may have power, but I have something you don't," I said, keeping my gaze locked on him.

"And what is that?" he asked, his eyes narrowing.

"Breasts," I said and flashed him the girls.

The angel stood stock-still, staring at my chest, his mouth open in confusion. So I made a fist and punched him across the jaw. He bent to the side, and I sent a kick to his sternum, sending him staggering back.

"Ha. Not bad for a mortal female, huh?" I said,

pleased with myself. I was wearing a bra, but the effect still worked.

The angel straightened, a hand on his jaw. "That was… surprising."

I grinned. "There's a lot more where that came from." My winning smile faded when I caught sight of Elsa lying flat on the floor. Her eyes were closed.

Damn it.

"You know," said the angel, his tone turning soft, sensual. "We could take a moment and rejoice in some mortal sexual pleasures."

"I'd rather drink a bucket of ammonia," I snapped. "You disgust me."

The angel's eyes blazed with anger. "You dare insult me, mortal?"

"I dare," I replied, feeling a spark of defiance.

The angel lunged at me again, his sword glinting in the dim light. I ducked and dodged his attack and tried to conjure up another blast of starlight, but my powers were still weak and flickering.

I was losing ground fast. His sword was too fast, too deadly. I had to think of something quickly before he landed a fatal blow.

The angel laughed, his eyes full of mockery and disdain. "Soon, you will feel the edge of my sword against that pretty neck. And you will die."

"Fuck you," I seethed.

Focusing, I tried to call up my magic again, but before I could move, the angel grabbed my wrist and twisted it behind my back. I winced in pain as he held me in place.

"Now, now, little Nephilim," he said, his breath hot against my ear. "Stop struggling. It's over. Your life is over. Accept it with grace. It's all you have left."

I struggled against his grip, but it was no use. The angel was too strong. I glanced over at Valen and Catelyn, but they were too busy trying not to get killed themselves to glance my way.

It's all you have left.

The angel's words hit me. It wasn't all I had left.

This was a moment of clarity for me. When all was lost. And I reached out for the only weapon I had.

I slipped my hand in my jeans pocket, yanked out Elsa's angel repellent—and sprayed the mother-fracker in the eyes.

The angel screamed and then stumbled away from me, frantically rubbing at his eyes. His face was an angry red, and his eyes were swollen with blisters as if I'd doused him with a can of bear mace.

I looked at the tiny bottle. "Thanks, buddy."

Not waiting for another second, I rushed over and kicked him in the stomach.

The angel stumbled back, yelping. "Bitch! I'm going to kill you!"

He moved forward, his sword gleaming in the darkness and a dark light emanating from his eyes. I could feel his power, his magic, and I knew I was in trouble.

But he did look stupid with the red blisters, like a

horrible tanning-bed experience gone wrong. It was a good look on him.

I'd have to thank Elsa later.

My eyes flicked to the sky again, and I saw a glimmer of hope. A tiny break in the clouds, just big enough to let a single star shine through.

It was enough.

I raised my hands, focusing on my magic, my starlight. It began to pulse once more, the warmth spreading up my arm and through my body. I felt my Starlight magic grow stronger, more potent.

The pale angel charged forward, his sword aimed straight at my chest. I sidestepped, just barely avoiding the blade. I thrust my hand forward, and a burst of starlight erupted from my palm, striking the angel in the chest. He grunted, his body recoiling from the impact.

But he wasn't done yet.

He stalked forward again, his sword whistling through the air.

I planted my feet, reaching out to my stars and holding my power.

A wail interrupted my thoughts. I spun around and saw one of the red-bearded angels run over to something on the roof near Valen. From what I could gather, it was his brother but resembled a bundle of disheveled clothing. In one swift moment, he hauled the angel's body over his shoulder, grabbed his brother's fallen hammer, and used it to point at Valen threateningly. We all knew what that meant.

And then his body shimmered, and he disappeared.

The roof under my feet shook as Valen and Catelyn rushed my way.

I faced the angel. A ball of starlight hovered over my palm, and the pale angel's eyes widened in surprise and anger.

I smirked. "Looks like your weather-tampering days are over, pal."

But before I could thrust my starlight at him, the angel's body shimmered and vanished.

CHAPTER 11

I sat in a wooden chair next to Elsa's bed. My butt was numb from sitting so long in the same position as I watched Polly, who skillfully stitched up the deep cut that stretched across Elsa's shoulder.

I hadn't been in Elsa's apartment that often. The scent of potpourri and incense filled the air. Her bedroom walls were covered in floral wallpaper, the same pattern matching the drapes. It was comfy, a room where I could just grab a good book, sit in a corner, and read for hours.

A sniff turned me around. Jade stood at the foot of the bed, her arms wrapped around her middle, looking pale and as disheveled as I'd ever seen her. The side of her face was swollen, as though she'd fallen face-first in a wasp's nest. Her eyes were bloodshot, and she hadn't stopped crying since Valen had used some of his healing magic on her to wake her up, and she'd seen Elsa.

Valen had also given Elsa some of his healing

magic in the hope that the older witch would regain consciousness, but she didn't. That's when we'd rushed her into her apartment, and the giant had gone to fetch Polly.

"Is she going to be okay?" My voice sounded thin, defeated. Elsa hadn't opened her eyes yet. Not since the battle on the roof with the angels.

Polly pressed a square of gauze over the stitches. "She's lost a lot of blood."

I waited, expecting to hear more. "But she will recover. Right? Does she need a blood transfusion or something?" I didn't think I could live with myself if Elsa died. This was my stupid plan to try and trap an angel. She was only there as backup because I had asked her to come.

I was a fool.

Polly heaved a heavy sigh and tucked the covers around Elsa's body. "No, not a transfusion. I'm sure that between my herbal remedies, ointments, and spells, combined with the giant's healing magic, they should all help."

Here we went with the "should" again. "What are you not saying?"

The healer met my gaze. "Elsa is not as young as you. She'll need more time to recover. More treatment. This could have been a killing wound. She was lucky that Valen was able to stop the bleeding."

My throat contracted, and when a sob escaped Jade, hot tears fell from my eyes. I wiped them away. "But she'll be okay. Right? *Right?*"

Polly nodded. "Yes. But she'll need a lot of rest."

"Okay," I said, my bottom lip quivering.

Polly eyed me from below her white toque. "Are you going to tell me why one of my best friends came close to dying tonight? Why she has a wound as though someone used her for sword practice?"

Polly's tone was accusing, full of resentment and anger. And it was totally understandable.

"She was helping me trap an angel." It sounded absolutely ridiculous when I said it out loud like that. It sounded insane. Maybe it was.

Polly blinked. "That's the stupidest thing I've ever heard come out of your mouth. Are you crazy? Do you have a death wish? What possessed you to come up with such an absurd notion? Don't you know that angels are untouchable? They're *angels*, for crying out loud."

I looked over to Jade before answering. "There's a guild of angel assassins after me." At her continued incredulous expression, I added, "Something about me has the Legion of Angels troubled. They want to kill me. So they sent ten of their best assassins to do the job. Three have died, so that leaves seven more that'll probably show up anytime now to try and do me in."

Polly grabbed what looked like antibacterial wipes from her coat pocket and proceeded to clean her hands. "Angel assassins are trying to kill you?"

"From that tone, I'm guessing you don't believe me." It was wild when I thought about it. And if I didn't know any better, I wouldn't believe me either. But I knew better.

"It's true," said Jade, coming to my rescue, seeing that Polly didn't believe a single word that vomited out of my mouth. "Her father told her. I mean, he should know, right?"

My angel father. Right. Only a few people knew that my father was an angel. Polly knew I was a Starlight witch and that my magic came from the stars, but she didn't know it was celestial and came from the angels. Neither did I until a few weeks ago. Maybe it was time she knew.

"Your father?" Polly dropped the used wipe into her pocket.

I took a breath and decided that it was high time Polly should know everything. "My father's an angel." I told her about my powers and where they came from, seeing her brows etching higher and higher on her forehead as I continued my tale until I got to the part where Matiel had shown up to tell me about the assassins. When I was done, I folded my hands on my lap and waited. I wasn't sure how she would react. Would she be angry? Fascinated? No idea.

The healer stared at us in turn, planting her fists on her hips and exclaiming, "Well, you should have told me sooner."

"That's true," I agreed, guilt pinching my insides. "I'm sorry about that. My life's been a little crazy lately. I haven't had time to sit and relax and settle into it."

Polly let out a breath. "I hope this idea of trapping an angel is over. You nearly got Elsa and Jade killed. Not to mention yourself, Valen, and Catelyn."

I felt Jade's gaze on me as I said, "Yes, it is. No more trapping." Total lie. The thing was, I still needed to figure out how to get the assassins to talk. If I couldn't trap them, how would I get my hands on that bit of crucial information? I needed answers. How else would I get them if not by trapping another halo bastard?

But one thing was for sure. This time, I'd do it alone.

I wouldn't risk getting any of my friends hurt or killed. Whatever I was going to do next, I'd do it on my own. I just didn't know *what* that was just yet.

My gaze fell over Elsa, and I felt another, more major, stab of guilt. Polly was right. Elsa could have been killed tonight. And it would have been entirely my fault. I wasn't taking any more risks with my friends' lives.

"I've done all I can for Elsa," said Polly turning around and fixing her gaze on Jade. "You sit," she ordered, pointing to the edge of the bed.

Jade wiped her nose with a tissue. "I'm fine."

Polly pointed to the side of Jade's face that seemed to keep swelling. "You're certainly not fine. You look like Mrs. Potato Head. Now sit. I need to take a look at your cranium. From what Leana told me, you took quite the hit."

Just when I thought Jade was going to resist, she moved and sat on the edge of the bed.

"Hmmm." Polly gently tipped Jade's head to the side. "An angel did that?"

"I think it was his fist," answered the witch.

I watched silently as Polly began to smear a purple ointment on half of Jade's head, seeing her wince whenever the healer pressed her fingers to her scalp. I was glad Shay wasn't here to witness this. She'd probably start crying, and if I saw her cry, I'd be a sobbing mess. Valen had gone to fetch her from Julian's place to take her back to ours. He and Catelyn had left together once Polly had arrived at Elsa's apartment.

"Tell her that the plan didn't work, but not that Elsa and Jade were hurt," I'd told the giant before he left. "I don't want her to know."

Valen had leaned over and given me a quick kiss. "Okay. Do you want me to come back to get you later?" His expression was tight, and he tried to hide his concern, but I could detect the worry in his voice. I knew he was concerned about the remaining seven assassins still chasing after me.

I shook my head. "I've sprayed myself with Elsa's angel repellent. I'll be fine. I'll see you in a bit."

"There, that should do it." Polly stepped back from Jade and began to wipe her fingers again with another cloth, though it looked exactly like the one she'd just used. Perhaps there was more to those coat pockets than she let on, like a magical washing machine.

I stared at her coat pockets. "What else you got in there?"

Polly turned and gave me a sly smile, a twinkle in her eye. "Wouldn't you like to know?"

"Yes. Yes, I would."

The healer laughed and stuffed her remaining ointments, jars, and gauze rolls into her pockets. "I'll be off, then. If you need me, you know where to find me."

"Thanks, Polly." I stood as she made her way to the door, grateful we had a healer in the hotel.

"You're welcome. Let me know if her condition worsens. It shouldn't. But I'd like to be kept informed."

"I will." I watched as the healer disappeared out the door.

"Are you staying here with Elsa?" Half of Jade's face was covered in that purple ointment. A waft of onion assaulted my nose.

I kept my face from showing the fact that the witch stank of raw onion. "If you want to go, go. I'll stay."

"Okay. Thanks." Jade stood up, wobbled, and then righted herself. "I think I'll go lie down for a while. My head feels like I hit it with a sledgehammer."

Again, that guilt gnawed at me. "Go," I said, rubbing her arm. "I'll stay with Elsa. You go lie down."

Jade forced a smile and wobbled out.

I let myself fall into my chair. Things couldn't have gone any worse tonight if I'd planned it. The only comfort I allowed myself was that, this time, it wasn't about Shay. She was safe, and the angels weren't interested in her. It was about me.

I really loved that kid, my little sister. And I wanted her to be happy, live a normal, paranormal life, and be a kid, as she deserved.

My thoughts drifted, and I wasn't sure how long I sat next to Elsa's bed. Probably hours, watching her chest rise and fall as she slept. Every time she moved, my heart would skip a beat. I didn't want to leave her side, but my body was beginning to ache from sitting in one spot for so long. And I was getting numb-butt. Trust me. There's nothing worse than numb-butt.

I stood up, stretched my arms and legs, and walked over to the window. The view out of Elsa's window wasn't as nice as mine, more like staring at neighboring rooftops, but I did get a peek of the sky. A thousand pinpricks in an otherwise infinite darkness. I sighed in perfect contentment as I basked in the muted beauty of the night sky. The stars were my friends, my family in a way. We shared a connection, and by that, I meant they supplied me with my magic.

Now that the sky was clear, I could appreciate their glowing beauty.

"Bastards," I muttered, remembering how the angels had somehow been able to control the forecast and had pulled thick rain clouds over the sky to hide the stars.

It told me they were resourceful, knew how to

manipulate my power, and were themselves powerful opponents.

I sighed through my nose. Tonight's events were starting to weigh me down. I knew I had to think of a new scheme soon, but I was tired. Exhausted. I wished I could take a nice, long hot bath with a certain giant rubbing me in all the right places.

Not tonight. Tonight I was on watch duty.

I took a deep breath, trying to calm my nerves, and turned around to face the room.

I froze.

Elsa was staring at me, her eyes wide open and fixed on my face. I gasped and quickly walked over to her bed. "Elsa, you're awake," I exclaimed, taking her hand in mine. It was still cold to the touch, but whatever. She was awake. That was something.

The older witch smiled weakly. "Yes, I am." Her voice was low and ragged like she hadn't used it in years. She blinked and looked around her room, seemingly to get her bearings. "How long have I been asleep?"

I looked at my phone. "Almost two hours."

Her eyes widened in surprise. "That long? What happened? All I remember was that angel bastard stabbing me with his sword. I fell, and then... that's when things went dark." She let go of my hand and clutched her locket like a lifeline, and my throat tightened when I saw her eyes filling with moisture.

I rubbed her arm gently. "Things didn't go as well as I'd hoped."

Elsa stared at me. "Did you trap him? Or one of the others?"

I shook my head, wondering if Elsa's memory had been affected. "No. The rain washed away my chalk circle. Remember? He stepped out."

Elsa blinked, her eyes slightly out of focus as she tried to recall the events. "The rain? There was no rain in tonight's forecast. No rain for another three days."

"I know." Clearly, she was missing time, but I wouldn't push it.

"But how?" Elsa winced as she tried to pull herself up. "I don't understand."

I let go of her arm and gently hauled her to a sitting position. "Let me get you another pillow." I dashed over to her wardrobe, grabbed an extra pillow, and placed it at her back. "That better?"

"Better." Elsa stared at the wound next to her shoulder. "Did Polly cut my blouse?"

"She did. And she bandaged you up."

The witch leaned back on her pillow. "Tell me more about the rain. I have a feeling something is missing. That I'm missing something."

I sat back down in my chair. "The angels did that. Apparently, they can control the weather. Did you know that?"

"I didn't." Elsa's expression turned grave. "What else? Did we beat them?"

"Not exactly," I answered, remembering how the pale angel had stabbed Elsa and could have easily killed her. "Valen managed to kill one of the twin angels. And then they just left."

Elsa rubbed her locket. "They'll be back for you. You know that."

I nodded. "With reinforcements."

"And you got nothing out of them?"

I licked my lips. "Well, the one that stabbed you did say something about the oracles predicting my death or some nonsense like that. I think these oracles came up with a prophecy about me. Something that's got them in a panic."

"A prophecy?"

"Yeah. Totally cliché. But there you have it."

Elsa's face screwed up in thought. "A prophecy sounds ominous."

"How so?"

"Well, prophecies are notoriously difficult to interpret. They can mean one thing, or they can mean several things at once. They can be true, or they can be false. But most importantly, they can have devastating consequences if they come true."

Elsa's eyes bore into mine with a newfound intensity. "They don't always foretell everything. They leave out important details. Things that could have changed everything. Things that could have saved lives."

I shivered at the intensity in her voice. "What do you mean?"

Elsa looked at me with a mixture of sadness and anger. "I mean that sometimes prophecies are crafted by those who want to manipulate the future. Those who want to achieve their own goals at any cost. Sometimes, innocent lives are sacrificed in the service of that goal."

I stared at her, horrified. "Do you think that's what's happening to me?"

"If the angels believe in this prophecy," continued Elsa, "we have to take it seriously. We have to figure out what it means before they do."

I nodded, feeling a wave of anxiety hit me. "But how do we even begin? We don't even know what the prophecy is about."

Elsa's lips thinned. "We start by going to the source. We need to speak to an oracle."

I stared at her while my brain tried to catch up to what she'd just voiced. "*Speak* to an oracle. Do you know where to find one?"

The witch gave me a tiny smile. "As a matter of fact, I do."

Okay then.

CHAPTER 12

I peeled off my clothes and tossed them on the bathroom tile floor. The steam from the shower fogged up the mirror so I couldn't see my reflection. Good. I didn't feel like seeing my new bruises, though I could feel them. From what I could see, I was probably spotted like a dalmatian. And I also felt dirty, somehow. Like the fight with the angels soiled me. Nothing a good hot shower couldn't wash away.

Julian had shown up at Elsa's apartment a few minutes after discussing this oracle situation and had offered to sit with Elsa.

"You look like shit," the tall witch had said. "Go home and rest. I'll take over."

"You sure?" I was reluctant to go, but he was right. I was tired as hell, and no doubt looked the part.

"I'll be fine," encouraged Elsa, looking small and weak in her bed. "You should go."

"Yeah. Go." Julian had pushed me out, and I'd let him.

After a long shower, careful not to rub too hard on my bruises, I reached for a towel hanging off the rack. My muscles felt sore after my night of fighting, but I welcomed the pain. It gave me something to focus on instead of my fear and anxiety.

The truth was, that tingling I felt in my limbs and now in my gut, was still there—only it was getting worse. It was hard to describe. It felt foreign yet familiar, like a cold, relentless energy fueling inside me. It was as though I were being pumped with a magical fuel, waiting to ignite, like the start of an engine. And it was only getting stronger.

I pushed the thoughts away, wrapped the towel around me, and tiptoed out of the bathroom so as not to wake Shay. She had school tomorrow. She needed sleep.

I sneaked into my room to find Valen sitting in an armchair beside the window overlooking the street below.

"Still up?" I moved over to the massive walk-in closet that could have fit my entire old bedroom back at the Twilight Hotel.

"Feel better?"

"Not really," I called out from the closet. I wasn't worried about how loud my voice was. Valen had equipped the bedroom with magically induced soundproof walls. I could scream at the top of my lungs, and Shay would never hear.

I yanked the towel off, tossed it in the laundry

basket, and snatched Elsa's angel-repellent spray from the shelf.

"Tell me more about this oracle," came Valen's voice.

I knew then that he'd been thinking about it since I came home ten minutes ago to find him sitting in the living room alone with the lights off. Shay had gone off to bed hours ago when Valen had picked her up from Julian's.

"Well," I said. Then I held my breath as I sprayed my face. After seeing what it had done to the angel, I just didn't want any in my eyes or my mouth. "She thinks if we find her oracle friend, he or she can reveal to us what prophecy the angel oracles predicted. I don't know how it works—damn, missed my arm completely—but according to Elsa, they'll be able to tell us." It was by far the best lead we had right now. And I was going to find this oracle first thing tomorrow.

"You missed a spot."

I flinched and turned, seeing the giant leaning on the opening of the walk-in closet with his arms crossed over his broad chest, eyeing my naked body with interest. Damn. I'd never heard him coming.

"You know, for someone so big, you move as silently as a cat. Not sure I like that."

Valen chuckled, pushed himself off the frame, and walked into the closet, giving me no time to react. His eyes roved up my body slowly, taking in every curve and line like he was memorizing them. I shivered as his eyes lingered on my breasts before traveling down to my hips.

My breathing stuttered when his gaze stayed on my lower half for a few beats too long before he finally looked away, leaving my body heating and my lower regions pounding. The smirk on his face spoke volumes; he knew exactly what he was doing to me.

"Here," I said, handing him the bottle and trying to get rid of my raging hormones. Though that was nearly impossible when such a man was staring at your naked body like he wanted to lick every inch of it. His gaze held me in place like an invisible rope. "Can you do my back?"

"I can." His eyes never left my body. "I can do *other* things as well. All you have to do is ask."

"Ha. Ha." My face flushed as I tried to focus. It wasn't working.

He smiled wider at that and shrugged nonchalantly before closing the distance between us until we were standing toe to toe.

"Do you know where the oracle is?" he asked softly, his voice sending shivers down my spine as he took the spray and moved behind me.

I swallowed. "Somewhere in the city. Elsa couldn't remember the address. She's too exhausted, but I'll swing by first thing tomorrow." The fact that this oracle was right here in the city was the best news. By tomorrow, I'd finally know why the angels wanted me dead.

And somehow, that scared the crap out of me too.

"I'm coming with you," came Valen's deep voice. "I'm not letting you out of my sight."

I shivered as a mist of the spray hit my back. "I figured as much." And I didn't mind one bit. "After we take Shay to school, we'll go."

"About that." Valen sprayed my shoulders. "Shay has an event at school tomorrow."

"An event? What event? How come she didn't tell me?"

"She was asleep when you came in."

"Right. So, what's this event?"

"A talent show," replied the giant. "The kids go onstage and show off their abilities."

I couldn't help the smile on my face. "And she actually wants to do this?" Shay was more of a reclusive kid, like her big sister, so I was quite taken aback by the idea of her performing her magic in front of an audience.

"She does. She's pretty excited about it too. She couldn't stop smiling. Couldn't stop talking."

I felt a warmth spread through my chest, knowing that Shay was growing up and exploring her talents. "Did she say what she was planning on doing?"

"She wants to surprise us. I tried to get her to tell me, but the kid is tough."

"She is. I wonder what she'll do." I pictured Shay standing under the spotlight, beaming like a sun, her eyes twinkling as she looked out into the crowd below her. She had grown and changed so much in such a short time. "When is this?"

A spray hit my back. "Tomorrow around four. At Fantasia Academy."

I sighed, feeling my heart pounding a little faster. I was nervous. Nervous for Shay. But I was excited at the prospect of seeing what she and the other kids could do. It was her moment to shine. I was happy for her.

Valen was silent for a moment. "I want you to be careful tomorrow with the oracle, Leana," he said softly, his voice firm but gentle at the same time. "We don't know what we're going to find. You might not like what this oracle says."

"I'm pretty sure I won't." That was an understatement.

"I don't want you to do anything reckless."

I snorted. "Me? Reckless? Never. Don't worry. I'll be the picture of responsibility."

Valen let out a soft growl, which was both arousing and scary.

"What?" I asked as I turned my head to look at him and saw how concerned he was.

He gently turned me around and sprayed my lower back, then my ass, and then he crouched to get the backs of my thighs. I was very *aware* of how close he was to my Lady V region, and it rejoiced at his nearness.

But I also prayed to the goddess that I didn't accidentally let out a tiny fart.

"I don't like oracles." The air moved behind me, and I felt the giant stand up.

"You've met an oracle before? You didn't say?" He was most definitely full of surprises tonight.

"I have."

"And? Care to share?" He didn't sound very enthusiastic about it. But I wanted to know. I needed as much information as possible before meeting the oracle.

"I don't trust them."

"Oka-a-a-y." I could sense the apprehension in his voice as he spoke those words. Valen was always a stoic man, but he couldn't hide a flicker of fear in his tone. It made me realize he was on edge about whatever we were about to face.

"Why don't you trust them?" I asked. He was going to make me pull it out of him.

"Oracles have a way of telling you what you want to hear," he said, "but not necessarily what you *need* to hear."

I nodded in agreement. It was true that oracles could be manipulative and often spoke in riddles that confused you more than when you started. But that's only what I'd read. I'd never met one before. The only oracle I knew of was the one in the *Matrix* movies.

I couldn't help but feel a shiver run down my spine at the intensity of his voice. Valen was not to be taken lightly, and the fact that he didn't trust oracles made me even more wary of them now.

"I get it. But I have to do this. I have to meet with the oracle. I need to know why the Legion of Angels is after me. I can't keep on like this. I need answers."

Valen was quiet for another long moment. "Remember one thing," he said, "that the future can be unpredictable and ever-changing. No one can possibly know what will happen, not even the oracles."

"I guess. Try telling that to the angel legion. They're taking their oracle's prediction to a T."

"Maybe. But I'd caution you to exercise some restraint with this oracle," he said firmly. "No matter what it tells you."

"I will." I nodded, feeling slightly reassured by his words. Yet I still had that lingering feeling of fear of what I would hear.

His hands were firm as he began to massage the spray into my skin, his fingertips pushing just the right amount of pressure. It felt heavenly, and I found myself leaning back into his chest, letting out a soft moan of pleasure.

Valen chuckled, his breath hot against my ear. "You like that?" he whispered, his hands moving down to my lower back, where the tension was the most severe.

I let out a contented sigh, feeling my muscles relax under his touch. "Feels amazing," I said, my eyes fluttering closed. My muscles were tight. They needed a little giant's touch.

"I love touching you," he breathed.

"I love it when you touch me too."

The giant laughed, but then his hands stilled for a moment, and I could feel his breath hitch. When his hands moved again, they were tracing lazy circles down my spine, and I knew he was just as affected as I was.

"I can't help it," he murmured, his lips brushing against the shell of my ear. "You're so soft, so beautiful. So tempting."

I'd never considered myself as tempting or attractive, but whatever floated his boat. I was all in.

As he continued to work on my back, his hands moved lower and lower until he was dangerously close to the curve of my ass. I inhaled sharply as he leaned in close, his lips brushing against my ear. His expert hands were heavenly. His touch was electric, making me feel alive and wanted in a way that no one else ever had.

Valen's strong hands began to knead my tense muscles, sending waves of pleasure through my body. His touch was both gentle and firm, and I closed my eyes, losing myself in the sensation.

"You're tense," he said his voice low. "Relax, I'll take care of it. I've got you."

I let out a soft moan, unable to control my body's response to his touch. Valen's fingers were like the perfect combination of hot and cold, and I could feel my body responding to each and every stroke.

"Where'd you learn how to do that?" I whispered, warmth pounding in my core. Probably with all the other girlfriends he'd had, not that it fazed me. Well, maybe just a little.

"A giant never reveals his secrets," he murmured, sending a shiver down my spine.

"As a witch, I can make you."

"Then you should make me," he growled.

"Maybe I will."

The next thing I knew, I let out a screech as my feet left the ground. I was in his arms, and he was moving out of the closet toward the bed.

He laid me down, his eyes traveling over my nakedness as he pulled off his shirt and ripped off his jeans.

My heart melted a little bit as I looked into those dark depths of his eyes that were full of concern for me and my safety.

"Hurry up. I need more relaxing," I teased.

The giant chuckled as he stepped out of his briefs, his long manhood standing at attention. It was always a shock, no matter how many times I'd seen it and the damn thing's size.

He lowered himself over me and kissed me for a long time, a feeling of something more than passion behind it. His lips moved over my neck, raining kisses and gentle licks that tempted and tormented my senses. I felt the heat rising within me as Valen's calloused hands slowly slid down my body to my thighs, sending jolts of pleasure through my veins as he found my secret spot. With every expert touch, I trembled and moaned in perfect pitch. It was almost too good to be real.

I never knew sex could feel like this, but now I was addicted to it.

The sight of this gorgeous man moving above me combined with the raw passion radiating between us ignited pools of desire within me.

Wrapping my legs around his waist, I clung to him, determined never to let go. We moved together in an embrace of emotion and desire, becoming acutely aware of each other's need for one another. And when Valen finally thrust inside me, I welcomed him entirely into myself.

But even as our bodies intertwined in passionate lovemaking, I couldn't shake the feeling of unease that lingered in the back of my mind.

What would this oracle reveal to us? And would it be something I could handle?

We'd see.

CHAPTER 13

Have you ever met an oracle? Yeah, me neither.

I couldn't help but imagine a kind of fortune teller, the cliché madame with a turban on her head and a crystal ball on a round table cluttered with tarot cards set in a cigarette-smoke-infested room in some dingy apartment building in the worst part of the city.

Turns out, we headed to Hell's Kitchen, a part of Manhattan I visited regularly. It was one of many paranormal neighborhoods or, rather, an area where they seemed to congregate. There were many districts like this one in the city. Off the top of my head, I counted twelve, but Hell's Kitchen was probably the largest after the Twilight Hotel.

I shifted in my seat and took a deep breath, trying to calm my fluttering heart. The truth was, part of me didn't want to hear what the oracle had to say because I had a horrible feeling it would be bad news. Of course it was. Why else was the Legion of Angels after me?

"You okay?" came Valen's voice next to me.

I turned and looked over at the giant, his handsome face set in a worried cast. I thought I was a professional at keeping my feelings hidden, but he knew me too well.

"I'm fine." Total lie, and from the twisting of his mouth, he knew it too.

Valen slowed his SUV at the next red light. "You look nervous."

"Just a bit jumpy. That's what two cups of coffee in under five minutes can do to a person."

Valen turned to look at me, and I turned away, knowing he'd see the lie on my face. I didn't want him to think I was afraid of what some oracle had to say. I was a Merlin, for crying out loud. Oracles were just seers, visionaries, not demons or even assassin angels.

"So how do you know this oracle?" The leather pulled as I turned around in my seat.

"Well," began Elsa, sitting in the back seat with her hands folded in her lap, "let's just say I've picked up a few tricks after living so long in this city." The witch had refused to stay in bed after being stabbed and nearly dying last night. I tried to reason with her, and Polly did, too, but Elsa wouldn't have it. She refused to tell us where the oracle lived unless she came with us. Stubborn old crone.

"Yeah, like how to be frustratingly pigheaded,"

Jade added, sitting next to her. She'd also come for moral support.

Elsa glared at Jade before turning around and looking back at me. "I met the oracle a few years ago when I was dealing with some troublesome spirits. He helped me out of a tricky situation, and ever since then, we've been in touch."

I nodded, taking in the information. "And he's willing to help us?"

"He owes me a favor," Elsa said with a smirk.

I grinned. "What *kind* of favor?" I asked, making Jade burst out laughing.

Elsa wasn't laughing. "Not *that* kind. Really, Leana. You have a dirty mind. You know that?"

Only when it involves Valen. I shrugged. "So, what kind of favor? Seriously."

Elsa blinked at me. "I once saved his life when a rogue troll tried to kill him. Not everyone appreciates what oracles have to say."

"A rogue troll?" I asked, surprised and impressed. "How did you manage to handle that?"

Elsa shrugged, a ghost of a smile on her lips. "Let's just say I have my ways. But trust me, this oracle is the real deal. He can see things that no one else can. He'll tell you what you need to know. I'm sure of it."

Valen grunted in disapproval. I knew he didn't trust oracles, and I knew there was history there he didn't want to talk about. But I also had the feeling he wasn't in a hurry to hear whatever this oracle had to say because of me. Because of how I would react.

Maybe he thought I'd freak out or something. Maybe I would.

"And you trust this oracle? What's his name, by the way?" Maybe if I knew his name, I wouldn't be so nervous. He'd seem more like a real person and less like a dark prophet of doom.

Elsa blinked. "The Brilliant Herald."

A bout of nervous laughter escaped from my throat. "I'm sorry, what?" Looked like Elsa was trying to be a joker this morning. I glimpsed at Valen to see if he was smiling, but the giant was focused on the road, his expression blank.

"The Brilliant Herald," Elsa repeated as though I were hard of hearing.

I glanced at her. "No. I heard you. I mean, that can't be his real name? Is it his stage name?" Maybe oracles were like fortune tellers or gurus, with stage names and a huge social media following.

"Sounds like a character from a children's book," said Jade, a doubtful look on her face. "Is this guy for real?"

"He's real." Elsa gave an annoyed sigh. "It's his real name, or at least the only one he gives. I'll admit it sounds a little absurd. Maybe he needs to keep his name secret? You know, because knowing a being's real name can be used against him."

"Like a demon's true name," I guessed.

Elsa nodded. "Maybe. I don't know. All I know is that he's been going by this name since I first heard about him."

"Hmmm." Either this oracle had a sense of

humor, or he was going to be a handful. I was leaning toward the latter.

Jade shrugged her shoulders, unconcerned with the oracle's name. "Well, whatever his name is, it doesn't really matter if we need his help. Right? We should just be grateful that he agreed to meet us and answer our questions. At least we have an idea of where to go now." She stared at me with a bright smile on her face.

"He knows we're coming. Right?" I asked after a moment of silence.

The last thing I wanted was to show up unannounced and be turned away. As soon as Elsa had mentioned that she knew an oracle and that this oracle might be able to tell us what the angel oracles foretold, I couldn't stop thinking about it. It meant that if this seer could tell me what the fuss was about, I didn't have to go trying to trap another angel. We all knew how well that had turned out.

Elsa glanced out the window. "I called this morning."

I waited for Elsa to give me more, but she didn't. "And he's *agreed* to help, right?"

"Like I said," continued the witch and then winced when she shifted in her seat, having probably pulled the stitches in her shoulder. Her eyes met mine. "He owes me. It shouldn't be a problem."

"Hold up." I peered at her. "Are you saying he hasn't agreed to help?" I stared at the older witch, the realization of what she was saying slowly dawning on me.

Elsa paused briefly, not meeting my gaze. "He didn't exactly say no…" She trailed off.

I groaned, feeling the knot in my stomach tighten. "That's not very reassuring." Damn it. This was not how I'd planned it in my head. In my head, the oracle was welcoming and had solved the big, prophesied riddle. Looked like I wouldn't catch a break.

"I know. I know." Elsa's voice was laced with frustration. "But trust me, if anyone can get us the answers we need, it's him. He'll help. I wouldn't take us there if I believed he'd be of no use to us."

My heart sank. So much for getting some answers. It seemed like the oracle would make us work for every bit of information we needed. But then again, that seemed to be the norm in this city.

"He said he'll hear us out," pressed Elsa, having sensed my apprehension. "But I can't guarantee anything else. The oracle doesn't take kindly to people wasting his time. He's a busy man, Leana."

I nodded slowly, feeling a sense of dread creeping up on me. What if the oracle refused to offer any help? Or worse: what if he confirmed my suspicions about my father's words, that I was transforming into someone else—or *something* else? That something inside me would soon be revealed and change me forever. Yeah. Good times.

I took a deep breath, reminding myself that I was a Merlin and a grown-ass woman. I could handle whatever was thrown my way. I didn't have a choice.

I turned halfway, looking at the giant to see if he had anything to add. Valen kept glancing in his rearview mirror, the muscles along his jaw tightening and his frown deepening. I knew that look. Something was up.

"What?" I looked over my shoulder, not knowing what I was supposed to be looking for.

"We're being followed."

"What?" Elsa, Jade, and I chorused at the same time.

My heart pulsed against my chest. "Is it the legion? Is it the assassins?" Crap. When I thought I'd have the morning off from attempted murder by angel assassins, here they were, tailing us. "But I sprayed myself?" Okay, that sounded strange coming out of my mouth.

"Maybe you missed a spot?" offered Jade.

I didn't. And if it was them, it meant that Elsa's spray didn't work as well as she thought.

"Could be the angels," said the giant, his eyes flicking from the windshield to his rearview mirror.

"Can you lose them?"

"No. Traffic's too tight. We're barely moving as it is."

"And you're sure they're following us?" asked Jade, looking behind through the back of the Range Rover.

"I'm sure." Valen took the next right.

I glanced at my side mirror. "What car are they driving?" I wanted to get a good look at them and see for myself if they were really following us.

"The black MINI Cooper," answered the giant.

Yup. There it was, just one car between us and the

black MINI Cooper. It took the same right and kept following.

I didn't feel like fighting another group of angels this morning. Especially not when my magic wouldn't be of much help. Not to mention that Elsa was by no means in any shape to fight with defense magic, nor was Jade, whose head was still shaped like someone had taken a sledgehammer to it. It was less swollen, but her skin was marred with angry purple-and-red bruises.

Only Valen could make a difference. And that solely depended on how many of those halo bastards could fit in that tiny car.

Let's face it. This was not a good thing.

As we drove deeper into Hell's Kitchen, the streets became darker, and the buildings stood closer together. I could feel the supernatural energy pulsing around us, like an electric current that threatened to overwhelm me. Or maybe that was just my nerves freaking out at the prospect of battling more angel assassins. The fact was, they wouldn't stop coming, which only intensified my need to seek out this oracle.

Valen turned onto a side street. The buildings were made of brick and stone, but many were damaged with broken windows, busted doors, and signs that once hung on the doors but now lay scattered in the street.

"We're here," said Elsa, pointing to a nondescript building that looked like it could have been fabulous in the 1950s.

Valen parked his Range Rover at the curb and killed the engine. I glanced at my side mirror again. And, sure enough, the black MINI Cooper came up behind us and parked.

"Ohhh. I don't like this. I don't like this one bit." The worry in Elsa's eyes was unmistakable. I didn't blame her. I'd be the same if I'd been stabbed by a pale angel bastard.

Jade was unusually quiet, anxiety radiating from her as she ran her hands up and down her thighs. She was scared. They both were.

And it was all my fault.

Part of me just wanted to say screw it and leave. But then what? It's not like the angels would stop following or would stop hunting me.

"I'll take care of it," said Valen, as though reading my thoughts. "You three stay in the car."

Before I could object, the giant slipped out of his seat and shut the door.

I yanked off my seat belt, and the three of us all turned and watched as Valen made his way to the MINI Cooper, walking like the predator he was, about to whack a few angel heads.

God, he was hot.

He stopped near the car and just pointed at it.

Again, totally hot.

And then something happened that I didn't expect.

Three car doors popped open from the MINI Cooper, and three females stepped out. Not angels.

"No. Them? It's the women from *The Supernatural*

Lounge," said Jade, her tone the same amount of surprise as I felt. "What are they doing here?"

"They followed us." I sighed in relief. "They're annoying but harmless."

The three of us slipped out of the car, seeing Valen with his arms crossed, speaking to the three young females.

As soon as Daisy spotted me, she hurried forward, her phone pointing in my direction.

"Leana!" she said, the other three running behind her. "Are you here to see the Brilliant Herald? The viewers want to know."

I didn't know how she knew about the oracle, and I didn't ask. "You got a new phone?" I said instead, seeing the gleaming black, untarnished screen.

Daisy bolstered her phone closer to my face. "Does this have to do with the angels trying to kill you? Is it a prophecy? Did the Brilliant Herald foretell it? How does that make you feel?"

I frowned, irritation filling me. "No comment."

"Are you marked?" continued the female. "Are you going to die? Is that what the oracle predicted?"

I gritted my teeth. Assaulting a younger female in the middle of a human-infested street was not the way to go, even though every part of my being wanted to punch her in the mouth to shut her up.

I looked at Valen. "You think…"

The giant nodded. "I'll take care of it. You three go in. I'll be there in a minute."

"Thanks." I turned to Elsa and Jade. "Lead the

way," I said to Elsa, seeing Valen from the corner of my eye herding the YouTubers back toward their car.

My legs felt like rubber as I followed Elsa to the entrance, which was a plain wooden door with no markings or indication of what was beyond. Elsa knocked three times, and we waited.

A few moments later, the door creaked open, revealing a dimly lit room. The smell of incense wafted through the air, making me feel dizzy. I squinted, trying to make out the figure standing in front of us. I'm not sure why, but I'd imagined Gandalf from *The Lord of the Rings*, a tall, mysterious wizard dressed in a long, flowing robe that was embroidered with symbols and patterns.

But that's not what I got.

Yes, the man standing before us was old with wispy white hair and piercing blue eyes that seemed to stare straight into my soul. But he wasn't wearing a cloak or a robe. Nope. In fact, he wasn't wearing much.

He stood in only a tiny pair of leopard undies with a bulbous, protruding abdomen.

"Welcome," he said in a low, gravelly voice. "I am the Brilliant Herald. Come in."

Here we go.

CHAPTER 14

"Uh…" I looked over at Elsa. "Is this…"

"Normal?" Elsa gave me a wide smile. "Yes. In a matter of speaking. What *is* normal? But the described behavior that conforms to social norms. The Brilliant Herald is… eccentric."

"He's an exhibitionist," I retorted. Looked like I was going to get my prophecy told by Homer Simpson.

The oracle turned around, and I covered my eyes. Not sure why I did that. Yes, I am. Because I had a feeling this side of him would be even worse. I peeked through my fingers and exhaled in relief. His undies, though teeny weeny, weren't a G-string. Thank the gods. But his backside wasn't much better than the front.

With Jade's snorts and trying *not* to stare at the older man's droopy bottom, we followed him into the room, which was sparsely furnished with a few chairs and a table. The walls were lined with shelves filled with books and trinkets. I had the feeling this room held more secrets than I could ever imagine.

The room was lit only with flickering candles casting eerie shadows on the walls. The air was thick with the scent of incense, and I had to suppress a cough as we made our way farther inside.

"Why have you come?" asked the Brilliant Herald, turning to face us. He interlaced his fingers and set them above his belly.

He couldn't have been more than four and a half feet tall, reminding me of Olin, but that's where the resemblance ended. Where Olin had bright orange, wild hair, and a long, pointed nose, this man, this *oracle*, had wisps of white hair and a tiny flat nose. He was barefoot, and his toes had seen better days. Looked like he hadn't cut his toenails in years.

Elsa stepped forward, her hand clutching her locket. "We need your help."

The oracle made a grunt. His eyes flicked over to Jade and then rested on me a little longer than necessary. A lot longer than necessary.

"And who might this be?"

"This is Leana," Elsa replied, gesturing to me. "She's the one who needs your help."

The old man's eyes seemed to bore into mine, and I suddenly felt very small and insignificant, though I towered over him. My forehead itched, and I felt a prickling inside my head, kind of like when Nikolas had used his vamp mind-controlling skills, but different. I still didn't like it.

"And why have you come here, Leana?" asked

the oracle, the itchiness on my forehead intensifying. Was he trying to see if I'd lie?

I let out a puff of air. "Well, it's a long story, Mr. Herald, Mr. Brilliant, uh… sir." Yeah, we were off to a great start. "The short version is that angel assassins are trying to kill me because of something their oracles predicted—a prophecy. That's all I know."

The oracle pursed his lips. "I see. And you believe by coming to see the Brilliant Herald you could discover what the angel oracle predicted and then relate this to you?"

"Yes."

The oracle's eyes flicked over to Elsa, and I could see the unspoken tension between the two of them. He owed her, but maybe he didn't want to owe her this much. But then again, he did call himself the Brilliant Herald. It was worth a shot.

"Can you do it?" I realized that could have been constructed as rude, but the words were out of my mouth before I could stop them.

The Brilliant Herald's eyes narrowed, and I felt the pressure on my forehead increase. I tried not to squirm under his intense gaze, but it wasn't easy. I had never felt so exposed before. It was like showing up to a party wearing nothing but a smile and my modesty with all my bits on full display.

"Very well," he said at last, breaking eye contact. "The Brilliant Herald will help you, but I must warn you that the knowledge I possess is not always pleasant. Sometimes, the truth is a bitter pill to swallow."

I nodded, feeling a knot form in my stomach. "I like pills. They're my comfort food," I joked with a laugh. He didn't. "Right. I just need to know what I'm up against. Why they want me dead. The usual."

The sound of a door opening cut through the air, and I turned to see Valen stepping into the oracle's abode. I glanced at the oracle. He didn't look one bit surprised to see the giant. Maybe he'd *seen* him coming.

The giant did a double take at the sight of the nearly naked older man. And I had to bite the inside of my cheek to keep from laughing.

Valen met my gaze and gave a sheepish smile. I guess it was hard to take someone seriously when so much of their skin was visible.

I wondered what had happened to Daisy and the others. Had Valen scared them off, or were they waiting for us outside—phones drawn and ready the moment we stepped out?

Paying no attention to the tall, crazy-ass muscled man, the oracle gestured to me. "This way."

He led us, me, to a table in the center of the room. An old typewriter sat on the table next to a stack of blank paper and nothing else. I couldn't see a crystal ball, tarot cards, a ouija board, or anything that said fortune teller. Just the dingy typewriter.

Two chairs were positioned before the table—one facing the typewriter and the other directly on the opposite side.

The oracle pulled back the chair next to the typewriter and sat. He waved a hand at me. "Sit," he ordered.

I glanced at Valen, seeing his scowl, and did what I was told. I pulled out the chair and sat facing the oracle.

"This is *so* weird," came Jade's whisper. Though I knew she'd meant it just for Elsa, her voice had sounded loud, and we all heard it.

I couldn't help but nod. This was definitely weirder than anything I'd ever experienced, and trust me, I'd had my fair share of weirdness throughout my life.

My heart pounded in my chest as I kept fiddling with my fingers, not knowing what to do with my hands. First, I leaned them on the table, and at the oracle's glare, I snatched them off and squeezed them between my thighs. I felt like I was about to jump out of my skin. I was so nervous.

This was it. The moment of truth. The moment when I would finally learn why the angel assassins were after me. And part of me didn't want to hear it. Part of me wanted to run out of here and go as far as I could away from the oracle.

But it was too late, and it seemed as though my butt was superglued to that chair. I wasn't going anywhere.

The oracle fixed Elsa with a stare. "This will settle the Brilliant Herald's debt to you. You'll not solicit me or demand my services after this is done."

Elsa gave a nod. "Yes. Your debt to me will be paid. You have my word."

The oracle made a grunt of approval. Then he closed his eyes and took a deep breath, his body stilling as though he was entering a trance. I watched in silence as he remained motionless for what felt like an eternity, feeling my friends' and Valen's gaze on my back.

Magic assaulted my senses, a crap load of magic. It was like a supercharge had been turned on. Looked like the tiny oracle was very powerful. I felt a chill run down my spine, and I wondered if he was summoning something dark and dangerous.

The oracle reached out, cracked his fingers, and then settled them over the keys, hovering but not touching. I felt a strong surge of magic coming from his fingertips.

And then the old typewriter began to move, typing out letters as though it had a mind of its own.

"Holy shit." My eyes widened as I watched the typewriter spit out words with an ease that was almost supernatural. Hell, it *was* supernatural.

Like I said, this was the weirdest thing I'd ever encountered.

"I need a picture," came Jade's voice, and I turned to see her with her phone in her hand. "Jimmy's going to love this."

Elsa just looked in awe and, if I had to guess, a little jealous.

Valen, well, he still looked upset, pissed, and he was staring at the typewriter with a deep loathing. He probably wanted to smash it.

I leaned forward, trying to get a glimpse of what

the typewriter was typing. But I couldn't see past the paper, and I was left to wonder what secrets he was uncovering.

"So you're actually getting communication from up there?" I said and pointed toward the ceiling like a fool. "How does it work? Is it like a recording of a prophecy? You're pressing rewind?"

The oracle said nothing.

"Much better than a crystal ball. Right?" I laughed. "Or glancing at tea leaves? I never understood tea leaves."

"Quiet," snapped the oracle. "You must not speak until the prophecy is complete."

I clamped my mouth shut, staring at the typewriter as it continued to type, and leaned back in my chair. The sound of the typewriter filled the silence, the clack of the keys echoing off the walls. The oracle's eyes remained closed, his body motionless as though he was in a trance. I wondered how long this would take and whether I had any chance of escaping the angel assassins before it was too late.

Minutes passed, and the only sound in the room was the *click-clack* of the typewriter keys and the breathing of those behind me. I shifted in my seat, feeling the tension building inside me. What if the oracle couldn't find anything? What if he couldn't read the oracles up there in the heavens and was just writing gibberish to get rid of his debt to Elsa?

The air in the room grew thick, almost suffocating, and I found it harder to breathe. Sweat beaded on my forehead, and my heart rate quickened as the typing grew louder. My eyes flicked to the oracle's face, but his eyes remained closed. He was completely absorbed in whatever the typewriter was spitting out.

And then, suddenly, the sound of the typewriter ceased. Just stopped.

The silence in the room was deafening as we all waited with bated breath. The oracle finally opened his eyes and stared at me with a newfound gravity. I felt my nerves kick into overdrive as I waited for him to speak.

"The knowledge I possess is not meant for the faint-hearted," he said in a hushed, melodramatic tone. He yanked out the paper from the typewriter, and I watched as his eyes moved along the page. I had the sudden foolish notion to reach out and grab it from him to read it.

Instead, I leaned forward, my heart in my throat. "Can you tell me what it says?" I could feel Valen's gaze on me, but I kept my focus on the oracle, not wanting to miss a thing.

"Yes," agreed Elsa. "This is precisely the reason why we came."

The oracle cleared his throat. "It is foretold that a Starlight witch will be born on the day of the new moon. This witch will draw their strength from Alpha Centauri's triple-star formation."

Just like me…

"Once, every two thousand years, the stars will

align with the moon and further empower the Starlight witch to unfathomable levels."

"Whoa," came Jade's voice.

"On the night of the next full moon," the oracle droned on, as though Jade hadn't spoken, "in conjunction with the alignment of the stars, the Starlight witch will become the key that unlocks the gates of hell, bent on destroying all life."

The room fell silent.

"Am I the only one here who thinks this is a load of crap?" I waited for an answer from Valen, Elsa, or Jade, but no one said a word.

"This is a joke," I tried again. "You're joking, right? This can't be right?" My heart pounded in my chest, each thud seeming to reverberate through the room. My mind raced as I tried to process what the oracle had just said. That on the next full moon, with my stars aligning, and as a Starlight witch, I would open the gates of hell? It didn't make any sense. Why would I do that? I wouldn't.

No. This was crazy. I would never do such a thing.

"The witch's existence poses a threat to the Legion of Angels and our world," the oracle continued to read. "And she must be eliminated at all costs."

"Wait a freaking minute." I rubbed my eyes with my fingers. "Enough with the Obi-Wan Kenobi gibberish. I don't understand. What does this all mean?"

The Brilliant Herald leaned back in his chair.

Holding the paper, he gave a flick of his wrist, and I swear I saw the ink vanish. He placed the now-blank prophecy over the pile of papers. He then glanced at me from across the table and said, "It means that if you do not die, you will bring the end of the world."

Awesome.

CHAPTER 15

My very existence was about to bring the end of the world. Wonderful.

Not exactly the happy-go-lucky prophecy I was hoping for. Not that I thought it would be a cheerful prediction. I just wasn't expecting it to be so ominous, doom and gloom, and final. But there you have it.

Me, Leana Fairchild, Merlin extraordinaire was about to bring on the apocalypse.

Nice.

"You okay?"

I gave the giant a shrug. "I've always wanted to be special."

Valen sighed, staring at me, his expression almost sick with fear. "This isn't funny. I warned you about them. Oracles are full of shit. I wouldn't believe half of what he said."

"Elsa and Jade do," I told him, staring at the floor. And so did I. For some reason, I believed every word the oracle read on that paper. Was that foolish? Guess I was foolish, then.

I had been silent on the ride back to the apartment above the restaurant, listening to Elsa and Jade argue about the "true meaning" of said prophecy. I couldn't bring myself to speak. I was in shock, in denial, and totally confused. I didn't want to be a *key* or whatever the hell it said in that prophecy. I didn't want to be responsible or involved in something so disturbing as opening the gates of hell. Yes, I had a few moments of self-pity and the "why me's." It was a lot to process. So yeah, I had a bit of an internal meltdown on the ride home.

We saw no sign of the YouTubers when we stepped out of the oracle's residence. The MINI Cooper was gone. Valen's doing, no doubt. Good. Not sure I would have been able to deal with them with the way my ears were still ringing with white noise. Because I might have done something a lot worse than smash their phones—like smash their heads.

"You look green," Elsa had said when we'd dropped her and Jade off in front of the hotel.

"You look like me the morning after I finished two bottles of wine on my own," Jade had added.

"I'm fine," I'd told them, and by Elsa's questionable frown, she didn't believe a word I said. Neither did I.

I'd forced a smile and a wave at the two witches as Valen pulled the Range Rover around and parked it behind his restaurant. I'm pretty sure my feet had some kind of magical autopilot mode because I didn't recall a single step I took up the stairs and into the living room before falling into the couch. It was like a hazy dream.

"I don't care what they think." Valen paced around the living area, a storm of emotions brewing on his face. He looked like a caged lion, ready to unleash his wrath on the moron who'd open his cage to toss in some meat. "Listen to me. Oracles can twist their words only to get a reaction from you. You need to read between the lines. Take their predictions with a grain of salt."

"But it wasn't *his* prediction. It was the legion's oracles. He was just reading it back to me, like reading an email." The images of the oracle's belly and the typewriter typing away magically were still very fresh in my mind. Yes, it had been the strangest experience in my life so far, but it had also been one of the gloomiest.

Valen shook his head. "Oracles are notorious for being cryptic and difficult to understand, including the Brilliant Herald. They don't always mean what they say. They get off on these riddles. The guy gave himself a title. Think of that. He's full of himself."

"Why do I get the feeling meeting this oracle dredged up something in your past?"

A deep breath sifted through Valen. He grimaced, and a dangerous glint flashed across his eyes. I couldn't tell if it was strangely endearing that he was so outspokenly opposed to the idea of oracles or if it had to do with some past experience. My bet was on the latter. But as I waited for him to go into more detail, he stayed silent.

"Valen?"

Valen hesitated, his sharp gaze scanning the apartment before returning to me. "You believe him?"

"I do." Unfortunately.

Valen's jaw tightened, and he stalked closer to me next to the couch. His hand cupped my cheek, his thumb brushing along my bottom lip. He looked tense. "You shouldn't."

"Easy for you to say. You're not the one who's the supposed key to end all life. Yeah, no pressure."

"You're stronger than that. You're not some puppet tangled in their strings. You're a Starlight witch. You're a badass. You control your fate. Don't let them dictate it for you."

I leaned into his touch, grateful for his comfort. Valen had become my rock in times of uncertainty. It's why I loved him fiercely. Wow. I really did love this giant. "But what if he's right? What if *I'm* the cause of the end of the world? That's kind of a lot to deal with at the moment." Give a witch a break.

"You're not," said Valen.

The words were spoken with such conviction that I almost believed him. Almost. I locked eyes with the giant. The worry lines on his forehead were a testament to how much he cared for me.

And in that moment, I thought I fell in love with him all over again.

Valen ran his hand through my hair. "Prophecies

are not set in stone. They're merely possibilities and not always the most probable ones. You're not the only Starlight witch. There are others. The legion might have descended upon them too. We just don't know."

I cringed at the thought. "Sure. But what if I *am* the Starlight witch in that prophecy?" Desperation crept into my voice. "What if I'm destined to bring on the apocalypse because my angel father decided to do the horizontal tango with a mortal witch?" Because, let's face it, that's exactly what had happened. A few nights of passion and then—bam! I was the Death Bringer.

Here I was, a child of the unholiest union in the history of celestial beings. But despite my unconventional origins, I was still a kick-ass witch.

Valen propped his hands on his hips. "And Shay?"

I met his gaze, knowing exactly what he was asking. "I have to tell her." My gut twisted just at the thought of adding more stress to that kid. But I had to tell her. "I won't lie to her, and I won't hide the truth from her either. She deserves to know in case… in case something happens to me." I swallowed hard, trying to shake the cloud of doom from my mind. It wasn't working. "And if something should happen…"

"Don't. Don't talk like that."

"It might. So I want you to promise you'll look after her."

"Nothing'll happen." Valen practically growled

those words to me. I swear he had some werewolf in him somewhere. A distant cousin? Perhaps a great-great-great-grandfather or something.

"I need you to say it," I pressed, my throat contracting. "Say it. Say you'll take care of her."

Valen let out a long breath through his nose. "I promise I'll look after Shay. But nothing will happen."

"I appreciate your confidence, but so far, it doesn't look good." It would have been nice to be able to call up my angel father and have a chat. Shoot the halo shit. Who knew, maybe he had the answers I needed right now. Too bad I couldn't reach him.

Valen stroked his chin. "Look, Leana. I know this is a lot to take in. But trust me, you're not going to bring about the end of the world. Yes, you're a powerful witch, but you can control your powers. You always have. You have ultimate control over what you do with them."

I nodded, trying to believe his words. But doubts still lingered in my mind. "What about the part where I open the gates of hell? Like I'm some key or something?"

Valen frowned. "Again, it could be a metaphor, or it could be something that can be prevented. We'll find a way to make sure it doesn't happen."

I cracked a faint smile. "How? You heard what the oracle said. It's possible that just by existing, I could be the key to unlocking powers I don't even have control over. It's no wonder the Legion of Angels wants me dead." If I were truly going to be responsible for the death of all things living, I'd want me dead too.

The giant placed his hands on my shoulders and forced me to look up at him. His dark eyes were intense, and I couldn't look away. "Leana, you can't let this prophecy define you. You're more than just a Starlight witch. You're strong, and you can control your powers. You'll beat this. Listen to me. You're not going to open the gates of hell. You hear me?"

I nodded, feeling a flicker of hope inside me. Maybe Valen was right. Maybe the prophecy was just a twisted version of the truth meant to scare me. But then, why was the legion so adamant to kill me? Yeah. That didn't make sense. What made sense was that the prophecy rang true, and I would have to die in order to save the world.

Nice.

I needed to focus. I needed to think. I needed to come up with a plan to save my life and, at the same time, *not* open the gates of hell. Good plan.

I sighed, feeling a weight settle back onto my shoulders. "When's the next full moon?" I asked, my voice low and filled with tension. I knew it had to be soon. Otherwise, the Legion of Angels wouldn't have sent their assassins after me.

Valen's jaw ticked. "Tonight."

I felt the blood leave my face. "I think I'm going to throw up." I let my head fall in my hands. Tonight didn't give me much time to prepare. Plus, I still had the assassins on my tail. Hopefully, Elsa's spray would keep them away until I figured this out. *If* I figured this out. So far, it didn't look good.

I bounced in my seat as Valen sat on the couch next to me. A big, strong arm wrapped around my waist as he pulled me tightly against him, holding me close. I closed my eyes for a second, taking in his scent of musk and aftershave and letting it soothe me.

We sat like this for a few minutes, the silence heavy with anticipation. With Valen's arm wrapped securely around my waist, I leaned into him, taking comfort in his warmth and strength.

"We'll figure it out," he promised. "I won't let anything happen to you."

The raw emotions in his voice had my eyes burning. "I know." What else could I say?

Valen let out a sigh and ran a hand through his hair. "All right. Let's say, for a moment, that the prophecy is true. What are you going to do about it?"

I shrugged. "I don't know. I mean, it's not like I can control when I was born or the stars aligning or the damn gate to hell opening. It's all a bit out of my control. Don't you think?"

Valen chuckled humorlessly. "That's not what I meant. I meant, what are you going to do to prepare? To prevent the prophecy from coming true?"

I frowned, considering his words. "I'm not sure what I can do. I don't even know what my powers will be and whether I can control them. And the gate to hell? How do you even close something like that?"

"Good questions," Valen said, nodding. "Do you

feel different? Have you started feeling this... change?"

"Like, do I feel suicidal or the need to kill? No." I took a breath, knowing exactly what he was implying. "But I do feel different. Like something's brewing inside me." Which only cemented my belief that the prophecy rang true.

Valen stared at the floor, and I could tell this bit of information bothered him. "Let's think about this logically," he said. "You need to find a way to stop the prophecy from coming true while protecting yourself from the Legion of Angels."

I sighed. "Right. But how do I do that? How do I stop this star alignment? I can control their power, the energy from those stars, but I can't *move* them. They're freaking stars. It's not how my power works."

"Maybe you can, and you just didn't know you could."

I blinked and stared at his face. "Come again?"

"If the prophecy can be changed with a simple alteration, then let's come up with a plan to do just that. If you shift those stars around so they don't align, the prophecy will cease to exist. It'll stop it from coming true." Valen's words were strong and reassuring. He was my anchor in the storm that was my life.

"Wait." I shifted in my seat, feeling a glimmer of hope inside me. "You honestly think I can move those stars?"

The giant traced a finger down the side of my

cheek. "I have no idea what you can and can't do. But since I've met you, you've been unstoppable. There hasn't been a situation where you didn't figure it out. Where you didn't kick some ass to get what you want," he said, a smile in his voice.

"I like kicking ass."

"I've noticed." Valen laughed.

"And if I can't? Move the stars?"

His gaze was heady. "Then you'll figure something else out. No matter what, we'll change the outcome. We'll break the prophecy."

I sighed. "That would be amazing." A nervous energy coursed through me as I thought through Valen's words. Could I really move those stars? It seemed impossible, but if there was a way, I had to find it.

The warmth of his hands around me and the passion in his eyes were devastatingly irresistible. Instinctively, I moved my arms to loop around his waist. It felt like the most natural thing in the world. His lips parted as he drew in a breath of my scent, taking in my face and mouth as he gazed at me with widening eyes.

Remembering how good his kisses were, I was tempted to grab his face and kiss the hell out of him. I had a lot of tension that needed some release. I needed something to ground me, even if it was just for an hour or so. And Valen's kisses and his love-making might do just that.

"We'll figure this out. I promise." Valen leaned closer and kissed one corner of my mouth. Then the other side, pulling gently on my lips and sending pools of warmth into my belly.

The sensation rippled through my body as his fingertips brushed against the small of my back. His lips pressed into mine, and he pushed a probing tongue between them. I tasted coffee on him.

A soft moan escaped me as my fingers entwined themselves at the back of his neck, bringing him closer to me. It felt wrong to be doing this during such a moment, but it reminded us both that we were in this together; it was worth it.

I pulled him close, my body responding to his like a magnet. I let my nails trail over the back of his neck and up to scrape over his scalp, and I threatened to pull out his hair. I scratched him gently as my tongue danced with his, my body flush with desire.

He was sexy as hell and turned me on just by looking at me with those damn fine eyes. Hell, he could melt my panties with just a kiss. I was a very lucky woman to have found such a man, such a giant.

Too bad I was about to end the world and couldn't enjoy more of him.

I didn't think I could move a star, not even on a good night with a clear sky. And I didn't want to disappoint Valen by telling him so. I wasn't a goddess. I was just a witch who happened to wield the power of the stars. I was nothing special if you didn't count the part where I happened to be a key to open the gates of hell tonight.

So, if I couldn't move the stars, how did I stop this

apocalypse from happening? What else could I do to stop the prophecy?

And then it hit me.

If I couldn't *move* the stars to keep them from aligning, I'd find a way to *close* the gates of hell. That's it. I was sure there was a spell or something. If this gate was similar to a Rift from the Netherworld, there was a good chance I could close it.

Yeah. Look at me making plans.

Now, all I had to do was live long enough to see it through.

CHAPTER 16

While I spent the rest of the day researching the Alpha Centauri system, trying to understand the mechanics behind star alignment and the cosmic energy that flowed through them—and not doing a very good job at it—I'd asked Elsa and Jade to look into a spell that could close the gates of hell. I needed all hands on deck for this one and might as well use the witch arsenal at my disposal. I wasn't ashamed to ask for help or to admit that some spells, magic, were just out of my depth.

"Yes, yes, yes." Elsa had gripped her locket, rubbing her finger along the pewter casing with a lock of her dead husband's hair a few minutes after I'd called her. "That part of the prophecy had me shaking with chills," expressed the older witch, staring up at the ceiling as though she were getting her own forecast from the oracles in the heavens.

"What gave me the chills was that dude in his tiny undies." I chuckled. The image was imprinted on my retinas—forever. I caught Valen smirking, and I smiled at him. He looked much more relaxed than before. It was a good look on him.

Jade doubled over, cackling with laughter. Her head shot up, and she wiped the tears of hilarity from her eyes. "Oh my god. I mean, come on. Seriously. I never would have expected an oracle to look like that. It's too absurd for words."

"Right?" I giggled. "Like flowing robes and a staff."

Elsa let out a puff of air. "That's a wizard in some fantasy movie. Oracles don't hold staffs. They don't need to. They have the power of divination."

I snorted. "There was nothing divine about the Brilliant Herald. But the typewriter trick was *interesting*." More like amazing. It was the kind of magic I wished I could do. He looked like a pawnshop owner, not an oracle who received words of wisdom from the heavens. Yet he'd given us the prophecy from the angels. That had to mean something. The dude had some skill. However, I did hate what he'd transmitted.

Elsa licked her fingers and flipped the pages of her tome. "So, you think if you can move a star or close the gates, you can stop the prophecy from happening?"

I nodded. "That's the general idea."

"And you'll be scot-free?"

"That's the plan. We go for two, and hopefully, we'll get one to work." I looked over at Valen, who'd been quiet this whole time, his attention focused on the book he was reading. I couldn't tell what he was thinking. His features were carefully smooth, but that didn't mean a cyclone wasn't brewing in that giant brain of his.

Elsa leaned back. Her face pinched in thought. "Well, considering the alternative, I think it's the only choice you have. It's not like you can speak to the Legion of Angels. If I could, I'd give them a piece of my mind," she added, tapping the side of her nose.

"I think it's a great idea." Jade skated to the kitchen, poured herself a glass of water, and rolled right back. "It's going to work. I can feel it." It was hard not to be charmed by her confidence when she wore those denim overalls and a red cap over her blonde locks.

I gave her a tight smile, wishing I shared her enthusiasm. I wanted this plan to work, at least one out of two, but I couldn't shake off the dread that had settled in my gut when I left the oracle's shop and stayed there like a festering wound.

"And *we* are just the witches to help you with that," announced Elsa. "If shutting down this gate is anything like closing Rifts, we shouldn't have a problem. Rifts can be closed. You yourself, Leana, have closed at least one that I recall, when that horrible janitor Stanley wanted to ruin the hotel."

"Raymond," I corrected. "Assistant manager." I remembered that night on the hotel's rooftop, battling demons and the poor bastard Raymond falling through the Rift right before it closed.

"Whatever," said Elsa, waving her fingers at me.

"The point is that gateways and portals can be closed. This is good."

"And if you're wrong?" asked Jade, zooming around the apartment on her roller skates. She did a pirouette and glided around the furniture like a character from *Disney on Ice*.

Elsa frowned and propped her fists on her hips. "I'm not. But we better get a move on and find a spell that'll work. Because we don't have much time until the full moon."

With a determined look on her face, Elsa quickly took out a dusty old book from her bag, set it on Valen's Brazilian pine dining table, and started flipping through the pages. Jade skated over to her and peered over her shoulder.

I knew Elsa and Jade were my only hope to close the gate at this point. I had already spent countless hours trying to figure out how to do it. But closing the gates of hell seemed to be a task beyond my witchy capabilities.

Beep! Beep! Beep!

I snatched my phone off the table and tapped the timer app to off. Then I reached over, grabbed Elsa's magical angel repellent, stood up, and moved away from everyone to spray my entire body with it.

"How often do you need to do that?" asked Valen, a comical arch to his brow.

I set the bottle back on the table. "I've set my timer to every three hours, just in case. So far, we haven't had any angels knocking on our door, so I'll take that as a good sign. Guess it works."

"It *works*," snapped Elsa with a slightly annoyed tone to her voice.

Jade met my gaze and gave me her "wide eyes," and I could tell she was trying hard not to laugh.

But I was grateful for Elsa's angel repellent. Being invisible or undetectable to angels was the only good thing I had going for me right now. I didn't want to mess it up.

It seemed like hours later, all of us deep in concentration, as we pored over old tomes, scrolls, and the Merlin database.

My eyes burned from the strain of reading my laptop's screen for so long without a break. I was close to numb-butt again, and I could feel pressure on my bladder. I seriously needed to pee.

Suddenly, Elsa slammed her hand on the table, making me jump, and I think I might have peed a little.

She turned to Jade. "I think I've found it," she said, a glimmer of hope in her voice. "This spell can only be cast during the full moon, which requires— oh. That won't work."

"Why? What is it?" I asked, swiveling my body to get a better view of her expression from where I was.

Elsa looked at me. "Because it needs at least two full days for completion."

My heart sank. "We don't have that."

"I know." Elsa sighed, her face compressed as she stared at the tome's pages. She drummed her hands on the table, a defiant sparkle in her eyes. "But... if we work hard and fast enough, we might be able to pull it off. No. We *will*. There's nothing here that we can't do. Nothing out of reach. Blood of a virgin, ashes of a demon," she read. "Pfft. Like taking candy from a baby."

I laughed, though it sounded forced. "Blood of a virgin? Do I dare ask where you'll get that?"

"My friend Edna sells that in her shop on Canal Street, Witchy Delights," said the older witch. "There's always a fresh supply of virgin's blood."

Ew. I didn't want to have to think about that.

"Barb can help too," said Jade, hovering next to Elsa. She jabbed a finger at the page, but I couldn't distinguish what she was pointing at from where I was sitting. "That old witch has more magic in her white hair than all of us combined. And we'll need to be prepared to banish those that might slip through. They'll wish they'd never tried to cross over."

Right. "Because some will have probably escaped through by the time the gates close." I realized this was a possibility. It wasn't ideal. But a few demons compared to the apocalypse… I took that as a win.

"These gates," I said. "They're just a metaphor for something like a portal. Right? They're not these giant iron doors that we need to push and lock?" The image of these massive iron gates as high as the empire state building had me nervous and laughing on the inside, but there was still a possibility that it might actually happen.

Elsa looked at Jade before answering. "That's what we think. Like a much larger version of a Rift."

"How much bigger?" Rifts were hard enough to

close, and they were about the size of a large door. Something twice or five times that size would be a real challenge.

Again, Elsa and Jade looked at each other. "Well," began Elsa, "let's just say... the size of New York? Possibly bigger?"

My mouth fell open as dread hit. "But... that's crazy." It was hard enough for a skilled witch to close a regular-size Rift. This sounded unattainable. I tried to keep my face from showing the defeat I felt in my bones. Even if we banded together all the witches in New York, I didn't think that was enough power to close this gate.

But Elsa's eyes narrowed determinedly. "We'll manage," she said, her voice firm. "We'll just have to pool our resources and work harder than ever before. Failure is not an option. Because if we fail..."

She didn't have to say it. We all knew the circumstances should we, or rather I, fail. I doubted the angel legion wanted this to happen, which explained why they were so adamant about killing me.

I sighed, toying with my thumb ring and wishing I had some magical item—a relic or something—that could help close the gates quicker, but that seemed like too much of a fairy-tale dream at this point.

I felt Elsa's gaze on me. "We will do this," she said again as if by doing so, she could make it come true. She waved a finger at me. "You concentrate on moving those stars of yours, and we'll take care of the gate."

I smiled. "Yes, ma'am."

It sounded insane, but at least we had a plan. With a plan, we could move things forward and make things happen.

So while Elsa and Jade were busy with that, Valen and I scoured through ancient texts and modern-day scientific papers from the Merlin database, trying to find a way to move stars. We looked for any information we could find on star alignments that was needed for the prophecy.

So far, after hours of research, I got a whole lot of nothing that could help me move a star. It sounded ridiculous. No one, as far as I knew, could move a star or a planet. That was science fiction, not real life.

And as the hours flew by, my anxiety increased, and the thought of having the power to move a freaking star seemed impossible.

I had about forty-five minutes left before I had to meet up with Shay at her school for the magical talent show. I could not be late for that. Since Valen had told me, I'd been curious about what she'd show as her "talent." It was cute that she wanted to keep it a surprise.

Once the show was over, I'd have to have a chat with her and get her in the loop on things with the angels and the prophecy. I was not looking forward to telling her. I wouldn't leave her in the dark. Not anymore.

Now, if only I could find something to help me move a damn star...

My eyes moved over the screen, and my heart stopped.

"Wait a second." I leaned forward and checked the screen again, my eyes going a little blurry from staring at the laptop screen for hours on end.

"You found something?" Valen stood up and came around to stand next to me. The sound of feet scuffing the floor sounded as Elsa and Jade bumped into my shoulder.

"What did you find?" Elsa leaned closer.

I tapped my finger on the screen. "This here. It says a mage in 1516 claimed to have the ability to move stars by using an old type of magic ritual and... look at this... using *star* magic."

"Starlight magic." Jade's eyes rounded. "Like you."

"That's right." I nodded slowly, feeling a sense of hope rising within me. Maybe, just maybe, there was a way to move the star and fulfill the prophecy.

"So what you're saying is that he used his Starlight magic to move a star?" asked Elsa.

"With a ritual," I said.

My heart began to race with excitement at the possibility. Could it really be that simple? Could I use my Starlight magic to move a star? It sounded crazy. It was a long shot, but it was the best lead we had so far.

"Do you have the ritual?" Valen asked, his eyes scanning the screen.

"Uh..." I scrolled down the screen. "I don't see anything. No."

"Do you have any information on this mage?"

Valen met my gaze. "The more we know about him, the closer you'll be to that ritual he used."

I typed in a few more search terms and quickly found what I was looking for. "Yes, his name was Alexander Nightthorne. He was known for his mastery of star magic—or Starlight magic and was a renowned mage in his time. Says here he was a Star mage." He was a Starlight witch like me, but back then, perhaps being a Star mage sounded more prestigious than being a simple witch.

"Star mage, my ass," said Elsa, pulling the thought right out of my head. "Sounds like a pretentious buffoon. He's just using fancy words to describe the same thing you do."

"Okay," I breathed, feeling a spark of hope. "Let's see what else there is about Alexander. See if I can find any more information on his star-moving ritual."

Because without that part, I basically had nothing.

My heart started beating faster. Could it really be possible? Could I actually *move* a star with my magic? My mind raced with possibilities and doubts at the same time. I had to find out more about this mage and his methods.

I saw an image that looked like a copy of an old scroll, and I clicked on the link. It opened to reveal just what I thought, an old piece of parchment. The title of the link read Alexander Nightthorne's grimoire.

Okay then.

My pulse thrummed as I glanced at the image and began reading what looked like instructions to move a star. This was it. It had to be. It was complex and dangerous… and the solution to my problem.

I looked up at the gang and took a deep breath. "I think I found a way to move the star," I said, feeling a mix of excitement and fear.

Elsa's face lit up. "That's amazing! What do you need to do?"

"Wow," said Jade.

I glanced at Valen before answering. "It says here that I need to gather a lot of power from my starlights and channel it through a specific pattern of spells. It won't be easy, and I can only do it at night. Obviously. I also have to make sure to control the star's movement and make sure it didn't cause any harm to our planet or any other stars." I didn't want to make matters worse. If I accidentally moved the moon, I'd be in a helluva lot of trouble.

"So, it's possible?" Jade was staring at me in awe like I was a singer from one of her favorite eighties' bands.

I nodded. "Looks like it. I mean, this guy did it. And if he had the same power as me, I should be able to move a star too." That's right. I could do this.

Valen frowned. "What if something goes wrong?"

"We have no other choice. We have to try," I replied firmly.

"I agree." Elsa nodded. "We have to try. We won't know until we try it." She reached out and squeezed my hand. "I have faith in you, Leana. If anyone can move a star, you can."

I didn't know what to say to that, so I just smiled.

It seemed like a long shot, but after reading more about it, I felt like it could be our answer. The only way to stop the prophecy from coming true and prevent myself from being hunted down by the Legion of Angels forever was to use this ritual and manipulate the stars into another alignment. I just needed enough power and energy to make that happen, which meant I had some major work ahead of me if I wanted to pull it off...

"So..." Jade leaned on the table next to me, her eyes glimmering with excitement. "When do we start?"

I grinned, feeling a sense of determination settling in me. "Tonight."

That's right. Tonight, little ol' me was going to move a star.

CHAPTER 17

Fantasia Academy looked exactly like it did every day of the week when I brought Shay here to study all things magical.

Wedged between two other buildings, the old and worn structure had an almost majestic appeal. The large castle-like building boasted towers and turrets that towered high into the sky, making it stand out from its neighbors. Though you couldn't see it at first glance, the glamour of this particular building was unmistakable, as though a veil had been pulled away from my eyes in order to reveal the truth: a paranormal school hidden from the eyes of regular humans.

The air around me crackled with magic as we passed through the tall iron gates.

"Ooooh, this is so exciting," shrieked Jade. "I've always wanted to come to this school."

"We know. You haven't shut up about it," said

Elsa, a tiny smile on her face as she walked next to Jade.

"My parents couldn't afford it." Jade ran her fingers tenderly along the iron gates like they were made of some precious metal.

Yes, it's true. Shay was very fortunate to attend such an elite school. And I knew she was grateful. She was a good kid. She deserved it.

When we reached the stairs, Valen stepped up the stone platform and knocked three times on the massive oak double doors with me, Elsa, and Jade coming up behind him.

"Stop fidgeting," snapped Elsa.

"I can't help it. I'm way too excited," said Jade.

"You look like you need to use the bathroom."

Jade stuffed her hands in her overalls. "I'm so excited. I definitely could pee my pants."

I laughed just as the front doors swung open to reveal a tall, thin-shouldered man with a balding head, an elongated nose, and an amused smirk.

"Yes?" The man spoke in a slimy voice, barely masking his arrogance. A wave of garlic mixed with something unpleasant broke over me, and I barely managed to stop myself from wrinkling my nose in distaste.

Irritation welled in my gut. "Cosmo, you know who we are. You know me." He gave us the once-over with a deadpan look, like when you meet someone for the first time and instantly know you're never going to be friends or when someone doesn't even bother trying to hide how much they can't stand you.

The teacher, caretaker, or however he was employed in this school glanced at us casually. "Tickets," he said.

"Tickets?" Oh, crap. I didn't have any tickets.

A twitch of a smile appeared on Cosmo's face at what he saw on mine. "Without tickets, I can't let you in. You'll have to leave."

"Here." Valen pulled out four tickets from his jacket pocket. He wore a dark suit with a crisp white shirt that pulled around his biceps as he moved. Not to mention his ass looked scrumptious in those pants.

Disappointment flashed over Cosmo's face as he took the tickets. He glanced at them longer than necessary, and I had a feeling he was making sure they were legit. I despised this guy.

Finally, he said, "These look adequate. You may enter." With the tickets still in his hand, he stepped aside, his eyes on Valen. Was that a little worry in his expression? Yeah. Yes, it was.

I heard Jade squeal as we followed Valen inside. The last time I was here, I'd accidentally killed the sorceress Auria by removing that pendant from her neck. I shook those memories away, not wanting to think about such ominous events when I was supposed to be here for Shay's special day.

We stepped into a grand marbled foyer with elaborate high ceilings like those of a luxurious hotel. The charm magic from the school's glamour filled the room, sealing the building off from any supernatural access. I could feel the tingling magic radiating from every corner of the room, shimmering around me in pulses that mimicked the beat of a giant heart—the heart of the school.

The room's main feature was a graceful, curving stairway that swept up to the second and third floors. The school was incredibly imposing. Everywhere I looked were gleaming wooden doors and railings, stunning curtains, chairs, and side tables.

It looked exactly the same as the last time I was here, all except for one major thing. It was packed with male and female paranormals.

Adrenaline stabbed through me as my gaze swept across the room at the crowds of assembled witches, weres, and shifters, wondering if I'd ever crossed paths with them. Nope. These were strangers. Some were dressed in modern clothes like us, and others were clad in rich, colorful clothing made of fine silk and embroidered with golds, silvers, and reds. They were all engaged in happy conversations, no doubt thrilled about seeing their kids performing onstage. The scents of strong perfumes mixed with the paranormal aromas filled the air along with the pulse of magic and energies.

My heart sank when I thought of Matiel, our father. Shay would have really loved to have him here today, and I knew she was hurt by the fact that he couldn't be here, even more that he was impossible to reach at the moment. Hopefully, our being here would cheer her up. Nothing in the world was going to stop me from attending this important day for Shay. Nothing.

As I took in my surroundings, I noticed a tall, handsome man with a shimmering glass of liquid in his hand flash me a flirtatious grin. His female companion, however, seemed less than pleased with the attention I was getting and gave me a sour once-over that made my cheeks redden. I quickly averted my gaze.

"This is so cool," came Jade's excited voice beside me, her eyes wide and spinning around on the spot, trying to see everything at once. "Where's Shay?"

"They're performing in the auditorium," announced Valen, his gaze on the same handsome stranger throwing smiles at me. "This way." He reached out and grabbed my hand, pulling me gently with him. It was like he was claiming me as his, like he wanted the other males here to know that I was his property, and he'd pound in their heads if they got too close.

I wasn't complaining. I loved it when he did things like that. It made me feel special, desired, and I wanted to feel like that all the freaking time. Who wouldn't? When a man like Valen showed interest in me, I could just break out in cartwheels.

I caught jealous looks from a few females watching us as we passed them by. Their envy of me was palpable. Valen had been the most sought-after bachelor in the paranormal community. Well, not anymore. Now, he was mine.

I followed him without a word, Elsa and Jade

right behind us, though I could hear their excited whispers along the way. I wondered how Valen knew his way around and had so much knowledge about this school.

A large sign draped over a large entrance declared, WELCOME TO THE FANTASIA ACADEMY TALENT SHOW.

Valen took us through the doorway that unveiled a spacious auditorium with several tiers of seats running alongside the aisles. The walls were a glossy, polished wooden paneling. At the end was an imposing stage where it seemed the children were going to put on a show. It was splendid and delightful—from the graceful ceiling and walls to the gleaming chandeliers and luxurious armchairs. The lighting was a soft yellow, and it was beautiful to watch the different shades of yellow and orange play upon the walls and the other students in the room.

The air was a mix of trendy, earthy incense with the musky scents of a hundred bodies. The rustling of quiet whispers and the shuffling of feet as they hurried to their seats were amplified by the walls and took on a strange warbling tone. More people were in here. Some were already seated, and others conversed in the aisles. The first row next to the stage was filled with anxious-looking kids. I spotted my sister, who sat still like a witch popsicle with only her wide eyes moving.

Oh, dear. She looked like she wanted to bolt.

"Look, there's Shay." Jade pointed. "She looks scared. You think she'll cave and run?"

I looked over my little sister's face. She did look pale and like she was about to throw up. Part of me, my maternal side, wanted to rush over there and hold her, to protect her. But I knew she'd hate that.

"I guess we'll see." Even if she did decide not to perform, I wouldn't force her to do anything she didn't want to. If she got stage fright and changed her mind, that was fine.

"Here." Valen pulled me along to a middle row with five empty seats. I sat, met Shay's frightened eyes, and waved at her.

Shay blinked.

Damn. She was worse off than I thought.

"Poor dear," said Elsa, taking the seat to my left while Valen took the one on my right. "Maybe you should go talk to her. You know, give her some courage?"

Jade sat next to Elsa. "I think you should. She looks like she needs it."

I looked at Shay again, not knowing if that was a good idea or not. I didn't want to embarrass her in front of her schoolmates. So when she made eye contact with me again, I pointed to myself, then to her, and stood up.

Her stiff, fast headshake was all the answer I needed. She did *not* want me near her.

"I think she's fine." Nope. She was *not* fine.

Just as I lowered myself into my seat, I jerked as an intense wave of energy swept through me like wildfire. It was the same feeling I'd felt before, like being fueled by a foreign power, but this time it was even stronger.

"You okay?" Valen eyed me with concern.

"Fine." I sat, my heart slamming against my chest. I didn't know what was happening to me, but I hated it.

"There she is," came a loud voice over the chatter from the crowd from somewhere behind us, pulling me out of my thoughts.

I turned around in my seat and cursed.

Daisy, Dina, and Demi came rushing down the aisle, phones and selfie sticks at the ready. I glared at them as they ran toward me. They were like vultures, swooping in to prey on whatever drama they could find. And this time, it seemed, they had set their sights on Shay.

These YouTubers really didn't give up. The words "viewers want to know" and "potential disaster" came flying out of Daisy's mouth. I wanted to punch that mouth. These girls had no sense of decency or respect for boundaries. They were just here for the clicks and the likes.

Jade looked over her shoulder at what I was glaring at. "Oh, no. What are *they* doing here?"

"I don't know, but if they screw this up for Shay, I'm going to lose it." I glowered at them and then glowered some more as I caught a satisfied smirk on Cosmo's face as he lurked across from us at the auditorium's entrance. "Tickets, my ass." No way did these three have tickets.

Unfortunately, Daisy, Dina, and Demi found a

row of seats right behind us, hovering around me and trying to get me to say something for their channel.

I took a deep breath and tried to calm myself. This wasn't the first time they had followed me, but it was definitely the worst timing. Shay's magical talent show was about to start, and I didn't want her to feel even more nervous with these sharks hovering around us.

I turned to face the three women. "What are you doing here?" I hissed at them, trying to keep my voice low.

Daisy flashed me a grin. "We couldn't resist. A magical talent show? Come on. The potential for views is off the charts."

"If you ruin this for Shay," I seethed, "you'll wish they never invented cell phones." My frustration gave my voice some anger.

Dina rolled her eyes. "Oh, please. We'll be discreet. And if anything, having us here is good for the school. There's nothing wrong with more publicity."

I glared at them but could see there was no point in arguing. They were already here, and nothing I said would make them leave. Instead, I turned my attention back to the stage.

Valen leaned over and whispered, "You want me to take care of them?"

Yes. "It's fine." The image of the giant grabbing the women by their necks, kicking and screaming, did bring a smile to my face.

Suddenly, the lights dimmed, and a hush fell over the audience as we all waited for something to happen. Then a male teacher came strolling onto the stage. He cleared his throat. "Welcome to the hundredth Fantasia Academy's magical talent show. We are all very excited to show you what our students have achieved in such a short time. It is our pleasure to introduce you to some of our students' brilliant displays of magic. We open this evening's event with Zander Willabee."

One of the kids from the front row stood and made his way up onto the stage. He had an awkward gait, like he wasn't used to walking in public or standing in front of people, for that matter. When he reached center stage, Zander straightened his shoulders and took a deep breath before beginning his performance.

His act consisted of hovering different colored fireballs over his palms. He was a cute kid, and the audience erupted in applause once he finished. Zander beamed widely as he bowed before stepping down from the stage.

The next two acts were similarly impressive, with one student performing a complex wall of ice and then melting it with her fire. The next student turned small stones into living insects through simple incantations. Each performance was met with cheers from the crowd, but I couldn't help but feel my eyes wander back toward my sister. She still sat nervously awaiting her turn onstage, which was coming soon enough. I could see her trembling from where I sat. I wished I could do something to ease her fears. She was just a kid, and performing onstage in front of an audience could be quite daunting.

"Here she goes," said an excited Elsa.

Jade took out her phone and began filming. I thought of doing that, too, as I watched Shay take her place onstage, but somehow watching it through the lens of a camera didn't feel right.

She looked so small up there, but she was trying her best to look confident. I could see her hands shaking as she stood there on the platform.

This was her moment to shine, to show off her unique talents as a sun witch. Valen had told me she'd been practicing for days, honing her abilities and perfecting her routine, which she'd kept secret from all of us. And now, it was finally time to put on a show.

But Shay just stood there, looking frightened, like she was about to run off the stage.

Uh-oh.

I watched as Shay met my gaze, seemingly taking courage from the fact that I was here, that we—all of us—were here. It seemed to do the trick.

She took a deep breath and closed her eyes. Suddenly, Shay's hands erupted in a blaze of sunlight, the intense heat and brightness filling the room and illuminating the entire auditorium. I squinted at the bright light. The parents in the front row shielded their eyes, but I could see the looks of amazement on their faces.

Opening her eyes, rays of light emanated from

Shay, dancing, swirling, and twirling in a dazzling display of magic. She began to move, her body fluid and graceful as she performed a series of intricate hand gestures. With each movement, the light around her grew brighter, illuminating her.

With a flick of her wrist, Shay directed the beam toward a group of pots filled with dark earth on the side of the stage that I hadn't noticed there. As the sunlight touched the dirt, shapes rose out of the pots. First, it was just a string of tall green shafts. But they began to glow and grow, bursting into a riot of colors. Sprouting into a row of crabapple trees, their red and pink flowers opened in full bloom at the same time as their leaves.

"Holy crap," I said, not caring how loud my voice was. I was seriously impressed. Shay had just given these seedling trees a boost of sunlight and made them mature in front of our eyes. I had no idea she could do that.

The sounds of gasps and applause rippled through the crowd as Shay's embarrassed smile covered her cute, very red face.

She looked at me, and I gave her a thumbs-up, just as my father's ring burned around said thumb.

I turned my head slowly, searching for the source.

There, lurking at the edges of the auditorium, was the pallid angel bastard.

Well, shit.

CHAPTER 18

Three things hit me at the same time. First, the pallid angel wasn't alone as I spotted the surviving red-beard twin accompanied by a tall female angel and four other males. The second thing was, while I was researching moving stars and closing the gates from hell, I'd forgotten to spray myself with the angel repellent. Whoops. And the third, the school wards didn't work on angels.

"We've got company."

Valen was the first on his feet, ripping his shirt off to the joy of many enthusiastic female observers. I caught a few happy squeals. There were even a few whistles and applauses. Even Daisy had dropped her phone to get an eyeful. Her mouth flopped open, and there might have been a little drool. I didn't blame her. He was quite the sight to behold.

"Get Shay out of here," commanded the big man.

As soon as Valen had pulled off his pants, he was already in his giant form, his *giant naked* form, and he hurtled over three rows of seats like he was taking an easy stroll in tall grasses.

The pale angel smiled as he yanked, not one, but two long, gleaming swords from his back.

That's when the screaming started.

As soon as the females shook out of their hormonal stupor at the sight of Valen's ripped and excellent naked physique, they noticed the band of angel assassins, though I doubted they knew what they were. As soon as they saw their weapons drawn, they realized they were not friendly and ran for cover, meaning anywhere outside of the auditorium.

Paranormal families grabbed their kids and made a mad dash for the doors. Most had the good fortune to make it out unscathed while a few unfortunate souls were knocked over, some deliberately trampled by the fleeing mob. It was crazy.

"Glowing bastards," hissed Elsa. "Why can't they leave us alone."

"Because they want me dead." I stood up. "You guys stay close. You're still not fully healed from their last attack. I can't let you get hurt again." Or killed.

"We're fine." Elsa pushed herself up, and my skin tingled as she called upon her elemental magic. "I might not be in my forties, but I'm not dead. And as long as I still draw breath, I can still conjure my magic and kick some angel butt."

"Amen," said Jade, giving her friend a high five.

I sighed. Elsa might not be showing any signs of

injuries, but that didn't mean she was completely healed. "Fine. Just don't die."

I didn't wait for their replies as I hurtled—more like tumbled headfirst—over the row of seats in front of me, only to get stuck halfway through. I somehow somersaulted over the seat and then half rolled into the aisle in an ungraceful heap. After a considerable amount of effort, I finally managed to make it onstage.

The only thought in my mind right now was to get to my sister. With the shouts and screams of the parents still ringing in my ears, I climbed up the steps and reached Shay.

"Are those the angels that want you dead?" asked my little sister, eyeing the angel assassins with more curiosity than fear. I didn't like that. She should be scared.

"Yup." I grabbed her and yanked her behind me, using my body to cover hers. "And we're leaving."

"What are you doing? I can fight."

Not this again. "I know. And I also know you're just a kid. Way too young for this kind of stuff."

I looked out. Valen was already in the thick of it, taking on two assassins at once with his massive bare hands. He was surprisingly agile for a giant of his size, dodging their blows with ease and landing powerful punches that sent his opponents reeling.

I noticed a few paranormals had stayed behind, maybe parents, maybe the school faculty, but they were definitely not intimidated by the angels as they advanced on them. They should have been.

One of the paranormals hit the ground on all fours. With a sudden flash of light, a massive grizzly bear stood in his place. Okay. They might be more equipped than I first thought. But it wasn't every day you had to battle a pack of angel assassins.

The other two whispered Latin, and soon blue and purple magic dripped from their hands. They were witches or mages—powerful, judging from the sudden influx of magic that crawled over my skin. Together, they sent volleys of magic at the angels.

A cry caught my attention, and then the red-beard angel smashed Valen's back with his mega hammer.

I sucked in a breath through my teeth as the giant stumbled. He whirled around, throwing out his arm, catching the angel's legs, and sending him falling to the ground. But he was up in an instant, swinging that damn hammer with deadly precision.

The sound of metal clashing against metal filled the air as the screams of the fleeing audience mixed with the battle cries of the assassins, creating a chaotic symphony that echoed through the halls.

Daisy and her crew were moving slowly toward the battle, phones up and recording the fight. I could see Daisy's lips flapping, no doubt talking to her "viewers." Wait. Was she recording this live?

"What are they doing?" I hissed. "They're going to get killed."

"Who cares," said Shay. "They're dumb."

"They don't deserve to die because they're dumb." Though that would mean an end to their filming. Still, they weren't my problem. Right now, I needed to get the hell out of here with my little sister.

As Shay struggled behind me, most of the families had left. Which gave me a straight open path to the exit.

"Let's go." Grabbing Shay by the hand, I pulled her with me to the ground and started running down the aisle. Without my magic, I couldn't do much to defend us. Fleeing was my only option. No shame in running either. And to get my sister to safety, that's exactly what I was going to do.

Movement flashed in my line of sight. An angel leaped into the aisle, blocking our way. I halted, my heart thrashing in my throat.

Well, well, well. My pale friend from before.

"Running away?" The angel made a show of his swords and then rolled his shoulders as though anticipating decapitating me.

"Yes." No point in lying. I shifted my body to the left to shield Shay from him.

The angel grinned, his teeth too white to look anything like normal. "You won't escape me again. I am going to kill you this time."

"You don't have to," I said, speaking fast. "I know all about the prophecy. About the stars aligning tonight and the gates of hell. I can move stars," I lied.

It was still a working theory, but if that other Starlight witch, mage, could do it, I had to believe I could do it too. Who knew. Maybe I could reason with the angel.

"I'll move the stars and change the prophecy. You

won't need to do anything." At this point, I would say just about anything to get Shay and me out of this situation.

The angel laughed, his eyes moving to the side, and I spotted Elsa and Jade making their way toward us.

I stiffened. I didn't want him to hurt them again, but I was stuck protecting my sister.

The angel focused on me again, moving his weapons menacingly, his body tensing as if ready to take a swing at my head. "That's not how prophecies work. But how would you know? You're just a stupid mortal witch. You can't undo them. That's not how they function. Once a prophecy is foretold, nothing can change it. You can try to move your stars, but it won't work. The prophecy will always come to pass. *Always*."

"Not this time." Fear and dread twisted my gut at his words. What if what he said was true? He could also be trying to trick me. "Once I move the stars, they won't align. That surge of energy won't happen. The gates of hell won't open. Your prophecy will be broken. So how about you just go on your merry way and leave us be."

The pale angel let out a short, rough chuckle. "You have no idea. It's too late. You can't beat me. You're powerless during the day, *Starlight witch*."

"Touché. But come closer, and I'll kick you in the balls."

Shay laughed as I felt her moving behind me. It wasn't a laughing matter, but I would use my legs to defend myself. On top of that, I was quite skilled with a finger jab or two in the eyes.

The angel regarded me with an annoyed expression. "Nothing you do, none of your efforts will make a difference. It's why we're here to kill you. We'll never let you live. It's inevitable." He raised one sword and pointed it at my face. "You're going to die now." He angled his head, looking past me. "And then after that, I'll kill the other Nephilim bitch."

The rage that overcame me made me dizzy. "You touch her, and I'll rip your fucking head off."

The angel let out a long whistle. "For that, I'll break every bone in your body, and then I'll slice your sister's neck and make you watch… and then I'll kill you." His gaze jumped to mine, delight lighting his eyes. "We are going to have some fun, witch bitch. You're—"

A fireball hit the angel, and his face and upper body were lost in a sheet of yellow-and-orange flames. He screamed as tall red flames rose from his chest and reached high above his head. His howl— guttural, not human—echoed against the walls and reverberated through me.

"I hate that angel." Elsa approached, her hand dripping with her elemental fire.

"I think I hate him more. His face is stupid." Jade stood with her arms splayed, ready to hit the angel with her magic arsenal.

I eyed Elsa. "How?" The scent of burnt flesh filled the air around me as the angel, now fully engulfed with elemental fire, thrashed and screamed. Wow. The angel was actually burning.

The older witch's gaze stayed on the angel. "I made a few adjustments after my first encounter with him. Now he's going to feel it."

Shay's head nudged me as she peeked around my middle for a better look. "Whoa."

I blocked her view with my body. I didn't want her to see that. I couldn't do anything about the screaming.

"Come on. Let's go."

Grabbing Shay by the hand, I pulled her with me in a run, veering around the blazing angel to avoid the flames.

The angel screamed one last time. Then through the flames, his eyes opened against the torment just as another sound came from his lips. Laughter.

I halted.

With a pop of displaced air, the flames that had been burning him a second ago vanished, revealing not a perfectly tailored suit but a scorched one. His face wasn't much better. It looked like an overcooked sausage from a campfire—blackened with some flaky bits.

And then he smiled.

Uh-oh.

CHAPTER 19

The pale, now barbecued angel turned his head and glared at Elsa.

Shit.

In a blurred motion, he threw one of his swords at the witch like a spear.

"Obice!" cried Elsa as a semitransparent purple energy wall rose up from the ground and over her head.

The sword hit.

And I held my breath as the tip pierced Elsa's shield and came within an inch from her face. But that was it. It was sticking out like a deadly toothpick.

Elsa blinked and leaned back, her eyes wide behind her protection wall, her head tilted and staring in fear at the sword's tip. Had she been any slower casting that spell, it would have pierced her face, and she would have died.

Jade screamed a word I couldn't catch, and a blast

of powerful wind hit the angel, throwing him back and giving me those precious seconds to turn around and run.

But I couldn't. My legs wouldn't move. I couldn't abandon Elsa and Jade.

I whipped Shay around by the shoulders. "Is there a back exit to this place?"

Shay nodded. "Behind the stage."

"Go." I pushed her hard. "Get out and run to the hotel. Find Julian and stay there. Got it?"

Shay opened her mouth to protest, but she saw something on my face that stopped her. "Okay. But you'll be okay. Right? You'll come back?"

My insides squirmed. "I will." What else was I supposed to say? Sorry, kiddo, I might get killed? "Go. Go!"

I watched as Shay climbed back up the stage and disappeared around the corner. My gut twisted that she was gone, but at least no one followed her. Shay would be safe.

Someone screamed. Jade.

I spun around in time to see Jade dangling in the angel's grip, her feet grazing the floor.

Elsa hadn't moved, her face twisting with effort as she held on to that protection shield as though if she let go, that sword would skewer her. It probably would.

Heart thrashing, I glanced over my shoulder for help, for Valen. I saw the parents and the teachers first. They were still alive. A cacophony of colors, red, blue, and green, sprang from their hands toward the group of angels. My clothes and hair billowed around me in the wake of their magic use. The smell of earth and grass combined with the stench of sulfur filled the air as I felt the power of the elements working together, interacting, dancing, and bursting with energy.

But when my eyes found Valen, I stiffened and forgot to breathe.

Blood smeared his front as well as part of his head and face. Four angels, including the red-beard one, took turns hitting and stabbing the giant like a party piñata. Their movements were quick, too fast for Valen to parry. For the first time ever, I feared he might not make it. Maybe the angels were too strong for him.

Fear stabbed deep. *Valen.*

I staggered forward, but the sound of Jade's gasp stopped me dead in my tracks.

I whirled around, seeing her red, tear-stricken face. He was going to kill her and then probably finish off Elsa.

And Valen would die if I didn't help.

Who did I try to save first? My friends or the man I loved?

But when I saw the angel lift his other sword, the smile on his charred lips, I knew what I had to do.

I rushed forward. I wasn't known for my great bursts of speed or my talent for one-on-one combat with my bare hands. But it's all I had. And I was going to use them.

With all the force I could yield, I pushed off with

my thighs and threw myself at the angel and Jade like a linebacker. Or a very enthusiastic hugger.

I hit the angel on the side, the surprise knocking the sword and Jade out of his grasp.

I felt her fall, but I was still using my momentum to tackle the angel on the ground. We rolled together, and I gagged at the rancid stench of burnt flesh. I might have swallowed a few burnt skin flakes. I flipped over and got to my feet just as the angel recovered and pushed himself up.

His eyes went to his sword.

But I'd seen it first.

I lunged for it.

Just as I felt a presence above me, I twisted and kicked out with my leg as hard as I could, hitting the angel in the shins and taking him down to the ground. No sooner did he crumple than my hand was wrapped around the hilt. I launched to my feet and swung out hard.

The angel had anticipated that and jumped back, laughing. The bastard thought this was a joke?

"Do you even know how to use an angel sword?" He eyed me—or rather—he one-eyed me—since his left eye was a melted mess that looked like egg white.

I gripped the angel sword tighter. It felt light in my hand, impossibly light, and I knew this blade was made of something not of this world. Didn't matter. It was sharp.

I shrugged. "Come closer and we'll see."

"No mortal shall ever lay their hands on an angel

blade, lest they be sentenced to death. It is a sacred item and must not be desecrated."

I flashed him a smile. "Looks like we already covered that." I flicked my gaze behind him and saw Jade on her knees, breathing hoarsely and staring at Elsa, whose body was trembling with an effort to keep her protective shield from collapsing.

The charred angel stepped forward. "I'll kill you for this."

"Get in line."

The odds were that he *was* going to kill me, but I almost always beat the odds. I was ticked. Pissed that these angels wanted to kill me, yes, but angrier that they wanted to kill Shay, Valen, and my friends. Hell no.

The angel didn't hesitate. He came at me with a kind of superhero speed that you only saw in the movies.

Panic surged, and I jerked, instincts moving in as I tried to remember my one day of training with a sword—wait a second. I didn't have *any* training with a sword.

I swung out. And missed.

Okay. So handling a sword was much harder than it looked on TV and in the movies.

Something hard kicked me from behind, and I stumbled forward. I righted myself and spun around, holding the sword out and slashed at—air.

The angel let out a breathy laugh. "You look like a fool. You have no idea what you're doing."

"I really don't."

A whimper, and then a strangled cry sounded loud in my ears. Elsa. She was going to lose her control of the shield. And when she did, that sword was coming straight for her.

I caught sight of Jade stumbling toward Elsa just as the angel threw himself at me again.

I deflected an attack and spun around, unleashing a punch from my left fist into his stomach. He hunched over in pain, and I followed through with a strike of my knee against his face.

A normal person, a mortal, would have been on their knees in pain. As this was an angel, the bastard only halted for a second. Then he was on me again.

I slashed with his sword, where I thought his neck was, but the angel was a slippery bastard, and my strikes went wide. He was right. I had no idea what I was doing. I was just swinging and hoping I'd get lucky and hit something.

My arm jerked as the sword made contact with something solid. A miracle!

Nope. As the angel's body stopped moving in a blur, I realized his hand was on the sword's hilt. Next to mine.

I blinked just as his other hand, his fist, made contact with the side of my head.

Pain seared as I stumbled to the side, carefully close to blanking out as darkness crept into my sight.

My adrenaline soared, keeping me from doing just that, and gave me just enough focus to step back.

The angel slashed his sword in an arc. "*This* is how you master an angel sword."

"Good for you."

The angel—let's call him Burnie—charged and swung his blade savagely at me.

I threw myself back—but not fast enough.

I cried out in pain as the sword ran across my leg, cutting through fabric and skin. A warm trickle of blood stained my jeans, and I was shocked at how quickly he had moved. Then I was even more startled when his fist collided with my jaw. My legs gave way beneath me, and I crashed to the ground. Spots clouded my vision, and I blinked repeatedly, trying to shake off the disorientation as the metallic taste of blood filled my mouth.

I spat the blood from my mouth. "That hurt, Burnie."

The angel narrowed his one functioning eye. "Burnie? Who's Burnie?"

"I had to call you something. It fits, doesn't it? You all burnt now." I waved my hand at him.

Burnie's jaw clenched. "You insolent witch."

"I've been called worse." I wiggled my jaw and winced. "I think you dislocated my jaw—"

He came out of nowhere. Even if I had magic to protect me, it wouldn't have saved me from his speed.

Everything spun around me, and I felt a searing heat from the blade as it sank into my body. I felt pain like never before, and a sharp cry escaped my lips. The intensity of it overwhelmed me, and I found myself crumbling to the ground in agony.

The pain concentrated in my left thigh. Instinctively, I reached out, my fingers finding wetness over my jeans—a lot of blood. He'd cut me with his angel sword. And he'd gotten me good. Nicked an artery, most probably. If that was the case, I didn't have long.

Laughter reached me, and I looked up to find Burnie standing over me, his eyes wide with excitement at the prospect of me dying, of fulfilling his quota and stopping me from opening the gates of hell with my death.

Through my pain and blood thumping in my ears, I could hear Jade's cry as she tried to pull out the sword that would, any second now, kill Elsa along with Valen's curses as he fought the angels.

"How naïve of you to challenge us," Burnie chuckled as he closed in. He swiped his sword through the air and added, "Don't worry. You won't be alone in death. Your friends will join you. It'll be a party."

"I really hate you. You know that?" I rolled over on my butt and pressed my hand on my wound. Blood seeped through my fingers. It wouldn't stop.

"Not bad for a witch," said Burnie. And now that I was looking straight at him, part of his nose had fallen off during our fight. Ew. Now he had just two slits where his nose used to be. "But you were meant to die. There's nothing you could have done to change your fate. You should have never been born. And now, I'll rectify that."

I struggled to breathe. "You're an asshole."

Burnie chuckled and smiled at me wickedly, seeing the fear in my eyes.

Was this it? Was this how I was going to die? Killed by some angel thug in Shay's school? Nothing was honorable about dying in this way. Bleeding to death.

Fear coursed through me like an icy ribbon and settled into my core. I was going to die. I might as well just accept it.

"I'm going to cut out those pretty eyes of yours," said the angel. "You won't need them anymore. And I might have use for them. Or sell them. Not sure."

"You're sick." Terror slid to my middle.

"And your time is running out. Time to say bye-bye, little witch," he said in warning.

His sword grazed the skin on my neck, my flesh tingling as the cold metal slipped along my jawline and then back, tracing a line along my neck. I felt the angel's grip tighten in anticipation of my death.

I struggled in my failure, in my panic, and then a new fear slid into place behind it. I didn't want to die. Not like this. Shay needed me. Valen needed me. Tears welled in my eyes.

I did the only thing I could at the moment. Sure, it was dumb. But I was going on instincts. I wanted to live.

So, I called out to my magic.

Blocking out as much pain as I could, I pulled on the energy from the stars, hoping, praying that this one time, they'd give me more power during the day.

And then the strangest thing happened.

They *did*.

Not just the usual daylight little trickle of energy. I'm talking the mother lode of power.

A gentle electric buzz filled the air as I was surrounded by the immense cosmic energy emanating from the stars, waiting and ready to be used.

But this time, it was different. Not only because I could reach that much power during the day but because there was more. A hell of a lot more than even during the night.

Was this because of the star alignment? Probably. And the growing unfamiliar strength in my core I'd been experiencing? Of course it was.

But I didn't have time to think about it. An angel was trying to kill me.

As I tapped into the power of the stars, current surged through me, each cold jolt sending shivers throughout my body. My back arched as a giant slip of that power ripped through me. I blinked and stared at the blazing white energy that hovered over my hands.

My awesome starlights. And in daylight.

The pressure of the blade on my neck released. "No. Impossible."

"Yes. Possible."

With a burst of my will, I fired my starlights at the angel.

The beam of starlight hit him. He gave a loud, pained yell as his figure dissolved into dust. His sword hit the floor with a loud thud.

Holy fairy tits.

Another sound of metal hitting the floor had my head spinning around.

Burnie's other sword lay flat on the floor. Elsa and Jade stood in an embrace. Guess his celestial sword didn't do much once he was dead.

Still on my butt, I wiggled around, seeing the other angels' attention all on me. Maybe because I was glowing. Maybe because I'd blasted their pal into ash. Yeah, that had to be it.

I sat in a puddle of my own blood, but I could barely feel the pain. I felt alive. I could finally do my magic during the day. And I was going to keep using it.

The angels stood stock-still for a second. Then a few vanished as they beamed themselves up to the heavens. Some weren't so lucky.

I sent another blast of starlights. The beam split, sending shoots of starlights in different directions.

The remaining angels froze as the starlights plowed into them until they were all consumed by the blazing white light. Like logs burning in a fire, the angels' bodies burst into flames and disintegrated into ash. Until all that remained of them were piles of gray dust, just like Burnie. The angel threat was over. For now.

I sniffed. "Okay. That'll work."

CHAPTER 20

"I'm fine. Quit it." I smacked Polly's hand away.

The healer glowered at me. "You are most certainly *not* fine. You could have bled to death. Now stop moving so I can finish the stitches."

"Fine." I sat on a chair back in my old apartment on the thirteenth floor of the Twilight Hotel. My jeans' left leg was cut to expose my thigh where I'd been sliced with the angel blade, my leg covered in blood. I stared at my hands. They were caked with dried blood.

After I'd obliterated the angels, Valen had rushed over and picked me up, carrying me in his arms as he ran out of Fantasia Academy while using his healing magic on me. Buildings blurred as the giant ran down the busy street. I knew he had some kind of glamour magic too. Otherwise, we'd have been all over social media. Me, dangling in the arms of a great, naked giant.

But I hadn't felt much pain. Whether it was the

adrenaline rush or the rush of Starlight magic, I didn't feel a thing.

Right now, the only thing I felt was elation. I could finally do my magic during the day. Yay!

"You were able to use your Starlight magic." Elsa stood next to Polly, staring at me curiously.

"I did."

"Cool." Shay's legs kicked up as she sat next to me on the table. "I wish I'd been there."

"I'm glad you weren't." I looked over at Julian, who was leaning on the couch, and he gave me a reassuring smile. Although Shay had killed Darius and some of his minions, I didn't want her to witness more death. I was trying to keep her as innocent as I could. Not sure it was working, though.

"Polly says you have to drink this." Jade handed me a glass of blue liquid. "It's to help heal you." Her face winced like she was trying to warn me about how it would taste.

I took the glass and sniffed. "Smells like rotten eggs—Ouch!" Polly had pulled a little too tightly on one of the stitches.

The healer eyed me under her white toque. "You used your magic during the day? I thought you couldn't do that? Unless you've been lying to me all this time." I could tell by the accusation in her tone that she was angry, possibly hurt, that I would hide that kind of information from her.

Jade and Elsa went stiff. Polly didn't know about the prophecy, and I didn't think she should know. Not when there was still a chance to stop it and not have a wild panic on my hands. It was a lot to process for anyone. And the fewer people who knew about it, the better. Or that's what I told myself.

"I couldn't before," I said, giving her a bit of truth. "For some reason, now I can. My father had said there would be some change in me. This is what he meant. That I'd finally be able to conjure my Starlight magic during the day."

Polly's skeptical stare told me she didn't believe a thing I said. "You're lucky Valen was there to stop the bleeding. If not, even your *special* magic wouldn't have saved you. You would have died." Her tone was hard, condemning.

"Right." Okay. She was angry. I cringed and then chugged the contents in the glass, figuring it might calm Polly if I drank her healing tonic. I swallowed. It tasted worse than it smelled.

"Well, I'm happy she used her magic," said Elsa, taking the empty glass from me and setting it on the kitchen sink. "I would have died if she hadn't removed that foul beast. I was barely holding on to my protection shield. A few seconds later…" She pulled a finger across her neck.

"Death by the sword," commented Jade. "I really hated that guy."

Shay leaned forward. "Can I see? Can you show me your magic?"

I smiled at my sister. I knew she loved my starlights, and they loved her equally. "Sure."

I tapped into my starlight, and again they answered as they blossomed into a luminous ball over my palm. With a nudge, I sent them around her, and she squealed in delight as my starlights zoomed around her like a horde of pixies.

It was hard to explain how wonderful it felt to be able to do that. To tap into my magic and use it during the day. It's all I'd ever wanted since I could remember, way younger than Shay. To be like the other witches who could conjure their magic whenever they wanted. Could this mean that I'd always be able to? Or was this just a reaction to the stars' alignment? Getting closer meant I could finally overcome the sun and reach my stars? I didn't want to think this was only a one-time deal. I had to keep believing that from now on, I could use my starlight whenever I wanted. Because why the hell not? I was feeling way too good to start doubting myself.

"You shouldn't be doing that." Polly cut the last of my stitches. I counted eight of them. That would most definitely leave a nasty scar. Nothing I could do about that. Some healing, magical ointments would help restore some of the skin, but it would never be smooth like before.

"It's fine," I told the healer. "They won't hurt her. My starlights love Shay."

Polly dropped her medical scissors in her coat pocket and pulled off her latex gloves. "You need to be resting. You shouldn't strain your body by doing more magic. It'll keep you from healing properly."

"It's no big deal. I feel fine." By her scowl, I knew that was the wrong thing to say to a healer. "Listen, I feel better. That drink helped a lot." I widened my eyes to add a bit of emphasis.

Polly stared at me for a beat. "Your funeral. If you want to overexert yourself and die, be my guest." And with that, the healer spun around and marched out of the apartment.

My mouth hung slightly open as Polly disappeared around the doorway. I could still hear her loud steps down the hall, like she wanted us to hear her, wanted us to know she was ticked. "What's the matter with her?"

Elsa sighed. "She's mad because she knows we're not telling her the truth."

Polly wasn't stupid. Obviously, she knew we were hiding something. But even if I did tell her, what good would it do? She couldn't do anything to help.

"She'll come around." Elsa patted my arm. "Just give it time. All healers have tempers. She stopped talking to me for a whole month when she heard me saying my pumpkin cookie recipe was better than hers."

"I don't doubt it."

Something occurred to me. "Did any of you see the YouTubers? Did they make it out?" I hadn't seen the YouTubers leave, but I had to assume they finally got their heads screwed on right and had left with the others.

Elsa shook her head. "I don't know. But they weren't among the dead. So, maybe they got lucky."

"Hmmm." They weren't my favorite people, but I didn't want their deaths on my hands.

Shay giggled as my starlights pulled her hair up. She looked at me. "I wish my magic could do that."

We all wished we had what others had. Didn't we? And sometimes, I wished we could just be happy with what we had.

"And I wish I could grow plants in seconds like you did," I told her and saw her face light up. "That was incredible. Imagine the garden I could have with that ability?" So true. I could picture us living somewhere in the countryside, surrounded by wildflowers and fruit trees as far as the eye could see. It was a dream.

"It was very impressive, Shay," agreed Elsa, smiling warmly at the girl. "Your magic surpassed those of your fellow schoolmates."

"Really?" Shay held out her hands as my starlights puddled into her palms. And then she hugged them, like they were a big, fluffy cat.

Jade leaned on the table next to Shay. "It was awesome. I've never seen that. Usually, it takes a spell or a potion to be added to the pots, and then that usually takes a few days for plants to mature. You did it in a few seconds with your sun magic. Very cool."

Shay's face turned a bright red. "Thanks," she said, staring at the starlights.

"And," continued Elsa, "my tomato plants might need some of your talent. I'd love to have fresh tomatoes in my salad tonight."

Shay smiled. "I can help make your tomatoes grow." God, she was so cute. I came close to never seeing that smile ever again. The thought terrified me. But it had worked out. My magic, my starlights, had saved us.

Still smiling, I turned my head and looked at Valen. My smile vanished.

Valen stood apart from us. He leaned next to the wall beside my desk, his face set in a hard cast, his eyes worried. He stared at my starlights bouncing around a happy Shay. His posture shifted to an uncomfortable apprehension.

He was the only one, apart from Polly, who didn't seem pleased at all that I could use my magic during the day. He was upset, and I knew why.

A part of me understood that the only reason, though I was trying not to think about it, I could tap into that well of Starlight magic was because we were getting closer to what the prophecy foretold. The stars were aligning, giving me that extra power needed to open the gates of hell.

Valen knew this too. It was why he was so worried, so reclusive.

Our eyes met, and I felt a ribbon tighten around my chest, my throat. Uncertainty and fear flashed in his eyes. Valen was afraid he was going to lose me.

Emotions flared. I swallowed hard and looked away. I didn't want to break down. It wasn't the time. I wanted to take a moment to celebrate our win against the angel assassins, though I knew more would come. And I wanted to celebrate this day, this one time I could do my magic during the day. I just wanted a moment.

Screams sounded down the hallway.

Guess I could forget about that moment.

I could make out the words "sky" and "doomsday." Well, *that* couldn't be good.

I jumped off my chair and cursed at the sudden sharp pain in my thigh, but I managed to shuffle into the hallway. It was empty, which was an odd thing on the thirteenth floor. I hobbled to the apartment across from me and spotted one of my neighbors peering out his window. "Wayne. What's going on?"

He looked over his shoulder as I approached, his eyes going to my bloody thigh, but he said nothing. "Look." He pointed at his window. "Look at the sky. What is that?"

"What's going on?" Elsa appeared, followed quickly by Shay, Jade, Julian, and then Valen, who still looked like he wanted to punch a few angels.

I searched the sky where Wayne had pointed. "Oh. Shit."

The sky looked like Armageddon was upon us.

It was like the sky had taken a beating and was bruised. It was blood red with sparks of deep purple, blues, and greens, like a bruise clotting beyond healing. It was choked with thick red and black clouds with the occasional lightning strike. The sun was covered, like an eclipse, but it wasn't an eclipse. It was only about six in the evening, but it was as if night had fallen in broad daylight, making it gloomy and dark. All the colors were still there, but a pallid shroud cast over the world.

It was obvious this wasn't something of natural origin. This was not supposed to be.

Shouts and cries came from the street below. Humans pointed to the sky. Some had their phones out and were filming. The crash of metal hitting metal shook the building as cars crashed into other vehicles, their drivers too preoccupied with the sky to pay attention to the road.

"It's starting."

Wayne looked at me. "What's starting? What's wrong with the sky?"

"Stay in your apartment. Don't go out." I hurried out his door and went straight to the windows of my place. I pushed the curtains back and stared at the same scarred sky I'd seen in Wayne's apartment.

I felt the air move behind me as the gang crowded around my window and peered out.

I thought about something. "Should we alert the community about the prophecy? So that they can prepare themselves?"

"It's too late for that now." Valen came to stand next to me. "They can't do anything to change this."

I forced away the pang of guilt and apprehension within me. "We don't have much time." I looked at Elsa and Jade. "Is the spell ready?"

Elsa set her jaw, determined, but I could see the fear lingering there. "It wasn't easy, but it's almost done."

"Good." I nodded. "That's good." I blew out a

breath, knowing what came next. I'd barely had time to prepare, but as it was, I was out of time.

Jade crossed her arms over her chest. "You're going to move that star. Aren't you?"

I flicked my gaze on Valen as I answered. "Yes. It's not nighttime, but I don't think that matters anymore." It wasn't like I'd practiced, but if that other Starlight witch, mage, whatever, could do it, so could I.

"Don't you think you should rest a bit?" Concern etched Valen's brow, but something else was also in his eyes, something restless, dark.

I hooked a thumb over my shoulder at the window. "Did you see the sky? There's no time. I need to do this now. Before the full moon… which is in… how long?"

"Two hours, more or less," said Julian, checking his phone. "Is that enough time?"

"Has to be." Goddess, I hoped so. Because I didn't want to think about the alternative.

I watched as my starlights were still dancing around Shay. I felt more powerful than I ever had before. I could do this.

Yes. I was going to move a star and stop the prophecy. Everyone was going to be safe. That's exactly what I was going to do.

But we all knew my plans never worked out the way they're supposed to.

CHAPTER 21

Move a star. Save the world. And live.
No problem.

We were back up on the Twilight Hotel's roof. I figured it was as good a place as any to test my theory. And I was comfortable up here. It was familiar. And I needed that. I didn't want to go somewhere new and have to worry about my surroundings.

The sky was even worse out in the open like that, hovering over our heads like a massive spaceship about to crush us all.

It didn't help that the human population was in chaos, screaming and flash robbing. From where I stood, I could make out humans packed into their cars with their belongings cramped in the back seats, trying to flee the city. Unfortunately for them, Manhattan traffic was a nightmare without the apocalyptic sky. Now, nothing was moving. I could see traffic out to the horizon.

And, of course, a few groups of humans thought this was just awesome, like the neighboring building. A group of happy, drunk people were dancing to music on the roof of their building, and I spotted hundreds more on the other rooftops. Some were partying, and others were staring at the sky in awe.

It wasn't just our lives—we, the paranormals—at stake here if we should fail, if *I* should fail. It was also the humans' lives.

Yeah. No pressure.

But I felt strong, more powerful than ever before. Not only could I feel an extension of my power, like, say, another branch, but also an increase in its supply. A mega one. I was electrified with starlight; I had gone from simply being a regular electrical wire channeling magic to becoming the source of power itself.

I was supercharged with starlights.

For the first time in my life, I felt invincible, like I could do anything at all, even move a freaking star. It was intoxicating. I was on a high, and I never wanted to step down.

I could do this. I could feel it in my bones, the starlight's power pounding in me.

And with that surge of unfathomable power, I was going to move a star. Or nudge it. Well, I just needed to kick it off its course so it wouldn't align. No alignment, no opening of the gates of hell, no apocalypse. Easy peasy.

"Looks like the gates of hell have already opened,"

said Julian, carefully setting down vials and pouches that I could only guess contained poisons and potions, next to Elsa's and Jade's working area. The two witches were on their knees, Jade grinding a blue powder in a ceramic mortar with a pestle while Elsa was bent down, her nose nearly touching the pages of her spell book.

Catelyn and Valen stood on the opposite side of the roof, staring at the humans getting sloshed on the rooftop of one of the neighboring buildings. I'd called the giantess for help, and I was relieved she came to help without question.

"This is really something," said Julian as he lifted his head and stared at the sky. "Never seen anything like it."

I couldn't argue with him that it was a scary sight. A dark cast had settled over the sky, covering the sun and making it feel like it was ten o'clock at night when it was about six forty in the evening. But according to that prophecy, I still had until the full moon, which meant at sunset, so we had less than two hours left.

I was restless. Two hours might seem like a lot of time, but it wasn't. Not when you were trying to prevent some doomsday apocalypse. I was comforted knowing that Shay was safe with the twins in Cassandra's apartment below, though she had been livid about it.

"You always leave me behind," she'd said, her face scrunched up and her eyes round on the verge of angry tears. The pretty were had walked away to give us some privacy and joined her daughters in her living room.

I sighed through my nose, trying to think up a good excuse. I decided to go with the truth. "I don't want you to get hurt. Angels are still after me. You saw what they did back at your school."

The faculty members were probably angry at us for ruining the event and bringing angel assassins to their school. I didn't know if they'd allow Shay back in after what happened. It was another issue to add to my long list of things I needed to fix—one at a time.

"I won't. I can fight. You know I can." Her tiny jaw was set in determination, her eyes brimming with tears of defiance.

I pinched the bridge of my nose, feeling a massive migraine on its way. "I can't have you there distracting me. This is important, Shay. If I fail…" I couldn't bring myself to say the words. Cassandra's head snapped in my direction. Julian had told her. How much of it, I wasn't sure, but by the way she grabbed her daughters, it looked like she knew everything.

"It's not fair." Shay raised her voice. She had a temper, this kid, just like me.

"You can be angry all you want. You can hate me. But you're *not* coming."

"You suck." Shay spun around, marched to the living room, and let herself fall into one of the armchairs. Her arms wrapped around her middle, her chin on her chest. Her face was red, and I could tell she was trying hard not to cry.

Damn it. I didn't want her to feel abandoned or like I didn't care. I did care. And it scared me to death. It was why I wanted her there and not on the roof with me. I'd turned and left, not wanting to stay any longer in case I changed my mind.

I tried to calm my nerves as I looked up to the sky again. I'd always been able to feel my starlights, especially at night, like a soft humming in the air that reached inside me.

Now, it was like a drumming, a pounding, and my ears popped with a sudden change in pressure every other minute.

I could feel the stars, my stars, the Alpha Centauri, moving as they prepared to align themselves.

And I had to stop it. Or move them apart. No biggie.

I stared at the printout of Alexander Nightthorne's grimoire and read the spell again, memorizing it.

Elsa rocked back on her heels, pulled off her reading glasses, and speared them into her red hair. "I've never seen anything like it either. What it means is that the Brilliant Herald was right. This prophecy is happening whether you believed him or not."

"Do you know if he does other clairvoyant... *things*?" asked Jade. "Does he like... Can he tell if a couple is meant to be together?"

Elsa scoffed. "He's an oracle, not a fortune teller.

He receives divine instruction and prediction. You want your fortune told, get a fortune cookie."

"Ha. Ha." Jade smashed her pestle into her mortar, and I had a feeling she was imagining it was Elsa's face.

I looked at the witch with the eighties' crimped hair and denim overalls. "You and Jimmy having problems?" I'd never have guessed that. I'd always thought they were perfect for each other. But even the best couples had their share of issues. No relationship was perfect.

Jade gave a one-shoulder shrug but wouldn't look at me. "I don't know. He's been acting weird lately."

"How weird?"

"Distant."

Hmm. That didn't sound like Jimmy. He was always around, even as a cursed toy dog, wanting to know everything and everyone's business. Kind of annoying, but it came in handy at times.

"All men need their space," said Elsa, pushing her reading glasses up on her nose again. "I wouldn't worry about it too much. You're overthinking things again. Focus on the spell. Would you?"

"I am." Jade's face was flushed, and she mumbled something under her breath. I knew this was bothering her, and I didn't take her for the overexaggerating type. If Jimmy was distant with her, there had to be a good reason for it.

"Guys. Look."

We all looked up to where Julian was pointing, and my heart skipped a beat.

"Oh my cauldron," said Elsa, clutching her locket for protection with one hand and the other covering her head as though the stars were about to fall on her.

"Are those *your* stars?" asked the male witch.

"Yup." I couldn't believe what I was seeing. Normally on a cloudless night, I could get a glimpse of those three stars, like bright dots of lights the size of peas. Now, they were the size of oranges and clearly visible, like smaller versions of the moon, only more brilliant. I'd never seen them that close before, but I could feel them. These were mine.

"That's trippy," voiced Jade. "It's almost like you can reach out and touch them. They're so close."

And they were lined up in a straight line. Well, almost a straight line. The last star was slightly off to the left. But any fool could see they were on their way to form a perfect alignment with the moon.

It was the strangest thing seeing them so near. I might even have been excited, had it not been a sign of our doom. It explained why and how I was able to reach out to them during the day.

But I was going to *move* them back. And everything would be right as rain again. You just watch me.

"Are you ready?"

I turned to the deep voice that belonged to a sexy man with a full mouth that curved up, promising mind-blowing sex. I could attest to that.

"As ready as I'll ever be." That was the honest

truth. How could anyone be ready to stop the apocalypse or doomsday, whatever it was called.

Valen surveyed me. "I wish I could do something to help you."

"You are. You're my muscle. Kick the ass of the angels. I know more are coming." Hell, I was surprised they weren't already here trying to decapitate me again.

The giant's gaze moved to the paper in my hands. "You think it'll work?"

"It worked for this Alexander. He was a Starlight witch, just like me. I have the spell he used. It's not that complicated. Besides, I've never felt so... powerful before." I smiled at him. "I feel amazing. I can do my magic during daylight. It's something I've always wanted." What I'd dreamed of.

Valen raised a worried brow. "Not sure I share your enthusiasm."

I lost my smile. "I know I can do this. Why do I have all this power if it's not meant to do something." Apart from opening the gates from hell, of course.

"What if channeling all this new power does something to you? Changes you?"

Aha. "It won't. Look. It's already happening, and I'm no different. I'm still me. Just more powerful. And I kind of like it. I get to do magic during the day, like the rest of the witches." I looked over his face, seeing the distress in the tightening of his eyes. "Look. I'll let you know if I feel the sudden urge to be bad."

The giant smirked. "I like it when you're bad."

Heat pooled in my middle at his comment as I imagined doing all kinds of *bad* things to him later— once we saved the world. "I know you do."

Valen chuckled darkly. "I don't want my very bad witch to get hurt."

"She won't. Off with you. I'm going to start." I pushed him playfully, and he moved away, joining Catelyn, who was waving at someone from the other building.

"Okay," I declared, having memorized the spell. "I'm going to start. Let's move a star."

Jade and Elsa both stood, Julian next to them. Their eyes were wide, expectant, excited. I could see it. They knew I could do this.

With my heart throbbing, I tapped into my will and reached out to the magical energy generated by the power of the stars. I'd barely grazed into it as a cool shiver of magic washed over me. The intensity made me jerk, and I staggered.

Holding that power and feeling even more confident in my abilities, I took a deep breath and focused on the spell.

"On this night and in this hour, I call upon the goddess and her sacred power," I chanted. "From universe afar in time and space, take this star and move it to a new place."

I closed my eyes as the power surged through me. I could see the stars in my mind's eye, hovering so close in the sky, and I felt their energy within me. With each breath, I could sense the magic expanding, growing ever stronger as I reached out farther. Then, without warning, the energy seemed to coalesce inside of me, a glowing ember that slowly began to pulse and vibrate.

Suddenly, I had the strange sensation of being held in the palm of some giant hand, as if the stars were hugging me in a warm embrace. I opened my eyes and felt my breath catch in my throat as the sky seemed to ripple and shimmer with an ethereal glow. The stars pulsed with a life of their own, and I felt a surge of joy I'd never experienced before—my connection to the stars.

Straightening, I focused on the last star, Runty, seeing as it was the smallest of the group. Then I did what Alexander had said he'd done, as was mentioned in a copy of his grimoire, and imagined in my mind the star moving, dragging it across the sky, and picking its new destination.

And so I did.

The air sizzled with energy as I imagined Runty moving over to the far left. Over and over, I imagined it, the images clear, my mind focused.

But Runty hadn't even budged.

Frustration hit. I gritted my teeth, straining, sweat trickling down my back and temples. I felt the magic gathering again. The air hummed with a buzz of energy as the power of the stars soared through and around me.

With a deep breath, I started chanting the spell again, this time more confidently. I pulled on my Starlight magic as I did and again repeated the steps.

I focused on moving that one damn star. That single star, which had been winking at me ever since I could remember, now became my sole purpose.

And... nothing. Or at least I couldn't tell if I'd nudged it.

But it didn't look like I did. Plus, I had a feeling I would have felt different. Felt *something* to indicate movement.

Despite my efforts, my magic, and my incredible influx of starlight, it wasn't enough to move a star. I'd failed.

Dread hit.

We were all going to die.

CHAPTER 22

I wiped the sweat off my brow with the back of my hand, my arms wrapped around my knees as I sat on the roof feeling more useless by the minute.

I'd been at it for over an hour, maybe longer, and I still hadn't moved a star. I'd even tried the other ones, thinking maybe I'd picked the wrong star, that I could only displace a *certain* one of them, Runty's brother or sister. But even those wouldn't budge.

Nothing happened, even when I cursed them and then when I picked up a broken roof shingle and let it fly. Nothing.

I'd been so confident. So sure of myself, like never before. I'd *believed* in me. Believed I could do it. But I couldn't. I was wrong.

I had more energy coursing through my witchy veins than ever before, but it wasn't enough.

Maybe this was all beyond me? That thought didn't make me want to cry. It made me angry and just a tad depressed when I thought about Shay. She was so young. She had her whole life ahead of her. What would it look like now with demons taking over? Would they even do that? I had no idea. Maybe I should have asked the oracle for more information.

After all, mastering this was supposed to give me power and control over my destiny. It was supposed to break the damn prophecy.

The roof shook, and I looked up to see Valen lowering himself next to me. Looking around, my friends, even Catelyn, were regarding me warily, giving me space. It looked like they thought I was about to lash out. Maybe I was.

"I don't get it. I followed the spell. I did *exactly* what Alexander did. Why isn't it working?" I might not be the most powerful Starlight witch that ever was, but I had some serious mojo. Especially now, having my own star system so close. But even that wasn't helping. Had I done the spell wrong? I didn't want to start doubting myself, but I couldn't seem to figure out why it wasn't working.

Valen shook his head. "I don't know. Maybe he kept some things hidden. Maybe he didn't want anyone else to know how to move a star. Keep all that glory to himself. Mages aren't known to share their secrets when it comes to magic and power. He didn't want anyone else to share that praise."

"Yeah, he was a sneaky bastard," offered Jade. "I know witches like that."

That was a possibility. But I had a feeling he was a witch, not a mage. Not that it mattered anyway now. "It's too late to try and uncover his secrets. It would take days. Weeks. And that's even *if* we find anything useful. We have about fourteen minutes left until the full moon. I have to move a star—any star from that system." I didn't want to admit it, but I was starting to have a bit of a panic attack if my thrashing heart was any indication.

"Maybe he lied."

We all looked at Julian. The tall male witch shrugged. "Maybe he never did move a star. He made it up. Wanted to get the attention, the credit for something that he might not have done. I mean, were there witnesses?"

I shook my head. "I don't remember reading that."

"Right. It was like a diary of his accomplishments written by *him*. He could have been bullshitting."

I didn't want to admit that, but maybe Julian was right. Maybe Alexander was full of crap. He boasted about the ability to move a star when he couldn't do squat. And if that were true, we were in serious trouble.

No. I couldn't let that happen. The fate of our entire world rested on my ability to move a star. Failure was not an option.

But if this Alexander had lied or kept parts of his spell hidden, how the hell was I going to move a star without all the elements?

I stood up, frustration boiling inside me. "We don't have time for this. I have to try something else."

Valen straightened and placed a hand on my lower back. "What are you thinking?"

"I don't know yet," I admitted, "but I can't give up now. Not when the apocalypse is staring at me in the freaking face."

Elsa looked at me with concern. "You've been pushing yourself too hard, Leana. You need to rest for a few minutes."

"I can't rest," I replied, my voice hard. "Not until I've moved this damn star." I felt my starlights coursing inside me, wild and motivated, wanting to help move this star.

Julian crossed his arms. "Maybe we need to think outside the box. What if moving a star isn't about magic?"

"What do you mean?" I asked, intrigued.

"Maybe it's about technology," he suggested. "Maybe a machine or device can do it."

I let out a frustrated breath. "Where are we going to find such a device in less than…" I checked my phone. "Twelve minutes?" I yelled.

The male witch rubbed a spot behind his neck. "I don't know, Leana. You need more power. Like a magical jump-start cable. But whatever you do, do it quick." His voice held traces of frustration, anger, and fear. I knew he was worried, thinking of Cassandra and the twins. Hell, I was worried too. The damn prophecy was about me, not him. And I was starting to lose my cool.

"I think I've got it."

We all looked at Elsa, and the witch added, "That's it. Julian, you're a genius."

"I try."

Elsa reached out and grabbed my hand, giving it a reassuring squeeze. "You need *more* power. You need us."

"Yes." Jade clapped her hands excitedly. "That'll work. With my power and Elsa's and Julian's, the four of us combined, that'll give you your boost."

"You're right." I felt stupid that I hadn't thought of it. Because I thought this influx of my starlights was enough. Because I'd mistakenly thought I was badass enough to move a star on my own. I was a fool. The biggest fool in the universe right now.

"Hurry. Take my hand," instructed Elsa as she reached out and grabbed Jade's hand with her free hand. I watched as Julian grabbed Jade's other hand and took mine to close the circle. "We'll say the incantation with you. What was it again?"

I repeated the spell slowly, twice, until everyone seemed like they'd memorized it. "Focus on moving Runty, the smallest of the three stars."

"Runty?" laughed Jade. "Because he's the runt? I like it."

My eyes fell on Valen, and I met his troubled gaze, not knowing what he was thinking. My stare lingered on his face, taking in the unreadable expression. He seemed like a sculpture carved from stone, but his eyes told a different story. They were raging, turbulent storms. I noticed a small muscle twitching in his jaw.

Valen was freaking out on the inside. We all were.

I pushed my dread and fears away. "Ready?" I looked at their faces, seeing the resolve there and feeling a sense of pride and courage now that my friends were going to help me.

"Ready," chorused the witches.

I took a calming breath and repeated the words again. "On this night and in this hour, I call upon the goddess and her sacred power," we chanted. "From universe afar in time and space, take this star and move it to a new place.

The air around us began to hum with power as our hands clasped tighter together. I felt a surge of energy coursing through me, and I knew my friends were channeling their power into mine.

The four of us closed our eyes and concentrated on the star, directing our combined power into the spell. The air around us shimmered, and I felt a tingling sensation all over my body. I knew Elsa, Jade, and Julian were feeling the same thing.

Elsa's grip tightened on my hand, and I could feel her pouring all her energy into the spell. Julian's eyes were closed in concentration, and I knew he was doing the same. I could hear Jade chanting under her breath and the excitement in my friends' voices as we continued to pour our energy into the spell. It was as if we were all connected, our minds and souls working together to accomplish something great.

As we continued to focus on the spell, I felt my body start to tremble with the effort.

The power of the spell roared through me, amplified by the presence of my friends. The roof beneath our feet trembled as we focused on the star, Runty. Energy pulsated through our connected hands, building with each passing moment. The air crackled with current, with power, and I knew we were close to achieving what we'd set out to do.

I opened my eyes as our magic seeped through our hands and flowed onto us. A feeling of joy drifted through me. With the combination of Starlight magic and elemental magic together, it would be sufficient to move that damn star. I could feel it in me. This was going to work!

And again, I focused on Runty, imagining moving the star away from the others, dragging it to another point in the sky, the universe. I shook, the blood pounding in my ears as I poured every fiber of my magic into this spell.

But after a minute or so of continued pouring of our combined magic and efforts, Runty didn't budge.

The star remained at the exact same spot as before. Actually, it looked like it was more aligned with the others than before. It was creeping up on us.

It didn't work.

"Damn it!" I cursed, feeling a wave of frustration wash over me as I let go of Elsa's and Julian's hands. I walked over to the roof's edge, a sense of failure taking hold of me. After all our combined efforts, that damn star still wouldn't move.

It dawned on me that if I couldn't move it with my extra influx of magic, combined with three powerful witches' magic, there was nothing more I could do.

"Leana."

I turned around, seeing Jade staring at me wide-eyed like I'd just stolen her roller skates.

"What?"

She flicked a finger at me. "Look."

"Huh?" I stared down at myself to where she was pointing, and my breath caught.

My starlights were pouring out of me, coiling in and around my body like a mist. But that's not what had my jaw hanging open.

It was because my starlights were *red*.

Dazzling red, like the most brilliant rubies, swirled in and around my body. They weaved around me like a whirlwind of red light, like thousands of angry red pixies.

It didn't take a genius to know that this was bad.

"What's happening to you?" asked Elsa, looking just as scared as I was.

I shook my head and locked eyes with Valen. "I don't know. I'm not controlling them."

No. It was like they had a mind of their own. Not like when I used my starlights, I always thought of them as an extension of myself. But I was always in control, calling them when I wanted. Now? They just emptied out of me without my command, like another entity.

"Why are they red?" Jade looked visibly shaken, and I swear I saw her take a slow step back.

"Hell if I know."

I could feel the power surging through my veins. It was almost as if my starlights had taken over, possessed my body as their own vessel. I felt their energy pulsing through me, making me feel alive in a way that I never could have imagined. It was both exhilarating and terrifying all at once. I was afraid that if I let go, I might never be able to regain control.

I closed my eyes, trying to focus on regaining control of my starlights. But the harder I tried, the more I failed. The red starlights just kept pouring out of me.

"Guys, I don't think I can control it," I said, my voice shaking with fear. "I don't know what's happening to me." Not true. I knew this had everything to do with the prophecy and my involvement in opening the gates from hell. I just didn't want to admit it.

This was it. It was happening right before my eyes.

I was becoming the key to unlocking the gates of hell.

I had to stop it. I had to do *something*.

Suddenly, a sharp pain shot through my head, and I doubled over in agony. I could hear my friends calling out to me, but their voices sounded distant like they were coming from another world. And then, just as suddenly as it had started, the pain ceased, and I found myself on my hands and knees, gasping for air.

Valen rushed over, but I threw out my hand. "I'm okay." Definitely not okay. I could feel the red starlights' energy pulsating through my veins, threatening to consume me entirely. Soon I would be lost to them, to it.

But all wasn't lost. I still had one card left to play.

I met Elsa's frightened gaze. "Is your spell ready? Can you use it to close the gate?"

The witch gave me a determined nod. "Yes. It's ready."

"Do it." Maybe that's all we needed to fix this mess. Perhaps it had nothing to do with me and everything to do with my friends' magic and closing the gate. One way or another, we had to stop the prophecy. It didn't matter who did it, just that we stopped it.

"Uh. Guys? Better make it quick," said Julian, and we all looked at him. "Looks like they sent the cavalry."

A low, loud bellow erupted around us. I turned at the sound of rushing feet.

There, on the opposite side of the roof, was a horde of about forty angel assassins. And they came rushing at us.

CHAPTER 23

I'd been wondering when the assassins were going to show up. Just not that many.

I flung my hand at Elsa and Jade. "Do the spell. I'll take care of them."

Okay, so my starlights were now red and wild, and I wasn't sure if they'd even *listen* to me. Yet, *I also* felt wild and uncontrollable and possibly a little… cocky?

I felt powerful. Enough to kick the ass of some of those angel assassins. And I was going to.

When I looked over at Valen and Catelyn, they were already in their massive giant forms. Anger creased Valen's expression as his gaze traveled over the angels, his fists clenching and unclenching like he was oiling them up. Then they both stalked slowly over to the horde of killer angels.

The wall of angels approaching looked like something out of this world and fit for the movies. Different in size, genders, and ages, these were immortal beings. Size and gender made no difference here. The smallest angel, a teen angel, could probably kick my ass.

This wasn't the handful of assassins I thought were on their way. This was like they'd called in the alumni from years before. I'd never seen so many angels. All so intent on killing me.

With their angel daggers gleaming, they bore straight down upon Valen and Catelyn in a terrifying rush. The roof shook beneath my feet. They were around us in every direction. An endless, merciless wave of soldiers, they advanced with one mission— to kill yours truly.

It was a goddamn angel stampede.

Valen broke through the mass of angels with brute force, his giant form shattering their weapons as he rammed through them like a bowling ball knocking down pins in a bowling alley.

The giant lurched forward, propelled by the force of his powerful hind legs. I heard a scream and then a horrible tearing sound as he threw himself into the sea of angels. He ripped through them ruthlessly, his wild movements unstoppable and completely terrifying.

A flash of silver and a dagger impaled Valen's thigh, sinking into the giant's flesh.

Valen bent down, plucked out the dagger, and clamped his hand around the throat of the angel who had presumably thrown it. The angel resembled a small child in his imposing grasp. With only one hand, Valen ended the angel's life with a quick snap of his neck and flung away the limp body.

Okay, that was kind of gross. But necessary, I guess.

The pounding in my ears gave way to the chimes and rasps of steel hitting the roof's shingles with the shrieks and cries of dying angels.

"Here we go." Panting, I stared, readying myself for a deadly battle.

"Leana?" Jade looked at me, her face etched with worry, knowing what I was about to do.

"Just, do your spell," I shouted to her and Elsa before rushing forward to meet the onslaught of angels.

As I ran toward the pack of angels, my red starlights trailed behind me like a blazing fire. I could feel their power coursing through my veins, making me stronger and more agile than ever before.

The air moved and shifted as the angel assassins charged and broke apart, a group barreling toward me, swords drawn.

But I was ready for them.

I leaped into the air, dodging their swings and weaving in and out of their attacks with ease. My starlights flared, sending streams of red energy shooting toward the angels. They cried out in pain as the energy connected with their bodies, sending them flying backward.

I landed softly on the roof, scanning the chaos around me. Valen and Catelyn were engaged in their own battle with the assassins, their massive forms wreaking havoc among the ranks of the angels.

Elsa's and Jade's voices rose all around me as they chanted the incantation, echoing in unison as they poured their magic into the spell.

The angels were vicious, their razor-sharp swords and daggers glinting in the dim light. I charged them, my red starlights swirling around me like a cloak of fire. I sliced through their ranks with ease, my starlights cutting them down like wheat before a scythe.

An angel stepped into my line of sight—a female with a double-edged blade hanging in her right hand. Her stark white hair and skin reminded me of an anime character. Her eyes burned like silver coins and focused on me.

"Nephilim brat," she snarled. "Your death will make me famous."

"Where I come from, fake boobs and fat lips make you famous."

She raised a brow. "I shall take pleasure in killing you."

"Potayto, potahto."

"Nothing personal." The angel snickered. Her perfect lips stretched across her flawless face. "A job's a job. Isn't that right, witch?"

I shrugged. "If I say yes, will you fly away?"

The angel female moved in a blur of white and gray, faster than any angel I'd seen before, tearing up the roof shingles as she came at me in a rush. For a moment, I was frozen, staring at the nightmare angel I had unleashed upon the mortal world.

I spun, slipping away at the last instant. My pulse quickened, and the adrenaline spiked, but I refused to let fear take over. As I dodged her next attack, I saw an opening and took it. I countered her move with a swift blast of my pretty red starlights.

But the bitch twirled like a ninja ballerina. My strike went wide. Damn it. She was too fast.

"Is that the best you can do?" she mocked.

"That *was* pretty lame." No point in lying.

"It was." The angel raised her blade and pointed it at me. "I've had enough of playing. I'll take what's mine now."

I made a face. "Are you asking me out?"

Anger rippled over the angel's face. "For a middle-aged human female, you're very immature."

"It's not that I'm immature. It's just that you started it."

She gave me a pointed look. "They'll be singing songs about me when I'm finished with you. The angel who saved the mortal world from the Nephilim brat. Cesticle the great, the savior of worlds."

I snorted. "You do realize that your name sounds like testicle?"

Her eyes sparked with anger. "Bitch."

"Right back at ya."

I yanked on my starlights and hurled a ball of bright red lights straight at her.

Laughing, she dodged to the side, but I followed

her with a barrage of ruby-colored starlights. And still, the angel female kept evading my attack with ease.

"You fight like a child," she taunted between laughs.

I shrugged. "I prefer to call it whimsical."

"I'm curious." The angel slid a finger down her blade. "How did you manage to kill my own? What did you use?"

"A little bit of this… a little bit of that." With a flick of my wrist, I sent a flurry of red starlights flying toward her. The angel twirled and batted them away with her blade. But this time, I'd almost gotten her.

I could see the anger in her eyes as she charged at me again.

She moved like a cartoon character, just some blurred lines that I could barely see.

She hit me before I could move. My face exploded into a fiery agony, and I crashed backward, onto the roof. Without pause, I sprang back into the fight and skillfully avoided the flashing of her double-edged blade.

"Hey. Not the face," I told her, standing with my legs apart, my red starlights coiling around my hands. "My boyfriend likes this face."

The angel snarled. "I was sent to kill you. I'm the best at what I do. I've never failed. Never. I've always gotten my mark. I'm paid highly for it. But in truth, killing Nephilim brings me joy, so much so that I'm willing to do it for free."

"You're sick."

"I'm an angel," she said, as though that made up for her twisted mind.

She sprang at me in a storm of limbs and blades. It felt as if I were fighting a shadow. No demon or paranormal could move the way she did. And if she wasn't trying to cut my head off, I might have been impressed.

The angel glanced casually at Elsa, Jade, and Julian. "Are you so selfish that you care nothing for your friends? Do you want them all to die?"

Ouch. "They won't die. We have a plan. We're going to close the gate. Problem solved."

She threw back her head and laughed. "But they will die. All will die because of you."

"Shut up."

"You never cared about them. You only care about yourself."

"I said *shut up.*" Anger flashed through me. That wasn't true. I loved my friends. I loved Shay and Valen. I was fighting for them. But her words cut into me deeply, as though she'd already sliced me with her blade.

"See," she continued, a smile on her face, "this is the difference between mortals and angels. An angel would have willingly died to save the legion or even this miserable realm you call home. But not you. Not you mortals."

Rage pounded in my veins. "Screw you and your legion. You don't know me. You don't know what's in my head."

"I know enough to know that you would sacrifice all these mortals to save your own pointless life. The only person you care about is you."

"I don't."

"If that's true, you would have given yourself up. You would die to save them. But… here you are. Fighting me."

"Because there's still a chance we can close the gate and change the prophecy," I said, though my voice lacked conviction. She was getting to me.

The angel laughed mockingly. "You're out of your mind. The prophecies of oracles are always fulfilled. There's no way to change them once they're spoken."

"It will this time."

"It won't." The angel watched me. The pleasure and excitement in her eyes at killing me was disturbing.

Her words rang in my head until I could feel myself losing confidence along with the focus on my starlights.

The angel beamed. "You must die, Nephilim. You must die for this world to live."

She shot forward like a shadow of white and black. Her blade out and swinging, a battle cry rang from her lips as she lunged, thrusting her weapon at me. I dodged it, only to feel the blade brush my neck. I ducked and spun away from her attack, but not before she left a gash in my skin. She flashed a smile as she saw the blood on my neck. Her movements were agile and lightning fast, leaving almost no time for a reaction from me. But I had something she didn't.

Starlight magic.

"Looks like you're determined to get that promotion, huh?" I jeered, my smirk mirroring the sudden lack of mirth on her face. "What happens if I beat you? What then for your promotion?"

"You won't," she growled, swiftly shifting her blade from side to side. She charged me with a fluid elegance and relentless attacks. I crouched and rolled away, stumbling onto the roof.

"You missed." I smiled at her frustration. I, too, could play this game.

I knew I'd hit a mark when her eyes narrowed. Her laugh didn't meet her eyes as she said, "I think I'll kill your little sister for an added bonus."

Anger bubbled up. "Now, why did you have to say that."

She raised her brows. "I hate children. They smell."

The angel's blade glinted in the dim light as she lifted it over her head. With a wild rush of strength, she flung herself at me. I dove and spun. Not fast enough.

I cried out as her knee drove up into my gut. The air knocked from me in a whoosh, and I swayed, falling to my knees. Coughing, I kept my grip on my starlights.

Not yet.

"Leana!" Jade's cry sounded over the blood pounding in my ears.

"Stay back!" I shouted. I didn't want her to get hurt. I didn't want any of them to stop from doing that spell. It was the only thing that mattered.

With a scream of fury, the angel swung her blade, the tip whistling as it came around directly for my face. But I leaped back and sprang to my feet. Grunting with effort and rage, I ducked and dodged her swift attack.

She was a mist of white as she thrashed her long blade. The angel was so damn fast. Too fast for me to block her. Too fast for my throw of starlights.

I just needed a moment, one moment when she was distracted and didn't see my starlights coming.

In that instant, all I saw was her eager, twisted face. She was angry that she hadn't killed me yet. She stilled, hesitating like she was trying to come up with a new scheme that would end me.

Now!

I blasted a beam of red starlights at the angel. And this time, she hadn't seen it coming. She tried to dodge it. Too late.

It hit her right in the boobs.

The angel toppled back, her shocking and terrible gasps crying out in heaving pants. She dropped her weapon, her eyes wide and her mouth open in a silent scream. Red starlights poured from her eyes, nose, mouth, and ears until her entire body was enveloped in a sheen of red light.

And then she exploded into a million brilliant particles.

"I *can* change the prophecy," I muttered as the

fragments of what had once been an angel assassin flickered and scattered away with a gust of wind.

"Leana!" howled Elsa, and when I spun around, she was pointing at something behind me.

I rushed over to where she was pointing and felt my knees weaken.

There, amid the bustling streets around Fifth Avenue, a massive black line appeared—a crevice in the Veil. It hissed and popped with an unfamiliar energy as it grew and elongated until a portal materialized before me, its edges sparking and alive. The portal was like nothing I had ever seen before, swirling with colors and pulsing with power. It was terrifying. But this wasn't just any portal.

The gates of hell were opening.

CHAPTER 24

The air was thick with rustling, guttural whispers, carrying the scent of rotten fruit, blood, and carrion. The portal, the gateway, pulsed like a constant humming from a power line. I'd never seen one so big before.

The group of angels seemed to have felt or noticed the gates opening, for they fought with a new urgency—a destructive one. They focused on me. I was getting a "now or never" kind of vibe from them.

Shit.

That foreign power in my being pounded. The energy thundered and echoed in time with the pulsing of the portal as though it was answering its call.

Something was awakening inside me. A key to unlock the gates.

I was going to be sick.

A glimmer of silver emerged from the deep-red

sky, partially hidden by thick clouds. I watched the edge of the disc, unsure how close it was to fullness. Soon the full moon would be upon us. And the gates would finally be open.

We were running out of time.

I pushed that new dread from me and rushed over to the witches. "Is it working?" I yelled, ducked, and sent another volley of my ruby starlights at an angel who'd gotten too close.

"We're trying here," called Elsa. "But having an army of angels trying to decapitate you does complicate things a little."

Jade's lips moved in some spell, but her eyes were round and staring at the ongoing battle with Valen and Catelyn.

"Can you keep them off us?" Julian tossed a vial over their ritual circle, causing a bang like a firecracker.

"That's what I'm doing here." Again, I flung out my hand, and my red starlights smacked into two angel females, which sent them flying off the roof. That white-haired angel had been a real badass and moved with supernatural speed that these other angels didn't possess. It seemed not all angel assassins were created equally. I was hoping to keep it that way.

"I think Catelyn and Valen need help," said Jade, turning her attention to me. "There're too many angels."

She wasn't wrong.

I looked out. The angels descended upon Valen

and Catelyn, their weapons raining down on the giants' massive forms. Valen roared in defiance, fighting back with all his might, but the angels kept coming, overwhelming him with their sheer numbers. For every one he put down, three took their place.

"I don't think they're going to make it."

"If I leave, the angels will come here and stop you from completing the spell." I hated to admit it, but right now, my priority was to stop the gates from opening or at least getting them closed quickly without any major complications like thousands of demon hordes slipping through and into Manhattan.

I jerked as a sound, like the clap of thunder, boomed over my head.

I whipped around.

Dark smoke billowed around the portal, creating a frame of sooty blackness at the edge of the whirling doorway. It glinted and shimmered, releasing wisps of inky mist that spun like a vortex of shadows.

If you stared long enough, you could almost see to the other side, into a world of darkness, blood, death, and pain.

With a sudden crack, the portal flickered again. A surging mass of liquid darkness pulsed with the fluid motion of waves on an ocean.

And then my worst nightmare came true.

Not one but *twenty* demons clambered out of the portal.

I sucked in a breath through my teeth as I watched an army of monsters from everyone's worst nightmares leak through the gates of their realm and into the heart of downtown Manhattan. Every time the gateway shimmered and pulsed, another ten demons poured forth, their deformed, horrible shapes even more grotesque and wicked. If there was a physical embodiment of evil, it had arrived.

The stench of sulfur and decay was overpowering, and my ears ached with the drop in pressure. A gust of air rifled through my hair, whipping it against my face. The air stung with its unnatural qualities, especially a peculiarly sharp, acidic aroma. I recognized this acrid scent as the air of the Netherworld emanating from within the gateway. And it was toxic to us mortals.

A chilling yell echoed below through the streets. It was distant, but the fear contained in the voice was unmistakable. It was trailed by an unintelligible gurgle and then nothing.

The scream sounded again, this time much closer than before. And then another shriek. And another. And another.

The demons were attacking the humans.

I squinted into the wind. Shapes moved beyond the boundaries of our world. Hundreds. Hundreds of shadows were spilling out from the portal. And soon, it would be thousands.

It was hell. Literally.

If the gate remained open, we were all as good as dead.

"Whatever you're going to do, do it quickly. You

need to do it now. Look." I pointed at the gate, which we could clearly see now. "We can't wait any longer."

"We're ready." Elsa pushed herself to her feet with a determined expression. Julian and Jade came to stand around her to form a circle.

Elsa lifted her hands as though in prayer and said, "Together."

"Down to the gateway, beneath the ground," the witches chanted. "Forever-entrenched, the magic is sound. To soothe the gateway and her thoughts, our charm encircles her in knots. Take our magic, your wounds to heal, by our words, the gateway is sealed!"

I watched, awestruck, as the witches' bodies began to glow with a bright white light. The light seemed to grow in intensity until it was blinding. It enveloped my friends, lifting them off the ground and suspending them in midair. The light swirled around them, growing brighter and brighter until it was almost too much to look at.

And then, just as suddenly as it had appeared, the light dissipated, and the witches lowered back down to the roof.

Then, the light in their eyes dissipated, and so did the pulsing of their power.

"Did it work?" I stared at the gate, still visible with no change. "Did it work?" I repeated, not able to see a difference.

Tears filled Elsa's eyes. "It's no use. The gateway should have closed. The spell didn't work. I'm sorry, Leana. We've failed."

I stumbled back like she'd hit me. I'd put all my faith in them, their spell. It was the only thing left to save us.

I checked my phone. Two minutes left until the full moon.

Desperation filled me, and I felt the tears prick my eyes. Valen and Catelyn were still battling the angels, keeping most of them from reaching us. But maybe they shouldn't.

I couldn't move a star. And we couldn't close the gates.

There was just one thing left to do.

I had to die.

CHAPTER 25

Don't get me wrong. I didn't want to die, not when my life was finally on track. I'd found the man of my dreams who adored me, and I had a family now with Shay.

But if I didn't die, not only would they die along with everyone else I cared about, but the humans would die too. Maybe not today or next month, but the demons would slowly take over until nothing was left of the mortal world. Until it became just another demon realm.

The gates of hell were almost open, but I still had time to save everyone. And to do that, *I* had to die.

I let my hands drop and moved away from the witches, giving a clear path for the angel assassins to come at me.

A few turned my way, but they wouldn't come closer. I could see anger and fear emanating from the stiff postures of their bodies. Their gazes were full of hostility, and their faces held an expression of dread.

Ah. They thought I'd blast them into bits with my pretty red starlights. I could have, but that wasn't the plan. Not anymore.

I raised my hands in surrender. "I give up. Come and get me!" I shouted, tasting the salt of my tears in my mouth. "Come on, you sons of bitches! Here I am. What are you waiting for? I'm right here!"

"Leana?" I heard Elsa yell. "What's the matter with you?"

"What is she doing?" came Jade's voice from behind me.

"She's giving herself over to the angels," I heard Julian say.

Yep. He was right.

"What do you mean?" Elsa's voice was filled with confusion and a tinge of fear. "Wait—no. Leana, *don't* do this. You can't do this! Someone stop her! Valen!"

Valen's head snapped in my direction. Our eyes met. If hearts could literally break, mine did at that moment when I saw the recognition on his face. He knew what I was about to do.

Panic filled his eyes, quickly followed by a deafening roar.

"*No!*"

Valen's roar shook the air, sending shock waves of power through the sky. And my heart broke just a little bit more.

His hatred for the angels radiated from every part of him. His muscles were tense with rage.

And then he was sending angels flying in every direction, swatting them out of his way as he tried to reach me. Barreling through them as they sliced and slashed at him with their weapons, but he kept pushing through. Desperation filled his gaze as he fought his way to me, his Starlight witch.

But it was too late. He wouldn't reach me in time. It was over. Time to make things right. I couldn't waste another moment.

"*No!*"

The sound of Valen's cry felt like a stab to my heart. Hell, I couldn't stop the avalanche of tears after that. Tears fell at the pain that seemed to have no end. The hurt was too deep. Too raw. Who knew loving someone would hurt this much, knowing I was letting them go. I'd never felt this kind of agony. Not with my ex-husband. Not with anyone.

A tiny whimper escaped me as I stepped closer to the rooftop's edge. I felt detached from reality like I was having an out-of-body experience. My limbs felt paralyzed, and my body felt drained. My bottom lip trembled, and I took a deep breath, just as the angels closed in around me. My body shook, not from the fear of dying but from never seeing Valen's face again or feeling his touch on my skin. Of never seeing Shay's smiling face, Elsa's frown, Jade's crazy hair, or Julian's smugness when he talked about all the hotties in his past.

I would never see them again.

But through the pain, I felt a sense of peace. I was doing this for the greater good, to protect the ones I loved. I was doing this *for* them.

I'd never been one to give up without a fight,

without throwing in a few starlight punches and kicks. I'd fight 'til my very last breath and take whoever I was fighting down with me. But not this time.

"Leana! Stop! Please! Don't do this!"

A chill ran through me at Valen's plea. But I wouldn't look at him. It was no use. This was the only way. He'd see that… eventually. When the gates closed, and everyone was safe. I hoped.

Through my bleary, teary eyes, I saw the angels close in on me, their swords glinting in the moonlight, daring closer and seemingly noticing that I wouldn't use my red starlights on them. I was an easy kill now.

"For Shay. For Valen. For my friends," I rasped, my voice cracking, ready to meet my fate.

But then, something strange happened.

A beam of white light hit the first line of angels. I heard a pop, and they burst like sparkling confetti.

Confused, I checked my hands to make sure I hadn't slipped accidentally. But my starlights swirled around me, my *red* starlights. I hadn't unleashed them.

I looked over my shoulder. Walking toward me was my little sister.

"Shay? What the hell are you doing here?" That damn kid had sneaked away from Cassandra. If I wasn't about to die, I would have killed her.

With her entire body shining like a miniature sun, she gave me her signature shrug. "Helping. I can help. You need me. Uh—why are your starlights red?"

"Long story." My jaw fell open when it hit me. "Yes. I *do* need you." Maybe… just maybe it would be enough.

With my heart thumping, I grabbed her hand and pulled her close. "Listen to me," I said, speaking quickly. "We need to move that star, the smallest one," I pointed to the sky at Runty. "Together. With our powers. You need to picture it in your mind, moving it across the sky. You think you can do that?"

Shay, still shining brightly, shrugged like this was no big deal, like I had just asked what she wanted to watch on TV. "Okay."

I don't know why I hadn't considered asking Shay to participate. Probably because I didn't want my little sister to get killed in the crossfire of angel assassins, but her power was like none other. It was strong. Uber strong. And maybe just the right amount of power I needed.

"I've never been this happy about you sneaking out before."

Shay beamed, her sun power radiating around her. "Yeah, I know."

Blinking my last tear, I squeezed her hand and, with my other hand, sent a beam of my red starlights at three angels who'd broken through Valen's and Catelyn's defenses. A loud crack echoed as they fell to the ground in a pile of ashes.

I checked my phone again.

Twenty-six seconds left.

I looked down at Shay. "Ready?"

"Ready."

"Okay then. Let's do this." I didn't recite the spell. I didn't think I needed to. My witchy instincts told me just to use my starlights—and Shay's sun power. Plus, I had the unmistakable feeling that Julian had been right and that this Alexander had lied about moving a star.

Twenty seconds, I counted in my mind.

Shay's body shook next to me as her sun power combined with my own.

"Just see it moving in your mind," I repeated. I took a breath and reached out to my Starlight magic. My body flooded with the tingling energy that gushed from my core, racing along my hands, my body. Shay's power wound its way through me, joining mine and pulsing with the force of another heart.

But it also burned. Not too much, like lowering yourself in a hot bath too soon. Hot, but I could handle it.

I peered into the portal and caught sight of an innumerable mass of demons. Long shadows got closer, revealing wings, tails, and tentacles all flailing about in their haste. Looked like the demons had figured out our plan and were now clamoring to get through. I could hear them screaming and wailing from a distance.

Ten seconds.

Adrenaline flooded me. I closed my eyes and

focused, drawing in more starlight. I let it fill me, every fiber of my being humming with energy.

The red starlights that had been swirling around me suddenly began to pulse with a brighter light. The light grew in intensity until it was blinding.

Feeling Shay's power coursing through me, slowly I extended my right hand toward the star. My fingers trembled slightly, but I forced myself to stay calm. From the corner of my eye, I saw Shay mimic my movement. Then I visualized the star moving and imagined its fiery mass shifting in the sky.

Five seconds.

And then, with a rush of power, I released my magic.

My body reverberated as Shay released hers too.

A beam of red-and-white light shot up into the sky, illuminating the darkness with its brilliance.

The star flickered, and then it began to move, a slow and steady drift across the sky until it was almost on the other side of the city.

One.

Too shocked and amazed and afraid to jinx it, I didn't say anything, nor did I let go of my little sister's hand.

The next moment, two things happened.

First, the city was rocked by a powerful shock wave that felt like an earthquake. Then slowly, the huge gateway that cut through the city's center, or rather, the gates of hell itself, began to close.

My ears popped with pressure as the portal

started to shrink and fold in on itself, again and again, until with a final pop, it was gone.

The gateway was closed.

"They did it!" screamed Jade. "Oh my god! They closed it!"

I didn't celebrate just yet, nor did I let go of the starlights still pounding in me. My eyes found the stronghold of angel assassins that remained. They were all just standing on the roof. Not fighting. Not attacking Valen or Catelyn, who were both staring at me and Shay with a mixture of pride and shock. Yeah, we rocked.

And then, one by one, the angels vanished.

CHAPTER 26

The thirteenth floor was alive with merriment. All the residents had emerged from their apartments and were congregated around several long tables, filled with delicious dishes and all sorts of alcoholic beverages as they were laughing, chatting, and celebrating.

Said celebrations were the festivities that doomsday hadn't come, my thirteenth-floor gang and I taking credit for saving the day. Some details were kept on the down-low, like my part in opening up a portal to the gates of hell. We didn't want another wave of hysteria, so some things were better left unsaid. And the demons that had escaped the portal had been taken care of by Arther and some of his pack, or so Valen had told me.

The human news described the portal opening as a severe weather phenomenon, probably because humans couldn't "see" the gateway. They'd only seen the disturbance in the sky. And we, the paranormal community, were going with the "giant Rift" scenario, and we were going to keep it that way.

Now, all I wanted was a well-deserved rest. I needed a month off. That's what I needed.

I spotted Shay next to Elsa, using her sun magic to grow the older witch's tomato plants. And sure enough, with just a flick of her magic, a tall green stem sprouted from the pot Elsa was holding. Big, juicy tomatoes hung from the branches. They both burst out in giggles.

"Hey."

I turned to see Catelyn coming over, a glass of wine in her hand. A few bruises marred her pretty face, but otherwise, she looked in perfect health.

"How are you feeling?" I asked the giantess, remembering the beatings she gave as well as the beatings she took.

"I'm good. Your man did his healing thing. The worst of it is gone."

"Thank you. Thank you for having my back." Catelyn and Valen had fought like champs, keeping the angel horde at bay while we tried to magic the gates of hell away and move a star. "We couldn't have done it without you."

A smile spread over her face. "Glad I could help."

I took a sip of my wine, enjoying the fruity taste. "You staying long?"

Catelyn sighed. "No. Arther and I are going back home tonight. He misses his pack. The woods. The quiet."

I nodded. "Yeah. I get that. It's a pretty special place."

"Unless you think you'll need me?"

I smiled at the giantess. "No. The threat is over." Well, *this* threat was over until the next threat showed up.

"Good. 'Cause I need some sex."

I burst out laughing. "I bet you do. And I bet it's awesome, too, with that pretty male specimen."

Catelyn flashed me her pearly whites. "You have no idea." Her eyes flicked away from me.

I followed her gaze. Arther was standing next to Valen, both men in deep conversation. Arther patted the giant's shoulder like he was trying to loosen him up.

"Valen looks pissed," said Catelyn.

"He is. He's mad at me." And I knew exactly why that was.

"Why?"

I opened my mouth to tell her when a generous woman with red cheeks, wearing a traditional white, stained chef jacket came marching my way.

"So?" Polly pressed her hands on her hips and glared at me. "I hear that your magic is gone. Is that true?"

"Later," snorted Catelyn, steering away from Polly and me.

"And?" Polly crossed her arms over her large middle.

"It's true." It was hard to keep the disappointment from my voice. For the first time in my life, I was able to use my Starlight magic during the day. Something I'd always wanted to do. But when I'd woken up this morning and pulled on my magic— nothing. My daytime starlights were gone. I was the same ol' dud as before.

The healer pinched her face in thought as she regarded me. "So, you can't do any more of that star magic? Nothing?"

"No. I can still do my Starlight magic but only at night. Like before. I just can't do it during the day." I'd also gotten a glimpse of my *white* starlights last night. The red starlight days were over. With the closing of the portal, I'd gone back to being the Starlight witch I was before all this nightmare.

Yes, I was a little disappointed. But I'd rather have my old magic back than none at all. It was who I was. I was a Starlight witch. And I wouldn't change it for the world.

"How do you feel?"

"Good. Same. I feel fine, Polly. Thanks for asking."

The healer made a disgruntled noise in her throat. "Well. You know where to find me should you start feeling a little… off."

"Thanks. I will." I watched the healer walk away and join Elsa and Shay, who were now eating and savoring those new tomatoes as though they were apples. Julian was there, juggling three tomatoes to the applause of the twins and Casandra, who looked like she wanted to take a bite out of Julian.

My little sister had more power in her baby finger

than all the witches in this hotel combined. Probably the entire state. And without her, I would have died.

Emotions flared, and I blinked fast. The last thing I wanted was to start bawling my eyes out when I was at a party and supposedly having fun.

Speaking of bawling my eyes out, I spotted Jade standing alone at the end of the hallway near my apartment, staring at her hands, her face flushed. Her outfit was a sight to behold—a pink-streaked black hairdo contrasted with a ruffled skirt and pink tights. And she finished the look with a Bon Jovi T-shirt. But despite the cheerful outfit, she still seemed despondent.

I made my way over. "Hey. You look upset. What's the matter?" I remembered her saying that Jimmy had been distant with her. Was that what had her looking so sad? "Where's Jimmy?"

Jade sniffed and hid her hands behind her back. "Over there with Basil."

I followed her gaze, and sure enough, there was Jimmy with a beer bottle in his hand, shaking Basil's with the other. What was that about?

I leaned on the wall next to her. "You guys okay? Is he still being distant?"

"No. I was wrong."

"About him being distant?" I waited for her to answer, but she just stared at Jimmy without blinking, a strange smile on her face.

"Jade? You okay?"

Jade thrust out her hand, and a pretty, antique-looking engagement ring winked at me. It was beautiful, with a smooth gold band and a single diamond set in the middle. It wasn't the largest diamond I'd ever seen, nor was it the smallest. It wasn't over the top, which I liked. It was perfect.

"You're engaged!"

Jade blinked. "I'm engaged."

I grabbed her in a hug. "I'm so happy for you," I said to her mass of hair.

"I'm happy for me too."

I laughed, letting her go. "You know what this means. Don't you?"

"I have to start having babies?"

I laughed harder. "If you want, but I was going to say we need to throw you an engagement party."

"Right." Jade beamed as she stared at her ring like she wasn't sure it was really there, and she was living a dream.

Warmth filled my middle. I was so happy for my friend, my friends. Jimmy and Jade deserved to be happy and have as many babies as they wanted.

"Congratulations, Jade."

I turned to see Valen next to us.

"Jimmy just told me," said the giant, looking scrumptious in a black dress shirt and pants that showed off a pair of muscular legs. He looked sexy and, dare I say, a little dangerous. I liked it.

"Thanks," said Jade. "Uh… Jimmy wants me to go over. I'll see you guys later."

I smiled and watched her go. When she reached Jimmy, he took her hand, pulled her against him, and planted a kiss on her mouth.

Hmmm. So cute and in love, it made me want to hurl.

I looked at Valen and lost my smile. "I guess from that frown you're still angry with me?"

"I am." Those two words had more emotions in them than if he'd yelled at me for a half hour.

Ah, hell. This was going to take some work. "Valen—"

"Leana!"

I spun at the sound of my name to find Basil standing behind me. "What did you do to the Youtoo girls?"

"Uh…" Shit, I'd forgotten about them. Maybe I'd gotten lucky, and the angel assassins had taken care of them. "Why?"

The hotel manager threw his hands in the air. "It's a success! The hotel's famous!"

I looked at Valen, but he was staring at Basil. "It is? You mean, they're alive?"

Basil clamped his mouth. "What do you mean by that? Did something happen? Did *you* do something to them? I thought I was clear with you. They were off limits."

I shook my head. "I didn't do anything. I was as sweet as a lamb." Except for the part where I'd destroyed Daisy's phone.

Basil narrowed his eyes at me, and for a moment, I thought he was going to scream. But then he just grinned and said, "Well, the show's a success. Over sixty thousand views already and climbing."

So they weren't dead. I wasn't sure how I felt

about that. I was numb. "That's great, Basil. Happy it all worked out."

"Yes, yes, yes." He tapped his chin in thought. "Which is why I agreed to have them do their show here once a month."

"What? You didn't!"

"I did."

"I won't let them follow me again. I did it for you as a favor. Once is enough."

Basil pointed a finger at my face. "If you still want your job, you will agree to let them follow you around once a month."

"I won't."

"You will. No amount of begging will change my mind."

"I don't beg." The nerve of this little witch. I was going to strangle him.

"The point is, it's good for the hotel. More exposure. More publicity. More paying guests. And you *will* do it. Valen." And with that, the hotel manager sauntered away. I heard him saying, "Have you caught the Youtoo show featuring the hotel?" as he approached someone else.

I looked at the giant, who thought a spot on the wall was very interesting. "Valen? Did you see their episode?"

Valen blew a breath through his nose.

"Still not talking to me? Fine. I'm going to strip naked right now in front of all these people. See if you'll speak to me then."

The giant's attention snapped to me, his mouth parted, and I swear I saw some heat in his gaze—

My thumb ring pulsed with warmth.

Fear struck, and my smile vanished. *Oh no. No. This can't be happening.*

"What's wrong?" Valen bent closer to me.

Before I could respond, Shay zoomed past us.

"Dad!" squealed Shay, the sound of her shoes flapping the carpet resounded as she galloped into my apartment.

"Dad?" I repeated, releasing some tension as I followed her in.

Sure enough, Matiel, aka my father, stood in the living room. Not another angel assassin.

The last time I'd seen him, he'd given me the worst news possible, and then he'd disappeared again, leaving me with more unanswered questions and a hell of a lot of uncertainty and fear. I wasn't sure how I felt about seeing him now. Should I be angry? Should I tell him to leave?

But when I saw my little sister jump into the arms of the angel, crushing her tiny body against his large one, I felt some of my anger crack.

"Hey, you." Matiel hugged his daughter and kissed the top of her head.

"Leana and me moved a star!" she blurted, her round and bright eyes like tiny suns. "And we closed the gates! And then, all the angels left!"

Matiel looked up and met my gaze. "Yes. I've heard. And I'm grateful. Pleased that everything worked out."

Without much of your help. "Yes. Everything did work out. I'm just glad it's all over and Shay can finally have some normalcy and some time for her. She deserves to have a normal life. Be a kid. Do kid stuff."

Matiel smiled, though his eyes shone with distress and maybe a bit of guilt. "Yes. She does." He paused and then added, "And so do you."

I pursed my lips. "I haven't done kid stuff in over thirty years. But I have been told repeatedly that I am immature."

Matiel laughed. I didn't remember ever hearing him laugh before, and I found myself enjoying the sound. It was hard to stay mad at him when he laughed at my jokes and when my little sister was bursting with joy at the sight of him. She truly loved her father. And I loved seeing her like this, like a real kid without the worries of the world on her shoulders.

Damn it. Maybe I was going to end up liking him.

"Will the angel legion leave Leana alone now?" Valen stood next to me. The scent of his aftershave and some musky cologne filled my nose.

"Yes," answered the angel, still holding on to his little girl. "You broke the prophecy."

"We moved the smallest star!" exclaimed Shay. God, she was cute.

Matiel smiled down at her. "That's right. And as such, there's no more reason for the Legion of Angels to fear you. I'm happy to tell you they will never bother you again."

"Mmm." I looked over my angel father. He did look a lot cheerier than the last time. "And I take it you can now travel freely to our world? There are no more *obstacles* in your way?"

Matiel let out a long sigh. "Yes. I'll be able to come visit you both as much as you want."

"Yay!" Shay jumped up and down. Her eyes widened as she added, "You missed my talent show. But maybe you can come to the next one?"

"I wouldn't miss it for the world," said Matiel, making an already happy kid all the more jumpy.

"So, Leana will never be hunted by your people?" Valen was still pressing my father for answers. "They will never come at her again? Can I have your word on that?"

My body pricked at the concern in his tone, and warmth pooled in my middle. He stood there, all hot and protective, staring at my angel father like he wanted to take a swing at him.

Any other man would have shit his pants at the giant's tone. As an angel, he barely even blinked. "You have my word."

Huh. Even I believed him.

Valen just nodded. And then, the next thing I knew, he grabbed my hand and pulled me with him.

I was too shocked and secretly too happy to object to his manhandling. Hell, I would love me some manhandling right now.

I caught a glimpse of Matiel pulling his daughter with him on the couch and heard him say, "Now. Tell me about this talent show," as Valen hauled me along with him toward the door.

"Where are you taking me?" I skidded behind the large beast of a man.

Valen stalked into the apartment facing mine and barked at Wayne. "Out. Now."

My mouth fell open. Just when I was about to tell Valen that we were in Wayne's apartment and he didn't need to listen to him, the fifty-year-old werecat jumped out of his armchair and hurried out of his apartment like there was a sale on Purina Cat Chow at the local grocery store.

"Valen. What are you doing?"

The giant kicked the door shut after the werecat, grabbed my waist, and pinned me to the wall.

"Are we going to have makeup sex? 'Cause if we are, I just wanted to say… *yay!*"

The giant made a sound in his throat that was part growl, part moan and had my nether regions applauding. "Don't ever do that again."

"Do what?" Though I had a feeling I knew what he meant.

Valen locked eyes with me. He was so close, the tip of his nose brushed against mine. "Never give your life away," he said, his hot breath caressing my cheek. "You're too damn important to me."

"Trust me. I didn't want to." I sighed. "It's not like I had a choice. If Shay hadn't shown up…"

Valen leaned his forehead against mine, the tension around his shoulders loosening a bit. "I can't lose you."

I swallowed, my throat contracting as moisture filled my eyes. Nope. I would not cry now. Not when I was about to have some mind-boggling sex in someone else's apartment.

"You won't. It's over. Done. We can move on with our lives."

He looked up. "I'm still angry with you."

I grinned. "Angry enough for a spanking?"

Valen raised a brow. "Oh, yes. Lots of spanking… and lots of *other* things," he said and dipped his head to kiss me.

His kiss was anything but gentle. It lit a fire inside me, and I succumbed to his touch. His tongue swept across mine as we kissed, setting off an explosion of emotions within me. I matched his intensity, pressing hungrily against him with my own kisses. Then I pulled back to give his neck and earlobe some attention, lightly grazing each with little bites.

He groaned, and it set my core on fire. The feeling of his hard body pressed against mine triggered something feral in me, and I pulled him tighter to me. His rough, calloused hands slid over my body, caressing me and sending shivers through me.

Yep, I'd moved a star with the help of Shay. The gates of hell were closed. The Guild of Angel Assassins were done with me.

But all I could think of right now was that I was about to have me some out-of-my-mind makeup sex, and that's all that mattered.

CHAPTER 27

I stood on the Twilight Hotel's rooftop, next to Shay, taking in the view of the cars driving on Fifth Avenue and people strolling along the sidewalks. The night sky was a black cloak with stars twinkling and sparkling like diamonds and gemstones. The wind was soft and gentle with the unfortunate stench of exhaust from the streets below.

"I'm sorry about your magic," said Shay, leaning over the railing beside me. "Sucks."

I sighed. "Sucks balls. But I'm okay with it."

Shay laughed. "You said *balls*."

"I know." I smiled at her.

Shay lost some of that smile and stared at the railing. "Are you sad?"

I thought about it. "I was at first. Like this morning when I tried to summon it, and nothing happened. But," I said, turning my body so I was facing her, "I'm not anymore. I am who I'm supposed to be. I'm a Starlight witch. My magic comes at night.

It's exactly what it's supposed to be. And I'm okay with that."

Shay shrugged. "Cool." She looked at me and added, "The red was cool."

"It was. Very cool."

"Do you think you can make your starlights red again? Or purple?"

I drummed my fingers over the railing. "I don't think so. I think that was a one-time thing."

"Oh." A flash of disappointment appeared on her face. I understood that. I was also disappointed not to be able to play around with different-colored starlights. But it was okay. Okay, to be back to the witch I was before. And nothing was wrong with that.

"Shay." I reached out and grabbed her hand. "I wanted to thank you for what you did last night. For sneaking out and helping me. You did good. Real good."

"I know."

"Even though it was dangerous as hell, and you didn't listen to me, you saved my butt."

"I know."

I searched her face, not sure if she fully understood the magnitude of what she'd done. But she was only eleven and a half, almost twelve. She shouldn't have to.

"You happy you saw your dad tonight?" I asked her.

"*Our* dad," corrected my kid sister. "I told him

about my talent show. And how I made those trees grow with my sun power."

I chuckled. "Bet he was impressed."

Shay's face lit up. "Yeah. He's coming by tomorrow night so I can show him. Elsa's going to bring over some pots with some peach pits. I'm going to grow a peach tree."

I laughed. "I believe you. I love peaches."

"Me too."

"You better save me some."

Shay bit her bottom lip but said nothing.

That just made me laugh harder.

The night air was cool and crisp, the kind that made your skin tingle with anticipation. It reminded me of the night when I'd asked Shay how she felt about moving in with me and Valen in his apartment above his restaurant. We'd joined the giant, perched on his shoulders as he took us on a wild ride through the city at night.

It had been the first time with Shay and the last time. And I hadn't thought about it until now.

"A giant told me that your birthday is coming up," I said, angling my head toward Valen, who stood a few feet away. Even in the darkness, he was illuminated by the moonlight, all eighteen feet of him.

He wore a black shirt and cargo pants made of some stretchy material that had expanded and lengthened magically as he shifted and took on his giant shape as though they were tailored to him in that form. Catelyn had gifted him the magical clothing before she and Arther left for his compound up north. Good. He needed something to cover up any unsightly areas, especially around an eleven-year-old girl.

"What would you like?" I had no idea what girls her age would want. And I didn't want to be one of those big sisters or parents who just handed off money. I wanted to do something special for her on her special day.

I leaned against the railing and watched as Shay turned to face me. Her eyes were bright, filled with excitement and mischief. I knew that look all too well. It was the one she always wore when she was planning on misbehaving.

"What? What are you thinking?" I asked, raising an eyebrow. "I know that look."

Shay gave a sheepish grin. "Can I play with your starlights?" She looked up at me, hopeful, with that damn cute smile on her face.

I was a weakling. I could never resist that face.

A smile crept across my face. "That's what you want for your birthday?"

Shay's eyes widened. "Yes. But can I play with them now?"

"Sure."

I pulled on my starlights, the power of the stars, channeling it from above. A bright white ball materialized in my palm, and with a single breath, it exploded into thousands of twinkling stars. The little stars spanned out over Shay, the sparkles circling around her and leaving behind a trail of glittery dust.

They moved at her command, lifting her hair, some even settling on her hands like glowing pixies.

Shay let out a squeal of delight. "Leana! Look!"

"I know." I watched as my starlights greeted her like a long-lost friend. They loved her just as much as I did.

"Can I name them?" She looked at me, my starlights whipping around her like a litter of puppies doing their zoomies.

"Uh… if you want. Sure." I'd always referred to them as my starlights. There were way too many of them. But if she wanted to give them names, I was all for it.

"So. Are we doing this?" asked the giant, stepping toward us. It was hard not to think about that makeup sex we'd just had—in Wayne's apartment—when he looked the way that he did, the strong, sexy man-beast. The giant, sexy man-beast who'd been unforgivably rude the very first time I'd laid eyes on him.

I looked at Shay. "I'm ready. You?"

Shay's eyes darted from Valen to me. "Ready!"

I glanced at the giant. "Guess we're ready."

The giant stepped closer and scooped up Shay, who was laughing with joy. He settled her on his left shoulder before picking me up and balancing me on his right.

Shay let out a shriek. "Can we do this every night?"

"Valen?"

Valen laughed. *"We can."*

I chortled as Shay did a happy dance on Valen's shoulder while my starlights zoomed around her body.

I stared down at the street below. "Let's go, big boy."

Valen let out a deep chuckle that reverberated through his chest. It traveled up my back and down my arms when I shifted my weight on his massive shoulder. Sitting there, I felt a combination of joy and exhilaration. I smiled at the night breeze against my cheeks. I felt content and complete. I had everything I needed—a good job, a wonderful life partner, and the best kid sister anyone could ask for.

And my magic? Well, I was a Starlight witch. And I wouldn't change that for the world.

And then, with Shay and me perched atop his broad shoulders, the giant leaped from the edge of the rooftop.

Check out *Shadow Witch*, the first in The Witches of Hollow Cove series.

ARE YOU READY FOR YOUR NEXT MAGICAL ADVENTURE?

Okay, so I'm in trouble. Big trouble. I'm broke. Worse, my boyfriend of five years just dumped me. What do I do? I move in with my three eccentric aunts in their family home, Davenport House. Sounds exciting, only this massive farmhouse likes to eat men. Yup. If I were a regular human, I would have run out screaming like a banshee. As a witch—I do absolutely nothing. Hey, maybe they deserved it?

I'm back in Hollow Cove, the flamboyant paranormal community, where nymphs, werewolves, trolls, shifters, witches, and other paranormals live comfortable lives—and away from prying human eyes. As I settle into my new life, I decide to accept my aunts' proposal and join the family business—the business of protecting our town and killing anything that would want to harm it.

But I've been away from the paranormal world for quite some time, and my magical abilities are a little bit rusty—heck, they're practically invisible.

Things soon spiral down the crapper when people in our community start dropping like flies. And when demons start showing up in Hollow Cove, it's up to me, to take care of them. Permanently.

Get ready for this heart-pounding and laugh out loud magical adventure! If you like fast-paced urban fantasy adventure with a kick-butt heroine and plenty of action, suspense, and humor, you'll love Shadow Witch.

"Desperate Housewives meets Practical Magic."

In the charming suburb of Moonfell, the women of the community are more than meets the eye. Behind the white picket fences and perfectly manicured lawns, lies a world of magic, mystery, and scandal. Freya, a recently divorced witch struggling to control her powers, finds herself entangled in the drama of her neighbors. From the coven of witches who will stop at nothing to protect their secrets, to the sexy and dangerously seductive Blake, whose dark past and mysterious powers make him irresistible, Freya must navigate the dangerous waters of Moonfell while keeping her own secrets hidden.

With a mix of humor, romance, and supernatural intrigue, *The Housewife Witch* is a thrilling ride through the hidden world of witchy suburbia.

BOOKS BY KIM RICHARDSON

THE WITCHES OF HOLLOW COVE

Shadow Witch

Midnight Spells

Charmed Nights

Magical Mojo

Practical Hexes

Wicked Ways

Witching Whispers

Mystic Madness

Rebel Magic

Cosmic Jinx

Brewing Crazy

WITCHES OF NEW YORK

The Starlight Witch

Game of Witches

Tales of a Witch

THE DARK FILES

Spells & Ashes

Charms & Demons

Hexes & Flames

Curses & Blood

SHADOW AND LIGHT

Dark Hunt

Dark Bound

Dark Rise

Dark Gift

Dark Curse

Dark Angel

Newsletter

Never miss a new release! Sign up for Kim's Newsletter to receive exclusive updates on upcoming releases and discounted books!
Click here to get started!

About the Author

Kim Richardson is a *USA Today* bestselling and award-winning author of urban fantasy, fantasy, and young adult books. She lives in the eastern part of Canada with her husband, two dogs, and a very old cat. Kim's books are available in print editions, and translations are available in over seven languages.

To learn more about the author, please visit:

www.kimrichardsonbooks.com

.

Printed in Great Britain
by Amazon

26077108R00175